Leap of Faith

Can't be more than a mile away now. . . .

He gave a quiet, rasping whoop, urging himself on. He climbed to his feet and ran through the brush, the branches whipping at his legs.

Behind him, the riders closed. Their horses seemed to be blowing in his ears. He could hear the men breathing, the leather squeaking like trees rubbing together, the bits rattling against the horses' teeth, the bridle chains jangling like rusty sleigh bells.

"Get the son of a bitch!" a man yelled.

Yakima lifted his head and closed his eyes, pumping his legs and arms.

Behind him a man yelled shrilly, *"Woooo-ahhh! Pull up, boys."*

Behind Yakima, a horse screamed. Hooves skidded across sod, snapping brush and grinding rocks.

Yakima's stride didn't slow.

His boots kept thudding. The ground disappeared.

For two strides, he ran through air, began falling, cool air from below wafting over him, lifting his shirt flaps, blowing his hair above his head.

He opened his eyes, looked down. Below, a narrow fissure of silvery-liquid darkness rose toward him. . . .

Praise for Frank Leslie
and *The Lonely Breed*

"Frank Leslie writes with leathery prose honed sharper than a buffalo skinner's knife, with characters as explosive as . . . slams readers with the impact of a . . . edgy, raw, and irresist . . .

—Johnny D . . . f *Camp Ford*

continued . . .

"Hooks you instantly with sympathetic characters and sin-soaked villains. Yakima has a heart of gold and an Arkansas toothpick. If you prefer Peckinpah to Ang Lee, this one's for you."

—Mike Baron, creator of *Nexus* and
The Badger comic book series

"Big, burly, brawling, and action-packed, *The Lonely Breed* is a testosterone-laced winner from the word 'go,' and Frank Leslie is an author to watch!"

—E. K. Recknor, author of *The Legendary Kid Donovan*

THE LONELY BREED

Frank Leslie

A SIGNET BOOK

SIGNET
Published by New American Library, a division of
Penguin Group (USA) Inc., 375 Hudson Street,
New York, New York 10014, USA
Penguin Group (Canada), 90 Eglinton Avenue East, Suite 700, Toronto,
Ontario M4P 2Y3, Canada (a division of Pearson Penguin Canada Inc.)
Penguin Books Ltd., 80 Strand, London WC2R 0RL, England
Penguin Ireland, 25 St. Stephen's Green, Dublin 2,
Ireland (a division of Penguin Books Ltd.)
Penguin Group (Australia), 250 Camberwell Road, Camberwell, Victoria 3124,
Australia (a division of Pearson Australia Group Pty. Ltd.)
Penguin Books India Pvt. Ltd., 11 Community Centre, Panchsheel Park,
New Delhi - 110 017, India
Penguin Group (NZ), cnr Airborne and Rosedale Roads, Albany,
Auckland 1310, New Zealand (a division of Pearson New Zealand Ltd.)
Penguin Books (South Africa) (Pty.) Ltd., 24 Sturdee Avenue,
Rosebank, Johannesburg 2196, South Africa

Penguin Books Ltd., Registered Offices:
80 Strand, London WC2R 0RL, England

First published by Signet, an imprint of New American Library,
a division of Penguin Group (USA) Inc.

First Printing, March 2007
10 9 8 7 6 5 4 3 2 1

Chapter 1

Yakima Henry heard the roadhouse's batwing doors shudder behind him. He smelled the sweet plum aroma of a familiar perfume wafting on the night breeze.

"Yakima?" the girl called.

He glanced over his shoulder at the scantily clad doxie standing at the edge of the porch. He himself stood at the edge of the roadhouse's front yard, partially hidden by a spindly cedar.

"Uh . . . yes, ma'am?"

"Would you do me a favor?"

"What's that, ma'am?"

"I was wondering if you would . . ." The whore let the sentence die beneath the din emanating from the roadhouse. "Hey, what're you doin' out there, anyways?"

"I beg your pardon, Miss Sabrina. I'm taking a piss."

She laughed. "How uncouth! Why don't you use the privy?"

Yakima shook himself, tucked himself into his fringed buckskin breeches, and buttoned his fly with a grunt. His voice was deep, and he spoke with little expression, giving the impression that he preferred solitude to the company of others. "Privy's off-limits to breeds."

He picked up the firewood he'd gathered from the shed and headed back to the porch and the smell of tobacco smoke and liquor tinged with the fragrance of the whore's perfume.

"You can't piss where everybody else pisses?" she said, frowning down at him, brown ringlets framing her face. "That's rotten."

Her willowy figure in a low-cut cream dress, hair feathers, and several cheap necklaces was silhouetted against the roadhouse's two front windows. Raucous voices and piano music drifted over the batwings.

Yakima's undershot boot knocked a stone against the bottom step with a wooden thud. "This is the best job I've had in two years. I'm not gonna start complainin' about where I piss."

"He works you like a slave."

"I've worked harder, and for a lot less than what Thornton pays me. Now, what can I do for you?"

She tipped her head toward the batwings. "Me and one of the soldier boys broke my bed. Think you can fix it? It's early. If my bed was fixed, I could get three more customers serviced before closing time. You know Thornton's quotas."

"The headboard or the frame?"

"A leg broke."

"I'll get on it as soon as I fill the woodbox."

"Thanks." She smiled, looked around, and pivoting coquettishly on one bare foot, screwed a finger into her chin. "I'll give you a free poke sometime, when Thornton's not around."

The planks squawked as Yakima mounted the porch steps. "You'd lay with a breed?"

"Don't tell anyone," said Miss Sabrina, "but I've laid

with plenty of breeds. Last whorehouse I worked was around Belle Fourche."

She ran her eyes across Yakima's broad, muscular chest, his thick brown hands curled under the split logs in his arms. Having watched him working with his shirt off, she knew his belly was flat and hard as oak, his shoulders stout as wheel hubs, his waist not much bigger around than her own. His legs, slightly bowed, were turned with hard, long muscles straining his buckskins' seams.

She returned her glittering eyes to his face, with its broad, flat cheekbones. His dark skin was marked from knife pricks, and his lustrous hazel eyes were framed by long, dark brown hair. He smelled of leather, tobacco, sage, horses, and something else, which she imagined to be the smell of wild things in remote, far-flung, lonely places—animals as well as men.

Sabrina felt a warming, tingling sensation deep in her belly. He'd no doubt be quite the lover, this taciturn half savage—thrusting between her legs, his fierce heart pounding like a tom-tom. She'd bet aces to eights she wouldn't have to fake satisfaction for a change.

Wouldn't that be nice?

Flushing, she nibbled a fingernail, cast him another admiring glance, then turned slowly and slipped through the batwings.

Yakima was about to follow her when two men staggered out the doors and brushed past him, nearly knocking the wood from his arms. One laughing, the other singing drunkenly, they stepped off the porch and headed for the corral.

Yakima turned away from them, pushed through the batwings, and threaded his way through the bullwhackers, miners, and drifters, most of whom were camped overnight in the field behind Thornton's barn. He headed toward the woodbox at the room's rear.

Too late he saw the hobnailed boot thrust out from a chair to his left. His own left boot clipped it. He stumbled forward and fell to his hands and knees as the logs tumbled from his arms.

Laughter erupted around him.

Tensing his jaw, feeling his face burn, Yakima glanced over his left shoulder. A snaggletoothed bullwhacker wearing a battered derby and a greasy cravat turned in his chair toward Yakima and threw his head back, roaring.

"Stupid nigger! Pick those up!"

"Goddamn half-breeds never could walk a straight line!" added one of his poker-playing brethren on the other side of the table, chewing a cold cigar.

Yakima's heart thudded. Staring up at the snaggletoothed gent, feeling the veins in his forehead bulge, he set his right hand down on a stove-length chunk of cottonwood. His fingers curled around the log, tightened till his knuckles nearly popped through the skin. He began lifting the wood.

A gun hammer clicked behind him. "I wouldn't do that, breed."

Yakima turned his head slightly. From the corner of his right eye he saw the tall man he'd seen earlier. Bearded, bloodstained, wearing a ratty sombrero and three big revolvers, and toting a shotgun in a saddle boot. Bounty hunter. At the moment, he was aiming a long-barreled Remington at Yakima's right ear.

The room's din had quieted slightly, everybody waiting to see the floor painted with the half-breed's brains.

Yakima's gaze fell on his stocky boss, clad in the customary checked suit and bowler, bushy sideburns framing his long, raptorial face. Staring at Yakima, Thornton shook his head, slid his gaze to the man who'd tripped him.

"Bardoul, leave the breed alone, will ya? I don't pay him

fifty cents a day to crawl around on the floor like a fucking cripple!"

Bardoul glanced at Thornton. He flushed, wiped his hand across his mouth, and turned back toward the table and his fan of pasteboards and quarter-full whiskey glass. "Just re-mindin' the breed his station."

Yakima heard the hammer ease down against the firing pin. Releasing his grip on the cottonwood log, he turned to see the big bounty hunter slip the revolver into a shoulder holster hanging loose beneath his duster.

"You heard your boss, breed. Get to work." The man smiled, showing two tobacco-stained silver front teeth. A strawberry-shaped birthmark darkened the skin just to the right of his nose. "Otherwise I might have to look through my wanted dodgers. I bet I'd find your big heathen face star-ing out at me—five, six hundred dollars' worth, no doubt."

"Oh, come on, Wit," said one of the girls, known as Kansas Jen, throwing her arms around the bounty hunter's thick neck. "Leave the man alone and buy me a drink. I'm thirsty!"

"Like I said, breed, get to work," Bardoul said. He lev-eled a hard glance at Yakima, then ushered the whore toward the bar and yelled for beer.

Yakima glanced again at Thornton, who stood surveying the room from beside the piano, his eyes hard and quick and rheumy from drink. The roadhouse owner patted the piano player, a one-time ranch cook named Cisco Squires, to get him playing again, and gave Yakima a brusque nod toward the woodbox.

"When you're done there," he called through the rising din, jutting a long middle finger at the ceiling, "hustle two bottles of rye whiskey upstairs, room three!"

Yakima gathered the logs, stood, and glanced back at the

man who'd tripped him. The man was still chuckling, blowing smoke at the ceiling and tossing chips onto the pile in the table's center.

Balancing the wood in his arms, Yakima continued his serpentine journey to the back of the room, warily watching the floor, and dumped the wood in the box. When he'd added several logs to the stove, he went to the left end of the bar, where the two rye bottles were waiting for him. He grabbed the bottles, retrieved his toolbox from the storage room next to the backbar, and headed upstairs.

He delivered the rye to room 3, then knocked on Sabrina's door and went in. He paused, the door half open. Sabrina was sitting naked atop her dresser, wearing only her necklaces. A sandy-haired drifter, his pants and underwear bunched around his jackboots, thrust his hips between her spread knees.

The two were grunting and sighing, the dresser hitting the back wall with repeated cracks. Seeing Yakima but continuing to grunt and sigh, groaning, "Oh, God, that's so *good*," Sabrina winked over the drifter's right shoulder and flicked a hand toward the bed. The half-breed shut the door, crossed the room, and inspected the broken leg.

He finished hammering a nail through the leg and wrapping it with rawhide about the same time the drifter dropped several coins in Sabrina's jar and bid her good night.

Yakima followed him out and was heading down the stairs when the blond whore known as Faith met him on the steps. Of Thornton's eight girls, Yakima felt closest to Faith, as she often smuggled him steaks from the kitchen and had doctored a festering cut he'd received while working at the blacksmith's anvil. The lithe, high-busted blonde was pulling a stocky gent along behind her, holding her pink see-through duster closed with her free hand.

She gave Yakima a wan, conspiratorial smile and continued her graceful ascent of the creaky stairs, the stocky gent behind her staring wide-eyed at her ass and cooing, "Damn, it's been pure-dee two months since my last mattress dance!"

"Well, you're due then, aren't you?" Faith said, unable to keep the boredom from her voice.

Stepping aside to let two other pairs pass, Yakima glanced at the top of the stairs. The man with Faith peered across the main hall. He nodded, as if to signal someone, then followed Faith down the hall.

Yakima shifted his own gaze to the saloon's main floor. Three men were making a beeline for the stairs, moving fast, one tripping over a chair and nearly falling. They were big, dusty, hard-eyed men. One wore bandoliers crossed on his chest and a big, bone-handled bowie in a sheath under his left arm. As they passed Yakima on the stairs, one was chuckling softly. They all stank of horseshit, old sweat, and whiskey.

Yakima looked around the room for Thornton. The roadhouse proprietor and the most notorious pimp on the Front Range was helping the two bartenders splash drinks into glasses. He was too busy to notice the three men bounding up the stairs alone.

No one was allowed upstairs without the company of a girl—one girl to each man unless otherwise arranged with Thornton.

Someone grabbed the collar of Yakima's shirt, jerked it violently back, twisting the half-breed's head around. It was the big red-faced man with the bowie in the shoulder harness.

"Listen, breed, you stay away from the second floor for a while. No half-breeds allowed, less'n you wanna be sent to the rock gods with a bellyful of bowie." He prodded Yakima's side with his knifepoint. It felt like a bee sting; Yakima's gut tightened against it. "Comprende?"

The man turned and, slipping the knife into its sheath, climbed the stairs.

Chapter 2

"Breed!"

Yakima turned toward the bar, before which the thirsty customers crowded four-deep, yelling and waving greenbacks. Thornton stood behind the rough-pine counter, a bottle in his hand.

He glared at Yakima. "If you got nothin' better to do than stand on the stairs with your thumb up your ass, get outside and help the hostlers with the stage that just pulled in. After that, clear tables. We're runnin' out of glasses!"

Yakima pointed to the second story, to indicate the four men who'd gone upstairs with Faith, but Thornton had already resumed slopping booze and cajoling the regular barkeep to hustle his fat ass. Yakima glanced back up the stairs, then continued on down. He could muscle his way up to Thornton, but that would take several minutes, and Thornton had a habit of not listening to what he didn't want to hear, anyway.

Yakima returned the toolbox to the storage room, then pushed through the crowd and stepped outside, the batwings squawking behind him. The idea of Faith upstairs with the four men, three of whom she obviously hadn't been expecting, gnawed at his gut.

He started for the stagecoach, before which the passengers stood, dusting themselves off while the driver and shotgun messenger smoked and issued orders to Thornton's hostlers. He had taken only two steps when he wheeled suddenly and headed around to the back of the roadhouse. He took the back stairs two steps at a time, walking lightly on the balls of his feet.

Thornton normally kept the second-story door locked, as that entrance was used only for hauling wood and laundry, but Yakima had a key. He opened the door, stepped into the hall lit by red hurricane lamps in which candles smoked and guttered. A greasy blue carpet runner ran the length of the hall. Seeing no one in the hallway but hearing plenty of action behind the doors, Yakima moved to the far end and paused at the door to room 9.

On the other side, a man was speaking with eager anticipation. ". . . I tell you she was the best-lookin' whore in the Territory. She used to work for Crazy Kate over to Fort Dodge."

Another voice, lower-pitched, said, "We're in for a real treat here tonight, boys . . ."

Faith said something Yakima couldn't hear, but her hard tone told him she wasn't happy. There was a sharp crack. "Told you to shut up, bitch!"

Yakima bent down, raised his buckskin cuff above his right boot, and removed his Arkansas toothpick—six inches of ugly, double-edged steel, bone-handled and boasting a brass hilt.

Straightening, he turned the doorknob. The latch clicked. Yakima swung the door half open and stepped into the nearly dark room. On the dresser to his left, a single candle offered the only light.

Before him, Faith lay naked on the floor. One of the four

men knelt between her spread legs, his back to Yakima. The man's cartridge belt was coiled on the floor beside him, and he was fumbling with his fly buttons. Two of the other three were kneeling on either side of Faith, pinning her down, one holding his hand across her mouth.

The fourth—the red-faced hombre who'd stopped Yakima on the stairs—stood before her. He had his boots and pants off and was removing his shirt.

Looking up, he saw Yakima, and his eyes snapped fire. "Told you to make yourself scarce, Injun!"

The man holding his hand over Faith's mouth snarled, "Step out and move off, breed. Thornton owes us for an overdue freight note. We're just settling the debt."

Yakima stayed where he was and closed the door without turning around. He held his toothpick down low at his side. "I don't think the girl much cares for the way you're settling Thornton's bill."

The man kneeling between Faith's legs, staring furiously up at Yakima, was inching his hand toward his cartridge belt.

Yakima's voice was even. "If you like that hand, keep it where it is."

"Careful, Horsehead," said the man holding his hand over Faith's mouth. "These breeds know how to wield a pig stick—ow!" He jerked his hand from Faith's mouth. "Bitch bit me!"

Faith's eye found Yakima's. "Get Thornton and Willie." Willie was the hardcase Thornton hired to ride shotgun on the saloon—and the girls and anyone else in Thornton's employ.

"Now, now, let's not get hasty," said the red-faced man standing over Faith's head, staring at Yakima. "Tell you what, breed, if you just sit over there in the corner, quiet as a mouse, we'll let you have her when we're done. How'd that be?"

Yakima held his stare with a dark one of his own. "Get out."

"That ain't sportin'."

"You got one knife," said the red-faced hombre, with a devilish grin, slowly turning toward the bed and his weaponry. "We all got guns."

"I'll tell you one more time," Yakima said, his voice an even, menacing purr. "Get out."

"Yakima, don't," Faith said, glancing fearfully up at the men kneeling and standing around her.

In the next room, a bed was pounding the floor, and one of the girls was laughing hysterically. The din from the saloon below caused a perpetual vibration in the puncheons beneath Yakima's boots.

The one-eyed man squatting at Faith's left shoulder slowly straightened and stepped back. His right arm moved suddenly. Yakima couldn't see it, because the man called Horsehead obscured his view, but One-Eye was obviously grabbing the six-shooter from his low-slung holster.

Yakima shot his left hand out, throwing Horsehead into One-Eye. Horsehead bolted back with a grunt, boots thumping and spurs chinging, and the red-faced man made a dive for one of his three guns nestled among the leather atop the bed.

In a blur of motion, Yakima tossed the toothpick end over end. As the red-faced man hit the bed and rolled to his right, bringing up a short-barreled Schofield in his right fist, the toothpick plunked into his middle upper chest, six inches below his throat. The man groaned and threw his head back, his pistol exploding, the slug sizzling to Yakima's right and plowing into the doorframe with an angry *whack!*

On the saloon's first floor, the din instantly quieted and the laughing woman next door fell silent.

The man to the right of Faith bolted up and forward, launching his head and shoulder toward Yakima, who turned at the last second, grabbed the man's collar, and, pivoting, rammed his head into the room's closed door, splitting the panel down the middle.

As the man fell straight down, hissing in pain, Yakima saw Horsehead pushing himself to his feet and grabbing the cross-draw revolver from his left hip. Yakima leapt three feet in the air, throwing his arms out, pivoting and bringing his left foot up and to the right, slamming the heel savagely against the man's left jaw.

The jaw cracked like brittle sandstone. The man cried out and flew across the room, smashing the washstand, knocking the porcelain bowl to the floor, and landing on top of the shards.

Watching One-Eye in the corner of his vision, Yakima leapt off his left foot and brought his right heel against the silvery flash of a pistol. One-Eye cursed as the gun flew against the wall, tearing the wallpaper and cracking the plaster.

Yakima slammed both feet to the floor, faced the wailing hardcase from a yard away.

The man threw a haymaker, yelling, "You fuckin' half-breed son of a bitch!"

Yakima brought his right foot up, ramming it squarely into the man's groin. As the man's head dropped, Yakima punched his forehead hard. The man twisted around and fell hard on his chest, then rolled onto his side, wailing and clutching his privates.

Yakima glanced around.

Faith was sitting against the far wall, near the end of the bed, knees to her chest, mouth gaping. All four hardcases were out of commission. The one on the bed, with the knife through his chest, didn't appear to be breathing. Neither did the one by the door, whose neck was bent at a strange angle.

The one whose jaw Yakima had smashed was kneeling in the corner, as though a naughty schoolboy being punished, his head down, shaking like a leaf in a spring blizzard. The only one making any noise was the man whose oysters Yakima had smashed. He cursed and groaned and miserably sucked air through his teeth.

Yakima reached down, removed two more pistols and a knife from a sheath on the man's cartridge belt. He dropped the weapons on the floor, kicked them under the bed.

"What the hell's goin' on up here?"

It was Thornton's voice, booming in the building's eerie silence. Even the piano had stopped. Yakima realized he'd heard the man yell twice before as boots pounded the stairs. Now, several men were marching down the hall, boots and chinging spurs getting louder.

"Yakima!" Faith said sharply. "You have to get out of here now. These men have friends downstairs. *Bad* hombres!"

Yakima moved to the bed, pulled his knife from the dead man's chest, wiped the blood on the man's long underwear. The door burst open, nudging aside the man with the broken neck. In stepped Thornton, holding a pepperbox revolver in his beringed right hand. The house bouncer—a big, walleyed hombre known as Willie—bolted in behind him, stepping to Thornton's left and swinging his sawed-off shotgun around the room.

Several men and two girls stood in the hall behind them, peering in.

"Jesus Christ!" Thornton exclaimed, glancing around the room. His eyes settled on Yakima. "What in the hell is goin' on up here?"

"They all tried to take me, Bill," Faith said, hugging her

knees to her chest. "Only One-Eye paid. They said they were gonna mark me when they were done—as a message to you."

"Fuckers," Thornton said. "They thought I underpaid 'em for that last freight run they made for me." He looked at Yakima. "Thought I told you to help with the stage."

"I saw these boys follow Faith up the stairs."

"That's what Willie's for."

"I didn't see Willie."

A man muscled between Thornton and Willie—a short, blond kid in a bowler hat, chaps, suspenders, and a thread-bare underwear shirt. "Christalmighty!"

"Get out of here, Bilk!" Thornton shouted.

"The half-breed done this?"

"You heard the man—get outta here!" Willie turned and shouldered Bilk out of the room.

Thornton turned his angry, sweat-glistening face to Yakima. "You, too, breed. Clear out."

"He saved my hide, Bill," Faith protested, pushing her back to the wall and slowly gaining her feet. "It ain't fair to kick him out!"

"He's trouble," Thornton barked, glaring at Yakima. "You heard me, breed."

Yakima held out his left hand, keeping the toothpick in his right. "I'll be drawin' my time."

Thornton glared at him, his face flushing. Finally, he reached into his jacket, produced a wallet, and withdrew several bills. He slapped the money into Yakima's hand.

"Don't let me catch your troublemakin' hide in these parts again, breed." Thornton gritted his teeth and slitted his eyes. "'Less you want it perforated with Willie's double-ought buck."

Yakima glanced over his left shoulder. Willie aimed the

barn-blaster at him, grinning. The shotgun's hammers were cocked.

Yakima stuffed the folded bills into a pocket, shoved past Willie, and moved to the door. He paused, glanced at Faith, who stared at him sadly, brows furrowed, the corners of her mouth turned down. Yakima pushed through the onlookers, and made his way down the hall toward the stairs.

The crowd consisted of several girls and their customers in various stages of dress. A string-bean saddle tramp stood naked before an open room, sucking a cigarette and holding his hat over his privates.

He grabbed Yakima's arm. His bloodshot eyes were wide with skepticism.

"It true what Bilk said? You killed all four of 'em with a *knife*?"

Yakima jerked his arm free of the man's clutches and rammed his face up close to the drifter's, showing the man the toothpick still flecked with blood. "Yeah, and I cut their livers out and ate 'em!" He lifted his boot, slid the knife inside, then continued down the hall and descended the stairs two steps at a time.

Another job shot to hell.

Where would he go? What would he do next? After eight weeks working here, he'd managed to save only twelve dollars. The flimsy roll of greenbacks, including what Thornton had just paid him, was tucked away with his knife in his right boot well.

Halfway down the stairs, he stopped. Under the cloud of webbing tobacco smoke, the main hall had gone quiet as Easter morning. The men and a few girls stared at him from tables or their positions at the bar. Even the piano player had turned to regard him over the right shoulder of his soiled brown suit coat.

Someone coughed.

A few men in the back corner to his right, near the smoky woodstove, were conversing in low tones. One of them stood—a spidery gent with coal black hair and a ragged slouch hat shoved back on his head. He swept both flaps of his antelope jacket back, revealing the smooth walnut butts of two Colt revolvers positioned for the cross-draw.

Staring over the railing, Yakima turned the corners of his mouth up. Damn—why hadn't he taken the outside stairs? After a lifetime of trouble, you'd think he would have gotten better at avoiding it.

The man on the floor slowly, deliberately, drew both guns, his jaw tight, his angry eyes fixed on Yakima. "Had you a little party up there, did you, breed?" He slid his gaze around the room. "According to Marty Bilk, the rock worshiper did a little sharp blade work on Smith, Snead, Dallymeyer, and Horsehead."

"Horsehead?" someone grumbled. A chair scraped back, and a big man at the bar set his beer mug down and turned toward the stairs. "That's my brother-in-law."

"*Was* your brother-in-law, accordin' to Bilk," said the man in the black slouch hat, aiming both long-barreled revolvers at Yakima. "All four were *my* business partners."

"Trick Dallymeyer's my half brother, you fuckin' redskin!" shouted a man up near the front of the room. He stood drunkenly, tossing the whore from his lap, and grabbed the old Springfield rifle leaning against his table.

"I'm thinkin'," said the man in the slouch hat, staring down his extended pistol barrels at Yakima, "it's time to invite this breed to a necktie party."

Yakima glanced around the room. More men were rising from their tables and drawing their guns, several moving to-

ward the stairs. The three half-dressed girls ran back behind
the bar, breasts jiggling, hair bouncing on their shoulders.

Dallymeyer's half brother drew his own pistol and
shouted, "Forget the rope. I'm gonna ventilate the son of a
savage bitch where he stands!"

Chapter 3

Cursing, Dallymeyer's half brother extended his cocked pistol. Yakima hoisted himself over the railing. The shooter's revolver popped, the slug slicing the air where Yakima's head had been a quarter second before and plunking into a step.

Four feet out from the stairs, Yakima dropped straight down, both feet smashing into a baize-covered table as the man in the slouch hat fired both his pistols at once.

As Yakima's boots rammed through the table, the four men who'd been sitting there drinking and playing cards leapt to their feet. In the corner of his eye as he jumped off the falling table, Yakima saw one of the shooter's slugs baste the head of one of the gamblers. The other men yelled as the wounded man stumbled back against the stairs, blood flying.

Everyone in the room seemed to be yelling now, and a good half of them seemed to be shooting.

Yakima hit the floor on his feet, took two running strides, and leapt onto another table. Pistols and rifles popped around him, slugs stitching the air over his head, smashing the backbar mirror and several pictures on the room's opposite wall.

Yakima sprang left and forward, bounded off another

table to his right, sprang again and headed for the faro layout behind a square-hewn support post.

Behind him, Thornton bellowed like a poleaxed bull, "*Hold your damn fire—you're shootin' up my place!*"

Several men screamed as cross-fired bullets found flesh.

The shooting and the shouting continued, the slugs plowing into wood and glass and plaster as Yakima hopscotched the tables and chairs, overturning two tables and breaking three chairs in his wake, twice nearly losing his footing.

"*Git* that goddamn half-breed!" shouted the man with the muzzle-loading Springfield.

He triggered the shot as Yakima bounded off the faro table. The ball burned across Yakima's left temple. Another bullet nipped nap from his buckskin tunic as the half-breed flung his arms up and wrapped his hands around the wooden ring of a chandelier. Yakima hurled himself forward, kicking the cocked pistol out of a shooter's hand and dislodging the straw sombrero from the man's head.

Yakima landed on his feet, knees bent, two yards from the front wall.

"Goddamn it, get him!" rose a brittle, frustrated screech above the din.

Yakima took two more quick strides and, throwing his arms above his head, dove through the window. He landed on the porch in a hail of glass and lead, and rolled off a shoulder. He bounded out to where half a dozen horses were tied at the three hitchracks fronting the roadhouse, the others having jerked loose at the sound of the gunfire.

The stage horses nickered and whinnied, skitter-hopping. The hostlers held their headstalls, trying to quiet them down.

"What is goin' on in there?" shouted the stage driver, running out of the barn.

Yakima ignored the man and, hearing boots thundering

across the porch, ripped a piebald's reins from a rack and jerked the animal onto the wagon trail. He aimed the horse westward and swung into the leather.

Behind him, a rifle boomed and a pistol popped. More boots pounded. Men shouted. Yakima ground his heels into the pie's ribs and yelled, "Gooooo, horse!"

Snorting and bucking, the pie lunged off its rear hooves and, well before reaching the edge of the yard, stretched its stride into a gallop. Behind Yakima, more guns barked and men shouted.

"Get that kill-crazy savage!"

Yakima lowered his head as bullets cracked into the ground around him, several whining loudly as they ricocheted off rocks. Two more plunked into a boulder on the right side of the trail. He put the boulder behind him, followed the trail's northward curve, and kept his head down as the roadhouse yard and lights faded.

In less than a minute he was winding into the foothills, shrubs and boulders stippling the hogbacks around him. Then the black columns of pines and Douglas firs pushed up along both sides of the steeply climbing trail, and the horse began to blow.

Ahead, the trail forked. He took the right fork and descended into a hollow. At the bottom the trail leveled out, and the pie regained its wind.

Yakima followed the meandering path for several minutes, then halted the horse on the bank of a trickling creek. He turned his head back the way he'd come, listening.

Two sets of hooves thudded in the near distance, the horses blowing and the tack squeaking as two of the riders broke away from the main group and headed into the hollow.

Yakima cursed and kneed the pie into motion. Five

minutes later he'd followed another side trail out of the hollow and onto a flat.

Hearing one set of hooves closing on him from behind—the second rider must've taken the other fork—he urged the pie into a shambling, halfhearted gallop. Yakima cursed again. No matter how much urging and coaxing he did, whipping the pie with his rein ends, the horse's pace remained plodding, frustratingly slow.

Behind, the sounds of the approaching rider grew louder. A pistol cracked.

Hunkering low over the pie's neck, Yakima glanced over his right shoulder.

The rider was fifty yards behind, a bobbing silhouette against the star-flecked sky. The man's pistol flashed. A half second later, the crack reached Yakima's ears, the slug spanging off a rock to his left.

He urged the pie forward. A minute later, he was descending a slope in the rippling prairie when the pie suddenly fell out from beneath him, screaming. Yakima's chest slammed against the mount's neck, his momentum throwing him over the horse's head. He hit the ground on his back.

The ground pitched to either side, and his ears rang.

Groggily, he rose to his elbows. The horse lay six feet away, on its side, head turned at an odd angle, its neck broken. Its right front hoof had plundered a gopher hole. On the sand and dirt that the hoof had ripped out of the ground as the horse's momentum had propelled it forward, the leg lay Y-shaped, the bone exposed, blood glistening.

The thunder of hooves drew Yakima's eyes to his back trail.

The dark shape of horse and rider grew, the man hunkered low over his horse's neck, extending a pistol straight out from the horse's right shoulder. Starlight winked off the barrel. The revolver flashed and popped, the slug throwing up dirt and grass two feet beyond Yakima's left shoulder.

Yakima flinched and scrambled onto his haunches. As the rider neared, extending his revolver at Yakima's head, the half-breed ducked. The gun popped, blowing up dirt at Yakima's boots.

Horse and rider continued past Yakima in a rush of wind and sifting dust, the ground vibrating beneath the pounding hooves. As the rider pulled back on the reins, Yakima bolted to the dead horse. It had fallen on its rifle boot, but he could see the rifle's stock sticking up in front of the hip.

Wrapping both hands around the stock, he glanced behind him. The rider was turning his horse toward Yakima, thumbing back his revolver's hammer.

Yakima dug his boot heels into the prairie sod and gave the stock a hard tug. Behind him, the rider triggered another shot. Yakima winced as the bullet seared through his right arm. He gave the rifle another hard jerk. It popped free of the sheath. Yakima swung around, falling back against the horse and levering a round into the Winchester's breech.

The rider thundered toward him, sneering, "Stinkin' goddamn *savage*!"

He'd just extended the revolver again when Yakima triggered the Winchester. The man grunted and winced. The pistol sagged in his hand, stabbing flames and drilling a slug into the dead pie's belly.

As the man's horse continued on past Yakima, nickering and skitter-stepping sideways, Yakima ejected the spent shell. He started to ram fresh brass into the breech when he realized he'd fired his last shot. The rifle was empty. He looked at the rider.

The man stared back at Yakima, the darkness obscuring the expression on his face. He held the pistol straight down from his thigh. The pistol tumbled to the ground. The man sagged slowly in his saddle and disappeared down the opposite side of his horse, hitting the ground with a heavy thump and a sigh. The horse bucked, wheeled, and ran.

Yakima tossed away the Winchester.

He clutched the bloody wound, halfway between his shoulder and elbow. Pain seared through him, lanced up and down his arm and through his chest.

He looked down at the rider, who lay with his arms and one leg splayed, the other leg curled beneath his body. Blood gleamed low on his chest. The pistol lay in a tuft of bunchgrass.

Yakima picked up the gun, turned it in his hand so he could see the back end of the cylinder. Only one shell was left.

Hearing men yelling and hooves thudding, he cast a wary gaze back the way he and the dead man had ridden. He couldn't see anything, but judging by the sounds, the others had heard the shooting and were heading toward him.

Yakima looked around. The bench was flat and sparsely stippled with bunchgrass and sage, occasional pockets of chokecherry. To the east, the direction he'd been heading when he'd lost the pie, the rimrock rose on the other side of a brushy swale. A man could hide in the rocks at the top of that butte.

Wedging the pistol in the waistband of his buckskin breeches, Yakima turned to the dead man. He crouched, jerked off the man's neckerchief, and quickly wrapped it around the bullet wound, tying it one-handed.

Pulling the knot tight, he ran toward the butte, leaping sage shrubs and the occasional rocks. He didn't sprint but held himself to a jog, not wanting to spend himself before he reached the butte's base two, maybe three miles away.

He wished he had his moccasins instead of the stockman's boots, which weren't made for walking, much less running. But the moccasins were back in his quarters in

Thornton's barn, along with his mountain-bred mustang and his prized Winchester '73.

Gradually, the thuds and voices got louder. Yakima increased his pace, sucking air through clenched teeth, every jolting step sending fire through his wounded arm.

The night turned around him, the ground rising and falling like a pitch-black, storm-churned sea. He was growing dizzy from the pain and the blood loss. Every third or fourth step he stumbled.

Behind him, gunfire rose.

He threw a quick glance over his shoulder. Five riders galloped toward him, yelling and whooping like flesh-hungry lobos, triggering pistols and rifles. The shots plunked the sod around Yakima, clipping rocks and snapping sage branches.

Yakima stumbled, ran, stumbled again, continued running, keeping his gaze locked on the black anvil-shaped rimrock looming before him, seemingly the same distance away as when he'd started running. His breath hissed in and out through his teeth, through his nose. It sounded like a dull saw grinding through green lumber.

Cutting wood had been his last job. At the moment, he wished he had kept it.

Sweat dribbled down from his forehead and into his eyes, obscuring his vision. It runneled the dust on his cheeks, soaked his back and chest, his shirt flapping like a wet sheet.

His right arm grew heavy. He looked down, half expecting to see a poison-tipped arrow protruding from the bone.

Guns popped, the bullets closer, whistling past his ears. Horses' hooves shook the ground beneath his boots.

He stumbled, dropped to a knee, pushed off the ground with his right hand, the pain searing anew, and continued running.

A bullet clipped his boot heel. It threw his stride off. He

fell, looked up. A line of brush appeared straight ahead, twenty yards away. Beyond it, the base of the rimrock.

Can't be more than a mile away now. . . .

He gave a quiet, rasping whoop, urging himself on. He climbed to his feet and ran through the brush, the branches whipping his legs.

Behind him, the riders closed. Their horses seemed to be blowing in his ears. He could hear the men breathing, the leather squeaking like trees rubbing together, the bits rattling against the horses' teeth, the bridle chains jangling like rusty sleigh bells.

"Got the son of a bitch!" a man yelled.

"Blow his head off!"

Yakima lifted his head and closed his eyes, pumping his legs and arms.

Behind him a man yelled shrilly, "*Woooo-ahhh!* Pull up, boys!"

Behind Yakima, a horse screamed. Hooves skidded across sod, snapping brush and grinding rocks.

Yakima's stride didn't slow.

His boots stopped thudding. The ground disappeared.

For two strides, he ran through air, began falling, cool air from below wafting over him, lifting his shirt flaps, blowing his hair above his head.

He opened his eyes, looked down. Below, a narrow fissure of silvery-liquid darkness rose toward him.

Chapter 4

"What a bloody mess," Bill Thornton said as he and one of his two bartenders hauled the fourth and last carcass out of Faith's second-story room. "What a bloody goddamn mess!"

"It shore is," said the barman. Avery Sykes was a square-headed gent with massive tattooed forearms and thick red hair and mustache. Like Thornton, Sykes was nearly covered in blood from all the bodies he and Thornton and the other bartender and hostlers had hauled out of the road-house.

"You ever seen anything like it?"

"Nope," said Sykes. "I've worked in saloons from Tucson to Fort Dodge, but I can't say as I ever seen a fracas like this one here." As he and Thornton descended the stairs, Thornton holding the dead man's arms while the barman walked backward, clutching the dead man's ankles, Sykes frowned thoughtfully. "You know, there mighta been one bad as this—in Abilene. Yes, come to think of it, there *was*!"

"Shut up," growled Thornton, slipping in dripped blood on the tenth step from the top. "I don't wanna hear about it. When I get my hands on that half-breed son of a bitch, he's gonna rue the day he ever set eyes on this place."

The roadhouse proprietor scraped his boot on a dry step,

then continued down the stairs, grunting and cursing. "Out of the goodness of my heart I gave that dog-eater a job, and this is the thanks I get."

He cast a glance over the stair rail. The saloon's main hall looked as though a pie-eyed waddie had gone through on a bucking bronc, triggering a brace of six-shooters. Thornton and the others had hauled out most of the broken tables and chairs before they'd removed the bodies.

Now, where three-quarters of the furniture had stood, blood was pooled. Lakes of it. The room was littered with broken glass, playing cards, coins, paper money, bottles, shot glasses, and beer schooners. A blood-splattered stockman's hat sat precariously atop a window ledge. Thornton hadn't yet gotten around to removing the wagon wheel chandelier the Indian had pulled out of the ceiling. It leaned against a four-by-four joist as though it had recently broken off a wagon axle. Only luck had kept the spilled coal oil from igniting and the entire saloon from going up in flames.

Not long after the dust had settled, half the bullwhackers, saddle tramps, and drummers who'd helped destroy the place had lit a shuck, while six men with saddle horses— drovers from the nearby Roberts Basin Ranch, the bounty hunter Wit Bardoul, and Thornton's two hostlers—had gone after the breed.

"Yakima saved my life, Bill."

The blond whore, Faith, peered at Thornton over the rim of her soapy water bucket. She and the other whores were scrubbing and mopping up the blood pools, their clothes disheveled, their hair in their eyes, injured expressions on their faces. "If it wasn't for him, I'd likely have been butchered."

"They weren't gonna kill you." Thornton chuckled dryly, casting a nervous glance at the other girls. He and Sykes crossed the main hall, weaving around the whores and the blood pools as they headed toward the tied-open batwing doors. He noted his own halting tone as he added, "They were just gonna steal a few pokes, that's all. I'd have sent Willie after 'em later."

"They were gonna kill me," Faith called behind Thornton. "I could tell by the looks in their eyes. They were gonna cut my heart out and leave it for you in my *washbowl*!"

"The girl always was a little on the hysterical side," Thornton said woodenly, covering his own chagrin as he and Sykes swung the dead man onto the wagon parked before the stoop. He hadn't convinced himself, however. The possibility of someone killing his best whore to spite him made his jaws lock in anger. He should have had Willie keep a closer eye on the stairs.

Half a dozen bodies already graced the wagon's bloody box. They were stacked like cordwood, the sightless staring eyes, belt buckles, and spurs glistening in the light. If no one claimed them by noon tomorrow, Thornton would have Willie and the hostlers toss the lot in a distant, deep ravine— a real smorgasbord for area predators.

The last body tumbled over the others, thumping and rustling, a boot smacking a sideboard with a hollow thud. Thornton brushed his hands on his breeches and turned to Sykes, who sucked a deep breath. "A little loopy, Faith, but she makes more money on a weekend than all the other girls put together. Somethin' about her makes men turn to sugar."

Hooves thudded in the darkness. Thornton turned his head toward the sound, watched as three figures took shape beyond the roadhouse yard. The thuds grew louder as the three riders trotted their horses past the corral and the hay barn, the mounts snorting and blowing, the tack squeaking.

Behind Thornton, the stoop's floorboards squawked. The roadhouse proprietor turned to see Faith move to the edge of the porch, clutching a light wrapper around her shoulders as she cast her expectant gaze at the riders.

The bounty hunter, Wit Bardoul, checked his buckskin down a few yards to the right of the wagon. Thornton's two hostlers, Ace Higgins and Roy Brindley—burly farmhands from Iowa who'd given up prospecting last year when they'd been burned by two bad mountain winters—did likewise. All three were breathing hard and sweating atop their lathered horses.

As Bardoul's buckskin dipped its muzzle into the stock trough between the hitchrack and the stoop, the tall, snaggletoothed bounty hunter poked his battered sombrero off his forehead.

"He's dead," he said smugly through a deep sigh.

"You kill him?"

The bounty hunter chuckled. "He killed himself."

"Fell into Bear Creek," said Roy Brindley, doffing his railroader's pin-striped hat and shaking sweat from his long brown hair like a dog. "This time of year, that creek don't hold more than two feet of water, and he fell into the gorge below Snake Butte."

Ace Higgins patted the old cap-and-ball pistol he wore in a soft leather holster on his right thigh. "I winged him first, though."

"That was a lucky shot, you stupid granger," the bounty hunter snorted. "Prob'ly a ricochet."

Higgins opened his mouth to speak, but Thornton cut him off. "Where're the other riders?"

Bardoul dismounted and tossed his reins to Higgins. "After we seen that breed get sucked down that gorge, they went on back to the ranch. Stable my horses, will you, boys? I'm gonna get me some shut-eye, then light a shuck at first light." He mounted the porch and smiled down at Faith. "How 'bout I get a free poke for my effort, Thornton?"

Faith had been staring westward. Now she turned to the bounty hunter, making a face as though she smelled something rotten. "I've taken my shingle down for the evening, Mr. Bardoul. Maybe next time you're through." She turned toward the saloon but kept her angry, defiant eyes locked on the bounty hunter for an extra second, then strode through the tied-back doors.

Bardoul shouted after her, "Bet you'd turn your shingle out for that breed!"

Thornton whipped his head around toward the man. "Shut up, Bardoul. Don't go startin' rumors, sullyin' my girls' reputations."

"Rumors?" the bounty hunter said, stepping off the porch, grabbing his saddlebags and shucking his .56 Spencer rifle from his saddle boot. Both hostlers still sat their tired mounts, watching Bardoul with vague, disdainful interest.

"Hell," Bardoul continued, running a hand down his oiled rifle to clean off the trail dust, "I thought it was common knowledge your purtiest whore's been makin' time with that half-breed." He mounted the porch. As he passed inside, he added with a throaty chuckle, "I can tell by that look on her face it's true, too."

As Bardoul disappeared inside, his boots thumping atop the puncheons and grinding broken glass, Thornton stared at the door. His mouth was open, as if he were about to speak. But he said nothing. He felt as though he'd been slapped.

Had Faith really been diddling the breed?

Fury grew in him, a rat gnawing at his guts. Thornton had never really acknowledged it to himself, but he was in love with Faith, had been ever since he'd bought her from that well-heeled pimp Ivan Platt, in Cheyenne. There was something about her intelligent, bemused eyes and the regal way she carried herself, her porcelain-pale, sumptuous body. She had an aloof air about her, as if she were just going through the motions of not only whoring but living, as if she were just biding time till her real life, her true, noble calling, suddenly swept her away. A mysterious, beguiling creature, for sure.

That she was a whore, and a damn good one, didn't lessen her attraction. Those were business transactions. Thornton made good money off of Faith, more than he'd made off of any other whore in his thirteen-year career. In a way, he saw himself and Faith as coconspirators even more than business partners. Their arrangement was their joke, and everyone else was being duped.

But the fact—or the rumor—that she'd been sleeping with the half-breed for free, and that Thornton himself had been duped, was something he couldn't get his mind around. His face burned with betrayal, and the rat in his guts was working its way up toward his throat.

The sound of hoofbeats jolted him out of his reverie. Heart pounding insistently, he turned toward the yard as Ace Higgins reined his steeldust toward the barn and corrals, jerking Bardoul's and Brindley's horses along behind. Brindley himself had climbed atop the wagon.

As Higgins trotted off across the yard, Brindley slipped the wagon ribbons from the brake handle and said without turning around, "I'll take these carcasses out behind the barn, boss."

Thornton glowered at the backs of both men. Their sheepish demeanors told him they, too, knew something he didn't.

"Haul those stinkin' stiffs off first thing in the morning," Thornton called, his voice betraying his fury. "Anyone wants 'em, they can go wrestle 'em away from the coyotes!"

Brindley raised a hand as the darkness on the other side

of the yard consumed him, the wagon rattling, the wheels squeaking under dry axle hubs.

"And while you're out there," Thornton added, "look around for that breed. I want to be certain-sure that bastard's dead before I call the dogs off for good!"

"You bet, Mr. Thornton," Higgins said, a thin shadow dismounting before the corral.

"First light, boss," assured Brindley, his voice almost inaudible as the wagon rattled off along the barn's north side.

Thornton spat and turned back to the saloon, finding himself alone out here. Just him and the wind lifting dust in the yard, jostling tumbleweeds. Somehow, the bartender, Sykes, had drifted off without Thornton's realizing it. Now the roadhouse proprietor raked a hand through his sweat-soaked mustache and goatee, mounted the stoop, and stepped between the doors.

Five of his six girls were still scrubbing at the bloodstains with mops and rags while Sykes swept glass to Thornton's left, near one of the woodstoves. Faith must have gone upstairs.

The other bartender, Devlin McNair—a dandy with thin, pomaded hair and a carefully trimmed beard—was picking unbroken bottles out of the mess atop the backbar and stacking them on shelves before the bullet-shattered mirror.

They were sneering at him. Maybe not outwardly, but they were sneering, mocking him.

Bunching his fists at his thighs but trying to keep a lid on his anger, Thornton strode wide of a long mare's tail of blood and brains on the floor and planted an elbow on the bar. "Give me a bottle, Mac."

The thin-faced barman turned from the mirror, his pale features flushed, thin lips stretched from his teeth in a wince. Or was he sneering, too?

How long had Faith been diddling the breed, anyway, and why was he the last to know? Thornton prided himself on keeping tabs on his help, from the whores to the two Mennonites he hired to haul away his trash.

McNair grabbed a bottle off the backbar, and the wince became a smile of sorts. "In luck, boss. Found a couple that didn't get shot to pieces."

Thornton grabbed the bottle and headed for the stairs. Around him, the girls and Sykes worked dutifully, keeping their eyes downcast. Except for the sounds of Sykes sweeping up the glass and the girls scrubbing the blood, the room was silent. The tension was drawn tight as razor wire.

Thornton stopped beside Kansas Jen, whose red-blond hair hung down both sides of her face, covering her freckled cheeks. Her flannel housecoat and bare feet were blood-splattered, as were her hands grinding the brush against the stained puncheons.

"Jen," Thornton said.

The girl gave a start, jerking her head up, peering at Thornton through her hair. "Yes, Mr. Thornton?"

The other girls snapped enervated looks at him. The swish of Sykes's broom stopped abruptly. The room was as silent as a sarcophagus.

Thornton waited a second, staring stone-faced at Kansas Jen. He gave a sadistic chuckle. He moved his right shoe ahead and to the right, tapping the toe on the floor. "Missed a spot."

"Oh, for godsakes, Mr. Thornton!" the girl whined.

Laughing, feeling as though he'd retrieved some of his former authority, Thornton clutched his whiskey bottle by the neck and mounted the stairs.

Now he'd fetch back the rest from Faith.

Chapter 5

At the top of the stairs, Thornton stopped and looked at the doors on both sides of the hall, light from a half-dozen bracket lamps shuddering across the pine slabs. Behind the second door on his right, deep snores rose, tinkling the red mantles over the lamps.

Bardoul was holed up in his usual room.

Thornton moved down the hall to room 9, Faith's room. He took a deep breath, again putting his anger on a short leash, and placed a hand on the doorknob.

He tried turning it. Locked.

He cleared his throat, canted his head toward the gilded number 9 and the tuft of dried wildflowers that hung there. "Faith?"

He waited. On the other side of the door, silence.

The odd thing about Faith—*one* of the odd things—was that she'd somehow managed to draw invisible boundaries for herself, no small feat with Thornton, who treated his employees little better than slaves.

But when Faith's door was locked, or when she quietly demanded a rare night to herself, or decided to take dinner to her room rather than dine with the other girls and Thornton, Thornton found himself respecting her wishes.

He rationalized his acquiescence by reminding himself that she was his most valuable whore. Actually, it probably wouldn't have mattered had she earned next to nothing.

Faith—if she had another name, she'd never mentioned it—was inexplicably different from the other girls, and Thornton was under her spell. The difference couldn't be attributed to her beauty alone.

And now, with a tooth-grinding amalgam of fury and chagrin, the roadhouse proprietor removed his hand from her doorknob and ambled away. Better to confront her in the morning, anyway, when the passions of the evening had dissipated and he could think through the situation with a clear head.

If she really had slept with the breed, he'd have to figure out a creative way to punish her.

Thornton turned left down the branching hall and stopped at his own door. He fumbled his keys from his pocket, paused to pop the cork from the bottle, took a long drink. He smacked his lips, swallowed, and made several unsuccessful attempts at poking the key into the lock. When he finally got the door open, he stumbled into his large bedroom/office, took another pull from the bottle, then cursed loudly and slammed the door behind him.

When the door opened again, yellow morning light angled through the dust-streaked window at the east end of the hall. A wind had risen during the night; it was still banging around the roadhouse, rattling windows and bracket lamps, shuttling chill autumn drafts, and pelting the walls with sand and tumbleweeds.

Thornton stood in the doorway, feeling a little wobbly, his buzzardlike physique clad in sweat-stained long underwear and a faded red robe hanging open to reveal a bulbous paunch below a hollow, bony chest. His hair and goatee were mussed, his eyes red and rheumy.

On the dresser on the far side of the room, the whiskey bottle stood empty beside an ashtray overflowing with slender black cigar butts. A water glass lay broken on the floor beneath it. Against the right wall, his broad bed was a mess of strewn and twisted covers.

Thornton looked down the hall to his left. His voice rose like the sound of heavy water pouring around boulders. "That lousy fucking bitch betrayed me."

He slipped his hand into the deep right pocket of his robe and walked along the hall. He took the corner too sharp, rammed his right shoulder into the wall. The blow staggered him slightly, but his face did not lose its stony expression. Like a zombie, Thornton set his right foot down and continued to room 9.

Not bothering to knock, he twisted the doorknob, was vaguely startled when it turned easily and the door opened. He thrust it back against the wall and moved forward.

On the floor before him, Faith knelt over a bloodstain, a scrub brush in her hand, a tub of soapy water to her right. She wore a flowered, lime yellow wrapper over a corset and pantaloons. She was barefoot, and a hand-rolled cigarette protruded from her lips.

When the door opened, she turned toward Thornton with a start. She frowned up at him, blinking against the curling cigarette smoke and the blond bangs in her eyes, her straw-colored hair pulled into a loose braid behind her head. Her cheeks were puffy and red, her eyelids pink, as though she'd spent a restless night herself.

"Bill . . . ?"

The words welled up from him like pressurized water

from a pipe, echoing like thunder around the room. "Did you diddle that dog-eater?"

She removed the cigarette from her mouth and scrunched up her eyes. "What?"

"Answer me—*did you*?"

"What are you talking about?"

"You heard me, bitch!" He staggered forward, spread his feet, and dropped his chin with menace. "Did you diddle the breed?"

The girl's eyes flashed like steel. She rose slowly, her voice bitter. "What if I did?"

"What if you *did*? What if you *did*?" Thornton stepped toward her, removing his right hand from his pocket. His fingers clasped an open, bone-handled razor. Light from the window behind her flashed across the blade. "Come here, bitch. I'm takin' you downstairs. Gonna show the others what I do to cheatin' whores!"

"Get away from me, Bill. You're drunk!"

"I said come here, bitch, or I'll cut you right *here*!" Thornton bolted toward her, wrapped his left hand around her neck. His left foot slipped in the blood and water, and he fell back against the dresser, knocking over perfume bottles and a lantern. A tortoiseshell comb hit the floor. Thornton's lips snapped back from his gritted teeth. "Damn you!"

Faith spun away from him, nearly falling onto her bed and grabbing a post. "You're crazy drunk, Bill. I didn't sleep with Yakima. I don't know what you're talking about. Now get out of my room!"

"Givin' it to that dog-eater for free, were ya? Or maybe you were just keepin' it all for yourself." Spittle flew from Thornton's swollen lips. He crouched before her, like an attack dog. "I gave you extra room here. I gave you *privileges*. And this is how you pay me back?"

"What privileges?" Faith screamed, bending forward at the waist, her own eyes flashing fire. "I'm a slave here, like all the others!"

"Come *here*!" Thornton shouted, lunging toward her once more.

Faith wheeled toward the door. Thornton grabbed her arm and threw her back against the wall. He swung his left hand behind his right shoulder, slung it back, the knuckles smashing the girl's mouth.

Faith screamed as blood from her split lips splashed her cheeks. She turned to the right and dropped to her knees, cupping her mouth with both hands, sobbing and cursing.

Growling like an enraged bear, Thornton grabbed a handful of her hair, jerked her head back and up. He pushed his face down close to hers, his eyes wide with animal fury. He lifted his right hand. The blade of the razor winked in the window light.

"This is what we do to cheatin' whores in these parts, Faith. *See how you like this!*"

He shoved the razor toward her mouth, carefully lining up the blade for a clean slice across her upper lip.

Faith jerked away. "No!"

Thornton's wet left foot slipped out from under him. He half turned and fell against the wall, grunting and cursing, both feet skidding as though the puncheons were ice. They pitched as Thornton's back hit the wall, and he piled up at the base of it, raging and clutching the razor.

Faith scrambled to her right, gained her feet, and leapt Thornton's outstretched legs on her way to the door. The roadhouse proprietor grabbed her left ankle, tripping her.

"Where you goin', you mangy bitch?"

She hit the floor with a groan, hands slapping the

puncheons. She lay there for a moment, head up, eyes closed, as though dazed.

Thornton grunted as he got his legs beneath him. Glancing up, he saw two of the other girls poking their heads around the doorframe—the Cajun girl, Nettie, and Kansas Jen, who slapped a hand to her breast.

"Oh, my God, Mr. Thornton!"

Thornton laughed. "You girls got here just in time to see what happens to cheatin' whores." He rose and staggered toward Faith, stretched belly down on the floor, to the left of the bloodstain. "Demonstration time, Faith."

Out the corner of his eye, Thornton saw several other faces hovering behind Nettie and Jen. He laughed again as he held the razor up for the others to see.

"Sharpened just this morning," he bragged, flicking his thumb across the blade and contriving an expression of mock pain. "And it is indeed sharp!"

The girls shuffled around on bare or slippered feet, several sucking air through their teeth.

"Shit," said Claire, a rangy Mormon from Salt Lake, holding a cup of coffee in her hand. Her tone wasn't entirely regretful. "If you cut her face, Bill, she'll never work again."

"Give the girl a cigar," Thornton grinned.

Chuckling, he dropped to his knees between Faith's legs, and grabbed the back of her head with his right hand. He jerked her head up and had started turning her around to face him when she suddenly turned of her own accord, rising onto her butt.

Thornton arched his right brow and his pulse quickened.

The girl's eyes were slitted and her lips were pursed. He looked down. Her right hand was wrapped around the pearl grips of a silver-plated derringer.

"Demonstration time, you pig," Faith spat, clicking the single-shot's hammer back.

Thornton's lower jaw dropped in horror. He was about to shout a protest when the peashooter cracked. Smoke wafted around Faith's fist, the tang of cordite instantly assaulting Thornton's nostrils. He wasn't sure if it was the smell that made him nauseated or the sudden cold burn in his right side.

As Faith kicked away from him, Thornton looked down. There was a small, ragged hole in the left flap of his duster. Gray smoke wisped like worms around the hole. He jerked the flap away, and his heart thudded when he saw the blood oozing from a matching hole in his undershirt.

His right hand opened, and the razor tumbled to the floor. His eyes wide with amazement, he looked up at Faith as she calmly but quickly removed the derringer's spent shell and replaced it with a fresh one from the small box on her night table.

"Bitch shot me."

Faith flicked the derringer closed and aimed it in the general direction of the girls filling the doorway. They were either half dressed or, in the Mexican Carmella's case, wearing only pantaloons and a blue night sock, her bare brown breasts partially covered by a goose-pimpled arm.

Faith heard a trill in her own voice as she waved the pistol. "Any of you have a quarrel with what I just did?"

They lurched back as a group, all eyes flicking to the derringer's silver barrel.

Claire looked at Thornton, who'd fallen onto his back, yowling and cursing while clutching his bloody side. Her cup was tipped, coffee sloshing over the rim. Turning her gaze back to the whore with the wheat-colored hair, she said, "You best light a shuck, Faith."

Beneath the wind, the sound of an approaching wagon rose from the yard below Faith's window.

Claire's brown eyes snapped wide. "That'll be Willie and the hostlers!"

Kansas Jen was staring down at Thornton, her features stiff with shock. "Is he gonna die?"

"I just winged the bastard," said Faith, opening a wardrobe and hastily shoving clothes into a carpetbag. "If one of you wanna stop gawkin' and shove a rag into the bullet hole, he'll be all right . . . after I'm long gone from here!"

"She shot him," murmured Kansas Jen as the wind wracked the house and a horse whinnied outside. "She shot Mr. Thornton."

"Shut up!" Claire said, wheeling toward Jen. "Carmella, Nettie—don't just stand there. Tend the man!"

"I'm gonna kill you, bitch!" Thornton snarled through taut jaws, trying to sit up while holding a fist to the bullet hole in his side. "I'm gonna gut you like a fish and hang you from the barn eaves!" He threw his head back, his eyes bulging from their sockets. *"Willieeeeee!"*

"Shut up, Bill!" Faith said, wheeling toward him and aiming the derringer. "If you don't shut up, I'll drill one through your eye!"

Thornton's gaze flicked to the derringer, and he closed his mouth. As Carmella and Nettie edged toward him, frightened of the man and repelled by the blood, Faith turned back to the wardrobe. Reaching inside, she scooped up a hide sack filled with coins and dropped it into her carpetbag.

Willie's deep voice rose from the stairwell. "Mr. Thornton?"

Claire squeezed Faith's arm. "Will you *go*?"

Faith threw a last pair of underwear and a frayed leather hat into the carpetbag, stepped into shoes without bothering to lace them, and turned toward Thornton. He lay on his back, the two grimacing girls working on him, his head lifted to peer with mute rage at Faith. His lips were pursed and his nostrils flared as he breathed, his chest rising and falling sharply.

"Mr. Thornton?" Willie called again.

"Faith," Claire wheezed, *"go!"*

Boots pounded the stairs, echoing.

Faith kept her derringer aimed at Thornton as she moved to the door and peered left. As the boots continued pounding on the stairs, Willie's massive shadow grew on the wall.

Claire sidled up to Faith. "Take the back stairs. I'll stall him."

"No," Faith said, pushing Claire back with her left hand, keeping an eye on the hall. "They'll blame you later. Stay here."

With that, clutching the carpetbag in one hand, pistol in the other, Faith bolted out of the room and turned right along the hall.

"Good luck!" Claire whispered behind her.

Faith turned the corner just as Willie gained the top of the stairs. Voices and footsteps rose behind her as she opened the outside door at the end of the hall.

Clicking the door shut, she heard Thornton shouting something she couldn't make out, followed by *"Get that bitch!"*

Faith jerked with a start. Hefting the carpetbag and squeezing the derringer, she started down the unpainted staircase that dropped to the yard on the roadhouse's east side. The wind caught her wrapper and blew it around her like gossamer wings, sucked her breath from her lungs and pelted her face with grit.

Halfway down, her right shoe hit a loose plank. Suddenly she was rolling down the stairs, the derringer flying out of her hand, the carpetbag bouncing along before her.

With a groan, she landed in a pile at the bottom of the steps. She looked around, dazed, the misery in her right knee and her left ankle overshadowing the multiple other aches and pains. Her carpetbag was wedged between the stairs and the railing, about six steps up.

The scrapes and bruises numbed by terror, she flung herself toward the bag, lashing out with her right hand. The door at the top of the stairs flew open. Willie bolted out so fast he nearly flew over the railing. Turning toward her, he stopped and raked the revolver from his holster.

His voice was pitched with sadistic glee. "Hold it right there, missy!"

Thumbing the revolver's hammer back, he aimed down the stairs.

Faith squeezed her eyes closed and wrapped her fingers around the carpetbag's leather handle. She jerked toward the railing as the pistol cracked. The bullet sliced the air a half inch from her right temple, barking into the dust at the bottom of the stairs.

"Goddamn it!" Faith cried, pulling the bag off the step and heaving herself to her feet. She was no longer aware of the barking cuts and scrapes as she sprinted awkwardly in the heeled leather shoes along the roadhouse's east wall, the carpetbag flapping against her right thigh. She ground her teeth, awaiting another shot from Willie.

Crack!

The bullet puffed dust to Faith's left.

Willie's voice boomed above the wind. "Goddamn it, girl, don't you run from me!"

P-shtank!

The bullet ricocheted off a rock as Faith darted around the corner of the roadhouse. Hearing Willie running behind her, she paused at the corner, staring at the two hitchracks fronting the stoop, her stomach sinking and her pounding heart climbing into her throat.

She'd vaguely hoped she would find a saddled horse tied to the hitchrack, but there was only the rein-polished hitchracks and the stock tanks, the hay-littered water rippled by the wind. The wagon Willie and the hostlers had used to haul off the dead men was parked before the barn, the tongue drooping to the ground. The horses had been put away.

Casting a glance over her right shoulder, Faith cursed, her heart beating faster. She turned to the barn creaking in the wind and shrouded with blown dust. One of the two big front doors was open and knocking against the frame. Behind her, a boot kicked a stone. Faith bounded forward and ran toward the barn.

"Faith, where the hell do you think you're going?"

Her stomach tightened at Thornton's voice. He must have followed her down the outside stairs. A gun popped twice, blowing up dust and gravel on either side of her running feet. She tripped over her wrapper's hem and sprawled in the dirt, losing one shoe but somehow managing to hold on to the carpetbag.

She twisted her head around to peer behind her. Thornton stood at the corner of the roadhouse, Willie beside him. One hand clutching his bloody side, Thornton extended Willie's revolver straight out from his shoulder, squinting as he aimed down the barrel at Faith.

He smiled.

Faith sobbed and shrank back toward the ground, slitting her eyes. "Oh, shit . . ."

Behind Faith there was the metallic rasp of shell being levered into a rifle breech. The revolver in Thornton's hand puffed smoke. At the same instant, the rifle behind Faith boomed three times in close succession.

Thornton's slug smacked the barn as the rifle shots blew up dust a foot in front of the roadhouse proprietor and Willie.

The men cursed and scrambled back around the building's corner. A strong hand grabbed Faith's arm, jerking her up with a surprised exclamation. Half a second later, she was being half dragged, half carried through the barn's open door.

"Get down!"

As Faith dropped to the ground in the barn's musty shadows, she kept her disbelieving eyes on Yakima Henry, who was triggering his rifle toward the roadhouse.

Chapter 6

Yakima lowered the Winchester and stared through the wind-shredded gun smoke. The top of Thornton's head appeared around the east corner of the roadhouse. Yakima rammed a fresh round into the rifle's breech and quickly aimed.

A half second after Thornton pulled his head back behind the building, Yakima's slug blew a dogget of wood from the sun-blistered clapboards an inch from where Thornton's eyes had been.

"That oughta give 'em something to think about."

Yakima ejected the spent shell, seated a fresh .44 round in the chamber, then off-cocked the hammer. He turned to Faith. The girl stared up at him, rubbing her arm where he had grabbed her.

His lips stretched a wry smile. "You and Thornton have a spat?"

"What gave you that impression?" Her voice was tough, but then tears flooded her eyes, and she convulsed in a sob. "He tried to kill me, and I shot him with my derringer!"

Yakima grabbed her arm again. She winced as he pulled her up. "Come on."

"Where're we going?" she asked as he led her toward the

other end of the barn. She kicked out of her one unlaced shoe, and straw and goatheads pricked at her bare feet.

"Ain't sure, but we can't stay here."

"What're you doing back here, anyway? I thought you were dead."

"Just took a little swim."

In fact, he'd plummeted into Bear Creek Gorge, but twenty feet down he'd grabbed a stout tree root protruding from the bank. The root had snapped, and he'd fallen into the shallow water, but the root had broken his fall enough that he'd suffered only cuts and bruises when he'd hit the rocky creek bed.

He'd holed up along the creek till first light, then made his way back to the roadhouse. He wasn't going to let Thornton's hostlers get their hands on his prized black mustang, Wolf, and his Winchester Yellowboy repeater. Aside from the clothes on his back and in his burlap bundle, the horse and the rifle were about all he owned.

He kicked open one of the two back doors and looked around. His horse stood to his right, the reins looped over a corral slat.

Near the horse, Roy Brindley was on his hands and knees, hatless, groaning and shaking his head, the holster on his right hip empty. Earlier, when Yakima had saddled the black and been gathering his possibles from the barn's lean-to addition, Brindley had led the wagon team into the back corral. When he'd pulled his revolver, Yakima had brained him with his Winchester's brass butt plate and tossed the revolver into a stock trough.

Aside from Brindley and Thornton's stock, the corral was empty.

"Don't mind him," Yakima said, leading Faith toward Wolf and nodding at Brindley, who groaned and grunted, rubbing the steel-blue goose egg sprouting on his forehead. "He's gentle as a newborn lamb."

When Yakima had slipped the reins from the corral slat and swung into the saddle, he reached down and pulled Faith up behind him.

"I should have my own horse," she said, casting a fearful look at the barn.

"No time." Yakima kicked the corral's rear gate open and booted the black outside. Hearing footfalls, he reined the horse around as Thornton poked his head out of the barn's rear doors.

"Steady, Wolf."

Yakima held his reins taut in his left hand and lifted the Yellowboy with his right. He thumbed back the hammer, fired.

Thornton's eyes widened. He withdrew his head into the barn as Yakima's slug punched slivers from the door. Yakima recocked one-handed.

"Come after us, Thornton"—Yakima drilled another slug into the barn door with an angry *thwack!*—"and you're dead."

Setting the rifle across his saddle bows, he reined the horse around and spurred it toward the low brown buttes south of the roadhouse. When he'd ridden fifty yards, cracks rose on the wind. He and Faith glanced back.

Thornton and Willie stood at the corral's rear gate. Thornton extended the revolver in both hands, his tattered red robe blowing about his legs. Smoke puffed around the barrel as two more cracks sounded.

The roadhouse proprietor took two lunging steps forward, brought his right hand back, and flung the empty pistol out before him. Suddenly, he clutched his left side and

dropped to a knee. He kept his head raised, lips stretched
back from his teeth, shaking his right fist.

The wind tore his shouted words, so that all Yakima could
make out clearly was ". . . get you . . . dog-eater . . . takes
me . . . *life!*"

Faith turned her worried eyes to Yakima.

"His thunder's more fierce than his lightning," Yakima
assured her.

As he turned forward and gave the horse its head, the
black lunged up a cedar-stippled slope and Faith's hands
tightened their grip around Yakima's waist.

"No, it isn't," she said, and canted her head against his
back.

Yakima and Faith rode hard for several hours, stopping
twice to rest and water Wolf before continuing their ascent
into the Rocky Mountains' towering, canyon-studded Front
Range. Yakima stopped also to listen to the wind and study
their back trail.

Around three o'clock in the afternoon, he stopped the
horse near a boulder snag from which a giant fir grew
crooked. He shucked the Winchester, swung his right boot
over the saddle horn, and dropped to the ground.

"What're you doing?" Faith said.

Yakima tossed her the reins over his shoulder. "Stay
here."

"Yakima, tell me what's happening," Faith urged as he
climbed the rocky southern slope, holding the rifle in one
hand and pulling at pine branches with the other.

"I'm gonna see if they're nipping at our heels," he said
without stopping, tipping his hat brim low.

"See if *who's* nipping at our heels?" She hadn't heard or
seen anyone behind them.

"Stay there."

Faith scuttled forward onto the saddle then, hugging her carpetbag to her chest. She watched Yakima stride fluidly up the slope, moving with the grace of a mountain lion, long hair bouncing across his shoulders.

He wore fringed buckskin breeches, brown boots, a blue wool shirt, and a red neckerchief knotted around his neck. A Colt was holstered on his right thigh, thonged above the knee. Near the crest, he stopped, stole a glance over the lip, then hoisted himself up and disappeared over the top.

Hefting his rifle, Yakima jogged across the crest of the wide ridge shelving up through pines and spruces. At the top of a low knoll, he dropped to a knee and stared southeast, along the old Indian trail he and Faith had been following before he'd pulled off a half mile back.

He squinted his keen eyes against the sun glare and smiled. Three riders appeared around an aspen copse. They were little larger than match heads from this distance, but there was little doubt who they were.

"Stupid sons of bitches," Yakima growled, running a forearm across his sweat-slick jaw.

He stood, hefted the rifle again, and continued jogging south along the ridge.

Ten minutes later, he'd crested a rise in the ridge and made his way down the other side through bunchgrass and sage, zigzagging between aspens and keeping an eye on the trail below.

At the base of the ridge, he climbed through a boulder snag and ducked between two flat-topped, wagon-sized slabs.

He waited, watching, hearing the hoof thuds grow louder until the three men appeared, their horses climbing a low rise. Thornton's henchman, Willie, took the lead, holding his double-barreled shotgun across his heavy thighs, the brim of his floppy black hat hiding his eyes.

Brindley and Higgins rode behind, old cap-and-ball pistols on their hips, Spencer carbines in their saddle boots. Brindley looked a little pale from the braining Yakima had given him. Higgins wore his usual high-crowned, Texas-creased hat. The three leaned out from their saddles, scrutinizing the trail as though looking for something.

"I tell you, Willie," Higgins said, "he must've turned off the trail. I don't see nothing but elk shit!"

"Shut up and let me do the trackin', ya dumb granger," said Willie with an annoyed air of distraction.

Yakima stared at Willie, anger boiling in his guts. Willie had never called Yakima anything but "dog-eater" or "rock worshiper," or, when on his best behavior, "mangy half-breed." How many times had Yakima wanted to kick the man's big pig-eyed face to a bloody pulp but held himself back to save his job?

Watching the three men move toward him, Yakima pulled his head back behind the boulders. Deciding on a course of action, he grinned. In seconds, he'd removed his stockman's boots and socks and was leaping over boulders toward the trail.

"Where the hell that damn Injun go, anyway?" Willie said, lifting his head to gaze over his horse's twitching ears. "There ain't that many damn trails through these mount—"

Brindley's cry cut him off. "*Hey!*"

Out of the corner of his right eye, Willie spied movement.

At first, he thought a magpie had lighted from the slope along the trail. But when he turned his head in that direction, lifting his chin, he decided a *big* bird—a wild turkey or a buzzard, maybe—was swooping toward him. A half second later, he saw the man's outstretched arms and legs, the long black hair billowing as two bare brown feet bore down on him.

Willie's heart had only started leaping, and he'd only just started raising his shotgun, when the heel of the right foot smashed his jaw with brain-numbing impact. Lights flashed behind his eyes as he flew out of his saddle, dropping his shotgun and hitting the rocks on his left shoulder and hip. With an indignant cry, he rolled down the slope, snapping sage and loosing gravel in his wake.

As Willie's horse gave a startled whinny and galloped up the trail, Yakima landed on a boulder, pivoting on his bare feet and snapping the Winchester to his shoulder. Before him, Brindley and Higgins were sawing back on the reins of their own startled horses while trying to aim their old Colts at Yakima.

The half-breed drew a bead on Brindley's right hand, squeezed the trigger. A quarter second after the rifle barked, Brindley screamed. The revolver flew from his hand.

"God*damn* it!"

He clutched the bloody paw to his belly, grunting and grinding his teeth.

"Ahhh . . . *fuck*!" Higgins shouted, triggering his Colt as his horse fiddle-footed beneath him.

The slug spanged off the boulder under Yakima's feet.

Ramming a fresh shell in his rifle's breech, Yakima aimed and fired, blowing Higgins's hat from his head. He fired three or four more quick rounds, blowing up dust and gravel at the prancing feet of both men's startled mounts.

The men grunted and cursed, fighting to remain in their saddles as the screaming horses wheeled and galloped back the way they'd come.

Yakima fired three extra shots over the men's heads, and Higgins's horse bucked furiously. Higgins slid down the horse's hip before grabbing the saddle horn with his uninjured hand and pulling himself erect.

Seconds later, the men and horses were gone, dust sifting behind them, hoof thuds dwindling into the distance.

Yakima heard a grunt behind him, and leapt around, lowering the Winchester's barrel. At the bottom of the slope twenty feet away, Willie rose up on his left hip and spat grit from his lips.

The beefy man blinked groggily. His eyes found Yakima, and his upper lip curled. His right hand closed over the grip of the .36 Remington on his hip.

Yakima levered the spent shell from the Yellowboy's breech, an angry rasp of steel, and shook his head. "Tch, tch."

Willie slid his hand away from the revolver's grip.

"Go home, fat man," Yakima said. "If I catch you trailing me again, you'll have more than a sore jaw."

Willie glowered up at him, his fleshy cheeks flushed with fury.

Yakima turned, leapt from the boulder to the trail. Faintly, he heard the click of a gun hammer. He ducked, wheeled, saw the revolver in Willie's hand, and fired.

The .44 round punched through Willie's chest, snapping his head back against a deadfall tree. He choked and sputtered for a few seconds, then his chin drooped to his chest and his eyes lost their light.

Yakima ejected the spent shell, looped the rifle over his shoulder, then climbed back up the ridge to where his boots sat atop a rock, socks stuffed inside. When he'd donned the socks and boots, he made his way back up and over the ridge.

Faith was waiting for him in the shade of a juniper tree, sitting with her knees up, Wolf's reins in her hand. The black whinnied and turned his head with a mouthful of bluestem when he heard Yakima hopscotching down the rocks.

"What happened?" Faith said, rising. "I heard shooting."

"Some people don't listen to reason." Yakima slid his rifle into his saddle boot and grabbed the reins. "Come on. We have a few hours of light left."

"Yakima?" she said, when he'd mounted the horse and extended his left hand to her.

His eyes met hers.

"Where are we going?"

"I never know till I get there."

Chapter 7

Roy Brindley and Ace Higgins were heading hell-for-leather back toward the roadhouse when Brindley jerked his head to one side and pulled back on his horse's reins. The claybank whinnied sharply and dug its back hooves into the sand and gravel, skidding.

Higgins, halted his own sweat-lathered mount. "What is it?"

"Heard somethin'," Brindley said, staring at the two-track wagon trail behind them, turning his head this way and that, like a bird. He'd wrapped his neckerchief around his bullet-grazed right hand.

They were in the foothills now, about five miles from the roadhouse. The sun had long since set. Coyotes yammered in the southern hills rising darkly toward a velvet, starry sky.

"What'd you hear?"

"I don't know. Somethin'."

"You think that savage followed us?" Higgins laughed. "Come on. I need a drink."

"Wait a minute. We turn around, we're liable to get back-shot, or—"

A rustling rose from the weeds right of the trail.

"Christ!" Brindley said, fumbling his pistol from its holster and ratcheting back the hammer, wincing at the pain in his hand.

The weeds parted and a small animal waddled onto the trail. It stopped and turned toward the men. Two white-ringed eyes flashed in the starlight, and a short, white-ringed tail whipped stiffly. The raccoon chuckled angrily and, its back arched, scampered across the trail and into the thick brush on the other side.

Higgins laughed. "There's your savage, Roy. Better ventilate that polecat before he backshoots you!" He turned his dapple gray up trail and heeled it into a trot. "Come on, goddamn it, I need a drink *bad*!"

Brindley cast another cautious glance along their back trail, then holstered his pistol, swung the horse around, and booted it up trail. When he was a few feet behind Higgins, he said, "What're we gonna tell Thornton about Willie?"

Higgins kept his eyes forward. "What d'ya mean?"

"Well, shit, we left him back there, Ace. Didn't even go back to see if he was dead."

"You heard the gunfire," Higgins growled, wrinkling his nose and running a gloved hand across his beard. "He's dead, all right. And if we woulda gone back, we'd be dead, too."

"Yeah, but what're we gonna tell *Thornton*?"

Higgins rode in pensive silence for thirty yards. As they began dropping downhill toward a black plain spread out before them, Higgins reined his horse to a stop and turned to Brindley.

"We tell him the savage bushwhacked us, shot Willie outta his saddle. We dismounted and returned fire, but the savage got away. By the time we got to Willie, he was dead."

"What if Thornton rides up there and finds Willie's body?"

"Shit, magpies and coyotes'll have his bones scattered by tomorrow noon—if a mountain lion don't find him first."

Higgins chuckled. "Besides, I don't think Thornton's gonna be in any condition to ride fer a good long time."

"Reckon you're right about that."

"I'm right about a lot of things," Higgins said, booting his horse downhill. "Now, come on and quit worryin'."

They trotted into the roadhouse yard a half hour later. Two Murphy freight wagons sat on the far side of the yard, tongues drooping, and five saddle horses were tied to the hitchrack. It sounded like Cisco Squires was pounding the piano inside. Beneath the dissonant notes of an off-key waltz, male conversation rumbled. The big window left of the front door was boarded up, letting little light out of the main room, so the yard was darker than usual.

"Not a bad crowd for a Monday night," Brindley remarked, checking his horse down between the roadhouse and the barn.

As he studied the roadhouse shouldering back against the winking stars, his heartbeat quickened at the prospect of reporting to Thornton that the Indian had gotten away and that Willie was dead. Thornton was a contrary sort even when his health was good. Now, with the whore's bullet in him . . .

Higgins must have felt the same dread. Before Brindley knew what had happened, his partner had ridden up on his right and grabbed his reins out of his gloved hands.

"Go on inside and tell Thornton what happened," Higgins said. "I'll put the horses away."

"You're the one who concocted the story, Ace," Brindley cried. "You report to Thornton!"

Higgins turned his horse toward the barn and stopped, staring at Brindley from beneath the bill of his high-crowned Stetson. "You get along with him better than I do. Hell, I'd go so far as to say y'all have a ree-pore!"

As Brindley opened his mouth to protest, Higgins said quickly, "I'll take over the wood-splittin' chores for one week."

"And mortar the well coping?"

Higgins spat down the far side of his horse and studied the ground for a few seconds. He turned to Brindley. "All right."

With a heavy sigh, Brindley swung out of his saddle, his hand aching, his head throbbing dully from its meeting with that crazy savage's rifle. As Higgins rode toward the barn, leading the claybank, Brindley stared at the roadhouse, light from the small window at the right of the front door angling onto the rough boards of the porch floor.

A shadow moved in the far right window of the second story—a man's silhouette, hips thrusting, head bobbing. Faintly, Brindley heard the squawks of bedsprings getting a workout and the low groans of a whore.

It didn't appear that last night's foofaraw had cut into Kansas Jen's business any.

Brindley took another deep breath, fingering the swollen knot at the back of his head. He mounted the stoop and pushed through the roadhouse door. Since most of the furniture was now stacked with the firewood out back, only a couple of men were sitting. Six or seven others were bellied up to the bar—a couple of regular freighters in canvas coats and suspenders, and denim-clad waddies from nearby cattle outfits.

The two freighters were playing two-handed poker while most of the waddies were gathered around the Mex whore, Carmella, who was selling peeks down her sheer red negligee for nickels. The waddies probably couldn't afford pokes again till they got paid at the end of the month.

"Hey, Brindley, you get that half-breed?" a freighter called from the other side of the room, his voice thick with drink.

Cisco Squires stopped pounding the piano, and voices hushed as all eyes shuttled to Brindley. The hostler kept his eyes forward as he elbowed past a couple of drovers and set an arm on the bar.

"Give me a whiskey, Sykes."

"Comin', Roy." Sykes set a fresh-drawn beer onto the bar before a bearded drover, then, wiping his hands on his soiled apron, moved toward Brindley, frowning. "What happened out there?"

"Just give me the goddamn drink!"

The bartender filled a shot glass and set it on the bar. Brindley grabbed the glass, threw the whiskey back, and skidded the empty glass across the mahogany. The scrape on the bar rose like thunder in the silent room.

Brindley ran a wrist across his mustache. "Boss upstairs?"

"Where else would he be?"

Brindley pushed through the wranglers gathered around Carmella. One of the men—a tall gent with long black hair and evilly slanted eyes beneath a torn hat brim—hugged Carmella from behind, nuzzling her neck. As he hefted the girl's breasts through her negligee, he winked at Brindley.

"He's feelin' right poorly, too, Roy. Sure hope you got the heads o' that whore and that savage hangin' off your saddle horn."

Tightening his jaw and trying to quell his pounding heart, Brindley moved up the stairs one step at a time, sliding a hand along the railing. He felt the stares of those below but kept his businesslike gaze on the wall at the top of the stairs, which was decorated with a painting of a voluptuous naked woman draped across a lush silk bed, a giant black horse rising on its back legs behind her.

Like a man marching toward the gallows, Brindley walked along the hall, boots clomping softly on the sour runner, ignoring the grunts, sighs, and squawking bedsprings emanating from behind closed doors. He turned left down the branching corridor, removed his hat, and stopped at the last door on the right.

He knocked twice.

Light footsteps sounded.

The door opened a crack. The pale, spindly whore, Jo-Letta, angled one blue, red-rimmed eye through the crack.

"I gotta talk to Thornton."

"He's asleep."

Behind her, bedsprings groaned. Thornton coughed twice, cleared his throat. "Who is it?"

Brindley shoved the door open. As the girl stumbled back, frowning indignantly, nearly tripping over the hem of her long flannel housecoat, Brindley strode to the bed. Best get this over with, then go back downstairs and have another drink.

He looked down at the bed.

Thornton lay on his right side, pillow wadded beneath his head, sheets and quilts twisted about his legs. His face was flushed and wet. The room smelled like a bear den. The slop bucket beside the bed was half filled with bloody bandages soaked with urine.

Thornton stared up at Brindley, the corners of his eyes crinkling as he tried to focus. "You get 'em?"

Brindley fingered his railroad hat. "Sorry, Mr. Thornton. That savage ambushed us. He killed Willie. We buried him in the rocks, and then it was dark, so . . ."

"So what?" Thornton snarled, angry eyes suddenly focusing. The hostler felt like a Gatling gun was aimed at his face. "You came back without him and that miserable *whore* 'cause you were afraid of the *dark*?"

"Boss—"

Brindley gasped as Thornton reached up and grabbed his shirt. The roadhouse proprietor pulled the hostler's head down to within a foot of his own. Thornton's breath was sour, tinged with whiskey and opium.

His grip was surprisingly strong, considering his weakened state. He squeezed the collar so tight that Brindley's face burned with trapped blood.

"I want you to saddle a fresh horse and ride out after Bardoul. Right now. Tonight. *In the dark.*" Thornton spoke slowly, his voice a taut, mocking rasp. "He's headed for Denver City. If you ride hard, you should be able to overtake him before he gets to Fort Collins. You think you can handle that, or should I send JoLetta?"

Brindley winced against the pain in his pinched throat. "Wha—what should I tell Bardoul?"

"Tell him to bring me the heads of that rock worshiper and the girl. Tell him I'll pay him a thousand dollars and throw in free mattress dances for the rest of the year!"

Thornton jerked Brindley's head closer to his own, as if to punctuate the order.

Brindley nodded, grimacing at the hot, fetid breath in his face. "Y-you got it, Mr. Thornton."

"You won't get scared in the dark and piss yourself?"

"No, sir."

Thornton released Brindley's shirt. "Bust ass!"

"Yessir!" Brindley wheeled and headed for the door, the pale whore sidestepping out of his way.

"Brindley?"

The hostler turned back to the bed, slitting one eye as if expecting Thornton to throw something at him.

"A couple of the girls took advantage of my injury and ran out on me. When the stage came through, bitches hopped it." Thornton coughed, wincing at the pain, fresh sweat popping out on his forehead. The bed bounced like a skiff in a storm-tossed sea. "If you run into 'em along the trail, my direct orders to you are to put a bullet in 'em both. Understand?"

Brindley glanced at JoLetta, who stood back in the shadows, eyes sheepishly downcast. Turning back to Thornton, Brindley nodded. "You got it, boss."

He wheeled back to the door and donned his hat, then strode into the hall and down the stairs. Heading across the saloon's main hall toward the front door, he didn't stop to entertain questions from the waiting crowd of waddies, freighters, barmen, and whores.

He pushed through the front door and leapt off the stoop, heading for the barn. Ace Higgins was walking toward him, hands in the pockets of his buckskin coat as he nibbled his mustache.

"How'd it go?" he asked as Cisco Squires began pounding the piano with strained jubilance.

"Next time," Brindley spat as he marched toward the barn, "*you* can give Thornton the bad news and *I'll* fix the well coping my ownself!"

Chapter 8

Yakima urged his horse across a wide, flat creek, the water resembling a giant black snake winking in the starlight. He put the horse up the opposite bank through buckbrush and wild mahogany and reined the black into a hollow amid monolithic, mushroom-shaped boulders.

He looked around and, satisfied the place was well sheltered and hidden from the main trail, swung his right leg over the saddle horn and dropped straight down to the ground.

Faith groaned as, sound asleep, she slumped forward toward the saddle. Yakima grabbed her arm and gentled her off the black's rump. She'd wrapped up in a blanket as the cool mountain night had descended, and now as the blanket slid off her shoulder, Yakima grabbed it. He carried her across the hollow, past an old, charred fire ring, and eased her down against a rock.

As he drew the blanket across her, she lifted her head and looked around. "Where are we?"

"South Fork of Crying Squaw Creek, if I remember."

Numb with exhaustion and shivering against the cold, she slid onto her right shoulder as she curled her legs and drew the blanket up to her neck.

"I'll get a fire going in a minute," Yakima said.

He turned to the horse standing hang-headed on the other side of the hollow. It had been a long, hard ride, with two people on his back. Wolf's lungs expanded and contracted, making the leather squawk, the sweat-lather bubbling around the stirrup fenders. He blew and rippled his withers.

When Yakima had unsaddled the horse and walked him around a little to cool him before watering him, he staked him in high grass. He rubbed him down with an old gunnysack, then gathered wood and built a fire. He grabbed his hatchet from his saddlebags, stalked off through the boulders, and returned ten minutes later with his arms heaped with cedar boughs.

Fashioning the boughs into a bed near the crackling fire, he spread his bedroll over them and set his saddle at the head. He lifted the sleeping girl into his arms once more and eased her down on the bed, so that her head lolled softly against the saddle.

She groaned. Her eyes fluttered but didn't open. Yakima adjusted the boughs around her, removing a couple of sharp stones from underneath, then grabbed his striped wool blanket and added it to the girl's bedding.

Satisfied that she would stay relatively warm if he kept the fire built up, he grabbed a battered tin pot and filled it at the creek. A few minutes later he crouched beside Faith, a steaming cup in his hand, and nudged the girl's shoulder.

"Better have some tea."

She groaned and smacked her lips, slid her head lower on the saddle. "I'm not thirsty."

"You need something."

Faith's eyes remained closed. After a few seconds, her lips parted, and her breath resumed its steady rhythm.

Yakima straightened, stretched his back, feeling his own

fatigue deep in his back and in the bullet-pierced arm. He fished a peach tin from his possibles bag, opened it with his bowie knife, then slumped against a rock on the other side of the fire from Faith, sipping the tea and plucking peaches from the can. The creek probably had fish in it, but he was too exhausted to string a line—more tired than hungry.

When he'd finished the peaches and tea, he chunked another log on the fire, drew his spare blanket up, stretched out his legs, and crossed his ankles.

He fell asleep as soon as he closed his eyes.

When Faith opened her eyes again, copper morning light angled over the dark, craggy buttes to the west. The cedar boughs rustled beneath her, rocking her gently, and she looked around, then down at the branches, trying to remember where she was and how she'd gotten here.

It all came rushing back through the stiffness in her seat and thighs, rising through the mental fog that lingered though she'd slept all night—Thornton, Yakima, the endless ride.

She looked at the two heavy blankets covering her, damp with dew and smelling of horse and pine smoke. Before her, a fire popped, the warmth pushing against her, the smoke stinging her eyes. A kettle of steaming water sat to one side of the flames. A single brown blanket lay twisted on the ground to her right, near scuff marks showing where Yakima had no doubt lain.

Holding the bottom blanket around her, she got her stiff legs under her and stood, looking around the rocks for Yakima. Except for the blanket and the steaming water, there was no sign of him.

"Yakima?"

She held the blanket closed with both hands as she moved through the boulders, the ground cool and damp beneath her feet. She followed a game trail down a hill. The breeze was fresh against her face, rife with the smell of water. She crossed a sage-stippled flat, climbed another rise, and stopped.

Below, a narrow creek rippled over rocks, the golden sunlight sparkling on the glossy, blue-green surface. On the shore, Yakima stood bare-chested, feet spread shoulder-width apart, knees bent, arms extended. In each upturned palm he held a tin cup full of water rippling about the rim.

Faith opened her mouth to call out, but then she saw the concentration on Yakima's face, the muscles in his flat cheeks drawn taut.

His buckskin breeches shifted across his flexing thighs. Corded tendons stood out from his neck, and his long black hair blew about his sun-bronzed face. His belly was flat, hard as a boardwalk, his hairless chest rising toward hub-sized shoulders in a nearly perfect V. His biceps bulged like giant goose eggs, the bandage on his right arm strained by the writhing muscles beneath.

Watching the muscles shift and slide under his scarred, ruddy skin, Faith felt a warmth move up from the back of her neck, spread across her head to her ears. Her heart speeded up.

Yakima's right hand quivered, and water splashed over the brim. Grunting, he turned his head toward Faith.

She gave a start. "Sorry. I didn't know where you were."

Yakima's arms relaxed slightly. He lifted his voice above the breeze and the creek's chuckle behind him. "Hungry?"

"I could eat a grizzly bear." She slid a lock of hair behind her left ear. "What are you doing there, anyway, practicing for a circus?"

"Flexibility training."

Yakima tossed both cups straight up in the air. He shifted

his arms slightly and caught both of them from above, closing his fingertips around their rims. Crouching, he set both cups on a flat rock before him, without spilling a drop of water, then straightened and grabbed his shirt off a boulder.

He ran the shirt across his chest and behind his neck. "Learned it from a Chinaman. A Shaolin monk."

"Chow what?"

"We worked on the railroad together. In our free time, he taught me kung fu—Eastern fighting."

"Looks right uncomfortable, if you ask me."

"Shaolin masters, includin' the hombre I knew, could hold that pose for hours. So far, I've only made it to twenty minutes and I'll be damned if I can make it to one minute more."

He donned the shirt. Leaving it unbuttoned, he wrapped his pistol belt around his waist, then strode to the edge of the creek, dropped to a knee, and pulled a braided rawhide cord from the water.

At the end of the cord, five brook trout flopped and twisted in the air, pale bellies flashing in the sunlight. He grabbed his hat and boots from a boulder and strode up the bank toward Faith, sand sifting beneath his bare feet.

"I was waiting for you to wake up," he said, brushing past her. "I'll get these fryin'."

Faith wheeled to follow. "Yakima, where are we going?"

"Denver City, I reckon. Where else?"

"He'll look for me there."

"He'll look for both of us there, but where else you gonna go?" He glanced at the blue peaks in the west. "It's comin' on winter. You can blend into the crowd in a city. Up there, you'll freeze to death." He added with a wry smile, "Or get stuck in a snowdrift."

Later, when he'd fried the fish in lard, they sat around the snapping fire, eating the tender meat with their fingers and drinking green tea from tin cups.

"Whatever made you return to Thornton's?" Faith asked him, dropping another morsel into her mouth.

"My horse and my rifle."

Faith widened her eyes at him. "Must be some valuable possessions, to risk your life for."

"They're all I have." Yakima swallowed, plucked a chunk of trout from the bowl between his index finger and thumb. "The horse I traded an old Arapaho for, when ol' Wolf was still just a colt. The Winchester was a gift from a friend."

He glanced at the Winchester, the morning sunlight glistening on the gold-plated breech and the oiled walnut stock. The side opposite the receiver bore an etching of a wolf fighting a grizzly in deep grass.

Old Ralph had given Yakima the valuable rifle—specially built for the governor of Colorado Territory—after Ralph had won it in a poker game. Being a Shaolin kung fu master from China, Ralph had had no use for rifles or weapons of any sort. He shouldn't have had any use for gambling, either, but he didn't deny himself the vice. It was his way of communing with his fellow man after long, brutal days laying railroad track in the unforgiving Western sun.

Yakima had met Ralph when he'd hunted meat for the railroad line.

Of course, Ralph hadn't been the Chinaman's real name, but that was the name he'd given everyone, including Yakima, grinning his shit-eating grin, his slanted obsidian eyes flashing beneath his peaked straw coolie hat. He'd claimed that no one but his fellow Sons of Han could have pronounced his real name.

So Ralph was the name he'd gone by . . . till Yakima had found him hanging from a big cottonwood on the outskirts of Yankton, Dakota Territory, his wiry body stripped naked, tarred, and feathered. His killers had stretched his neck a good seven inches, and his tongue had ballooned to the size and color of a ripe plum.

One gambling win too many, no doubt.

Yakima had spent untold hours with the man, learning how to fight in the Shaolin style, but he'd never learned—or couldn't remember learning—how Shaolin masters were supposed to be interred. So he'd cremated Ralph on a funeral pyre, then buried his remains under six feet of dirt and rock marked with a crude wooden cross engraved simply RALPH: A GOOD TEACHER.

He'd said a few words in both his native Lutheran and Cheyenne and hoped that Ralph found his way to wherever it was he was supposed to go.

"I thought maybe," Faith said now, wiping her fingers on her dress, "you'd come back to see how I was getting along . . . you know, after those four savages . . ."

Yakima shook his head. "I saw you were all right." He stopped chewing, glanced at her. "Why'd you shoot Thornton?"

She looked at him through a wing of hair fallen over an eye. "He thought . . ." She let her voice trail off, frowning down at her bent knee.

Yakima lifted his tin cup in both hands and stared at her. "What?"

She kept her eyes lowered as she said haltingly, "Someone must've seen me sneaking you food from the kitchen, I reckon, and . . . spread the rumor that . . ."

Yakima gave a wry snort. "Cavortin' with a half-breed. Bad for business." He threw the last of his tea back, then wiped his fingers on his buckskins. "Eat up. I'll saddle Wolf and bring him around."

Faith swabbed her bowl with a finger and watched his broad-shouldered, slim-hipped figure disappear in the brush and the rocks, long hair sliding across his back. She had a passing image of his naked chest forming an inverted V toward his corded neck, his thick arms gristled with taut muscle.

Her face warmed. It had been a long time since she'd felt anything but revulsion for the male form.

She licked the grease from her fingers, stood, gathered the dirty dishes, and carried them off toward the creek.

Chapter 9

Roy Brindley had blown out one horse and sent it home before he raced a sleek, long-legged claybank around a long bend in Ute Creek and reined up at the edge of a breeze-rippled cottonwood copse.

He took a deep breath and scrubbed sweat from his brow as he stared at Ute Creek Station—a dilapidated log-and-sod hut, log-and-sheet-metal barn, and peeled-log corrals. Ute Creek's hostler, Melvin Hanson, was currying one of the six sweat-shiny horses milling in the main corral. Over the yard, a thin sheen of dust lingered.

"Goddamn it," Brindley barked, heeling the claybank out from the cottonwood shade and into the yard. He turned in his saddle to yell at Hanson, "Melvin, the stage just pull out of here?"

The beefy hostler, who'd stooped to pry something from a dapple gray's right front hoof, straightened, glanced toward the far side of the yard, and nodded.

"Did you see two of Thornton's whores on it?"

The hostler nodded again.

"Shit!" Brindley spat and turned the clay toward the shack. He'd hoped to catch up to the bounty hunter, Wit Bardoul, before he caught up to the whores. If he caught up to

Bardoul first, he wouldn't have time to kill the whores, because he'd be too busy fetching Bardoul back to Thornton.

Brindley had never laid a hand on a woman, much less killed one. Killing a woman, even a whore, was just too much to ask of a man with Brindley's sensitivity. Besides, his salary of twenty-five dollars a month and found was hardly recompense for carrying a woman's death to his grave.

Brindley swung down from the saddle, slapped his hat against his thighs, puffing trail dust, and tossed the reins over the hitchrack. He mounted the sagging porch, opened the creaky wooden door, and stepped into the roadhouse's smoky shadows.

Glancing around at the five vacant tables and the wood-stove stoked against the lingering morning chill, he felt his heart fall. No sign of Bardoul. Shit. That meant he'd have to run down the stage and kill those whores. He probably wouldn't catch up to Bardoul before the bounty hunter was halfway to Denver City.

"What brings you way over here, Roy?" said an English-accented voice to his right.

Brindley turned. The tall, gangling Englishman who managed the Ute Creek roadhouse for the stage company stood on a ladder behind the bar. Dressed in a buffalo coat and gloves, Leo Black was resetting the banjo clock on the wall above a line of dusty brown bottles and below a moose head with two bullet holes in one of its paddle-sized antlers. One hand on the clock, he adjusted his silver-rimmed spectacles with the other. "Thornton hasn't had rustlin' trouble again, has he? I'm fresh outta spare horses."

Brindley opened his mouth to respond but stopped when a husky, Russian-accented female voice rose suddenly. Black had come to this country with a Russian he'd married back in Indiana. Brindley had once worked for Black, but he'd never been able to savvy the big woman's broken English, and he still couldn't. All he knew was that Black was being summoned pronto.

Black's narrow face acquired a pained expression. "Coming, Elga!" As he hobbled down the ladder on a foot in which he'd taken an Arapaho arrow, he said over his shoulder, "Be right back, Roy. Help yourself to a drink."

When Black had disappeared out the roadhouse's back door, Brindley sauntered up to the bar, jerked his gloves off, and tossed them down. He'd begun hoisting himself over the bar to feel around for a bottle below, when he froze and turned toward the back of the room.

What he'd thought was the wind moaning under the roadhouse's rear eaves wasn't the wind at all, but voices. A man's voice and a woman's voice. They rose from behind one of the two cribs Black had arranged at the far back of the room, behind two buffalo robes strung across the room on a rope.

Brindley stood staring at the robes, listening. He heard a man's low voice and then a girl's hushed chuckle. The man laughed. If that wasn't Wit Bardoul's laugh, Brindley was a two-headed zebra.

His heart thumping hopefully, he strode into the room's rear shadows, where the smell of sweat and sex overlaid the smell of pine smoke and spilled whiskey. Sidling up to the curtain, he canted his head to peek through the gap between the robes.

Inside, Wit Bardoul reclined on a broad, fur-and-quilt-laden cot. Bardoul could see the bounty hunter only from his waist up. Snugged against his bare torso, bare back to Brindley, lay a slender, sandy-haired girl, twirling her fingers in Bardoul's chest hair. Bardoul was chuckling, lips spread back from his two tobacco-stained silver front teeth as he stared down past his belly toward his feet.

Brindley cleared his throat loudly, shoved the right robe back about six inches, and peered through the gap. Bardoul turned toward him, frowning, his right hand reaching for something on a chair beside the bed—a gun, no doubt.

"Who's there, damn it?"

The girl gave a clipped shriek and turned her head toward the robes. Her eyes widened. Brindley's stomach fell, and bile churned. Mormon Claire, one of Thornton's runaway whores. Shit.

Brindley cleared his throat again, his eyes on the whore. "Uh, can I have a moment, Mr. Bardoul? It's Roy Brindley."

"Oh, shit," intoned another female from somewhere around the bounty hunter's knees. The other runaway whore, "Nettie the Pretty," shoved her head over Bardoul's hairy belly, staring wide-eyed at Brindley. "Is Thornton here?"

Brindley removed his hat and cursed once more. The hostler, Hanson, must have seen the women ride in on the stage and only assumed they'd left with it. A fine damn pickle. Now he had no choice but to kill them. If Thornton got wind of them and him being here at the same time, and he hadn't followed orders, his life wouldn't be worth fishing bait.

"No, ma'am."

Bardoul was still frowning angrily at Brindley, the birth-mark along the right side of his thick nose turning raspberry red. "What the hell you want, Brindley? Can't you see I'm occupied?"

"Sir, I've come to discuss business," Brindley said.

Then, before Bardoul could say anything else, he wheeled and strode back toward the front of the roadhouse. He tossed his hat on a table, retrieved a bottle and two glasses from behind the bar, and sat down at the table. Behind the robes, the girls were chattering frantically but too softly for Brindley to hear.

The cot creaked, clothes rustled, spurs chinged. There was the sound of a gun cylinder being spun, and then the robes parted, and Wit Bardoul ducked under the rope. He drew the robes closed, then, adjusting the cross-draw holsters on both hips and his big bowie on his right, he ambled stiffly toward Brindley. He held a half-empty bottle in one hand, a long black cigar in the other. His shabby sombrero hid the upper half of his bearded face, and the wang strings on his buckskins danced as he approached Brindley's table.

Pinching his buckskins away from his crotch, he set his bottle on the table and sagged into a chair across from Brindley. "Nettie needs to file a tooth down," he grunted.

Brindley splashed whiskey from his bottle into a glass and shoved it toward Bardoul. "Where's your horse?"

"In the barn. Had Melvin reset a shoe. While I was waitin', stage pulls in." The bounty hunter grinned, tossed back half his drink. "And guess who was on it?"

"They're runaways."

"I know. They offered me free pokes"—Bardoul winced as he slid his right hand under the table—"and other sundry pleasures if I escorted 'em both to Denver City. The stage driver was givin' 'em a hard time. I reckon he knew who they belonged to and didn't want nothin' to do with 'em." Bardoul tossed back the rest of his whiskey and slid the glass toward Brindley's bottle. "Anyway, what the hell you want, Roy? The girls? Less'n you got somethin' better, you can't have 'em."

Brindley waved the subject of the girls off for later and refilled Bardoul's glass. He slid the glass toward the bounty hunter, then reached inside his canvas coat and slapped a wad of greenbacks on the table. "The half-breed's alive. He came back to Thornton's. He's got Thornton's prize whore, and they're heading into the mountains. Thornton's offering you a thousand dollars for their heads."

Bardoul was lighting his cigar, puffing smoke. His eyes were on the money. "Just the heads?"

Brindley nodded. "He's right piss-burned."

Bardoul stared at Brindley as he continued lighting his cigar, smoke puffing around his head, the match flame leaping, flashing in the bounty hunter's close-set eyes. He blew out the match, tossed it on the floor, and sucked a deep drag from the cigar. "That damn dog-eater got away after all, huh? Well, that rubs my fur in the wrong direction. It sure does. Wouldn't want it gettin' out I let a quarry slip away. This is a competitive business. A man's gotta guard his reputation."

"You'll do it?"

Bardoul lifted a shoulder. "Can I finish my cigar first?"

Brindley threw up his hands. "You can finish anything you want." He glanced at the buffalo robes. The whores had gone quiet.

"I'm done with that," Bardoul said, sipping his drink and sagging back in his chair. "Sometimes a man just wants to enjoy a drink and a good cigar. Study on things . . ."

Brindley shifted uncomfortably, glanced at Bardoul sitting sideways to the table, a boot crossed on a knee, his brooding gaze canted toward the floorboards, his birthmark crimson. Brindley splashed more whiskey into his glass. Outside he could hear Black and his wife arguing about a skunk trapped somewhere—in the henhouse, probably.

When Brindley had taken another sip of his whiskey, he squeezed his whiskey bottle in both hands and regarded the bounty hunter reluctantly. "There's one more thing, Mr. Bardoul."

Bardoul glanced at him, one eye slitted, blowing smoke through his nostrils.

Brindley leaned forward and flicked his eyes toward the buffalo robes. He kept his voice low. "Thornton wants the whores dead."

Bardoul lifted a shoulder. "So kill 'em. My plans have changed."

Brindley cleared his throat. "Would you do it?"

"Why can't you do it?"

"I don't think I could shoot a woman."

"Why the hell not?"

"I ain't sure. There's somethin' inside me that makes me kind of sick to think about it."

Bardoul chuckled and tapped ashes on the floor. "Close your eyes and pretend they're men."

"Please, Mr. Bardoul. You've probably killed a woman before, but—"

The bounty hunter turned to him sharply, brows ridged. "Only ones that deserved it. I don't abuse women for no good reason—slappin' 'em around and the like."

"I understand, I understand. That's damn commendable. But since killin' those whores would cause you less strife than it would me, couldn't you do it?"

"How much is it worth to you?"

"Huh?"

"You don't expect me to do it for free, do you? My gun's for hire, mister. I don't do charity work."

"Well, hell, I don't have any money."

"Would you shovel shit from Thornton's barn for free?" Before Brindley could respond, Bardoul slapped his left hand on the table, palm up. "Give me what you got in your pockets."

Brindley looked at the thick, callused hands forever etched with grime. "I don't have but a few dollars in change."

Bardoul rapped his knuckles on the table. "Come on, come on."

Brindley leaned back, shoved his right hand into his pocket, and dropped a cartwheel and a few nickels on the table. They rattled around, spinning and rolling and bumping against the bottles. "That there's all I got till payday."

"Christ, man!" Bardoul said, glowering down at the coins. "You need a different line of work."

The bounty hunter sighed, took another deep puff from his cigar. He set the cigar on the table so that the coal hung over the edge. "You're beholden to me, Roy." He threw back the last swallow in his whiskey glass, then rose, shucked one of his big Remingtons, and spun the cylinder.

Brindley stood, sliding back his chair. "I'll wait for you outside."

"Fetch my horse from the barn," Bardoul grumbled, shoving his sombrero back from his freckled forehead as he began sauntering toward the buffalo robes, holding the big Remy straight down over his right holster.

Brindley turned and hurried outside.

As he jogged down the porch steps and headed toward the barn, he rammed a finger in each ear, wincing, steeling himself for the pop of the bounty hunter's pistol. He hadn't heard a single report by the time he reached the barn.

Keeping a finger in one ear, he used his right hand to open the barn's double doors, then hurried inside, looking around for the bounty hunter's big Appaloosa. When his eyes adjusted, he saw the horse standing near the back door, reins tied around a stall post. Keeping his fingers in both ears, he walked down the barn alley, removed his finger from one ear to slip the reins free of the post, then began leading the horse toward the open front doors.

Brindley's face muscles were bunched, eyes slitted, waiting . . .

What the hell was he doing in there?

Maybe the bounty hunter wasn't as tough as he thought. Or . . . maybe the whores had turned the tables on Brindley and were hiring the bounty hunter to kill *him* instead.

When Brindley and the Appaloosa were halfway across the yard, heading for the roadhouse, he removed his other finger from his ear and stopped, staring at the front door, one hand hovering around his own pistol butt.

He was glancing at the claybank tethered to the hitchrack at his left, considering whether to make a break for the horse and get the hell out of there, when a pistol popped inside the roadhouse.

Brindley leapt back, heart racing.

A girl screamed shrilly. The scream was clipped by another shot.

There was a thud, as though of a body hitting the floor.

A rumbling, Russian-accented, female voice bellowed, "Vot's diss? Vot da hell you tink you do here?"

Boots pounded and spurs chinged loudly toward the front door. Wit Bardoul bounded through the door, and in two steps he was across the porch and leaping into the yard. With a sheepish grin on his face, shaded by his sombrero brim, he grabbed the Appy's reins from Brindley.

"Mount up, mount up!" the bounty hunter laughed, swinging into his own saddle as Brindley ran to the claybank. "That big Russian's goin' for her shotgun!"

"What the hell took you so long?" Brindley said, slipping his reins from the rack and grabbing his saddle horn.

"Figured I'd have me one more French lesson," the bounty hunter chuckled as he turned the Appaloosa into the yard. "Since they was free an' all. *Hyahh!*"

"Wait for me, blast it!" Brindley yelled as he swung into his own saddle and reined the claybank away from the road-house.

Hearing the Russian's rumbling, incoherent bellows echoing inside the roadhouse, growing louder as the woman stormed toward the front door, Brindley slapped his hat against the claybank's rump and raked his spurs against its flanks.

The horse whinnied shrilly and lunged forward in an instant, ground-eating gallop.

He was passing the last corral on his left and a dilapidated springhouse on the right when he heard the woman shout in Russian behind him. He lowered his head and winced as the claybank galloped after Bardoul, a tan smudge racing through the cottonwoods ahead.

"You tink you can make a mess in my house?" the Russian screamed.

Brindley kept his eyes forward, lowered his head another two inches. A shotgun blast frightened blackbirds from the cottonwoods on both sides of the trail.

"I'm gonna make a mess out of *you!*"

Chapter 10

Yakima gigged Wolf up an easy incline through sage and fading wildflowers. Faith rode behind him, arms around his waist, head resting against his back. He could tell from her rhythmic breathing that she was asleep. She'd slept for a good hour or longer.

He halted the black at the top of the ridge and looked down on a narrow valley bordered on the opposite side by a steep sandstone ridge. A cottonwood-sheathed creek meandered along the partly shaded valley bottom. A small herd of mule deer loitered along the creek's far bank, the does and two bucks foraging while a wily old bull with a huge rack stared up the hill at the interlopers on the ridge.

As Yakima heeled the black forward and down the ridge, letting the horse pick his own way through the piñons, talus slides, and Spanish bayonet clumps, Faith lifted her head from his back.

"Where are we?"

"About five or six miles southeast of where we were the last time you asked."

"What're we doing?"

"We're gonna give the horse a blow. He's been needing one for a long time. We'll build a fire, make tea. I'd shoot one of those deer down there, but we're too close to mine diggings to risk a shot."

Yakima figured that by tracing a roundabout course, avoiding mining camps and main roads and keeping to the foothills of the Front Range, they probably had about four more days to Denver. That was if the weather held. Today was warm and clear—Indian summer with bees buzzing and songbirds singing in the shadbark scrub—but it being early October, a mountain snow could hit at any time.

He'd like to find the girl a horse. Riding double in the mountains was hard on even a stalwart mount like Wolf. But Yakima didn't see how they could appropriate one, short of stealing it and risking a necktie party for them both. Miners tended to be even more proprietary about their livestock than farmers and ranchers.

Yakima stopped Wolf at the edge of the creek, amid the sun-gilded cottonwoods, and slipped fluidly out of the saddle. He reached up, took Faith under the arms, and lifted her down.

"You do that like I don't weigh anything," she said, keeping her hands on his shoulders and staring up into his face, a shy smile tugging at her mouth.

"When you've tossed as much freight as I have, a woman doesn't feel like much."

Faith removed her hands from his shoulders and turned away with a wry curl of her upper lip. "Thanks for the compliment."

As Yakima loosened Wolf's latigo strap, Faith cast her gaze along the creek, her dress buffeting lightly around her legs. The day was warm, so she wasn't wearing a blanket around her shoulders. She was as dusty and sweaty as Yakima, which meant she was covered with damp mud from head to toe.

"I'm gonna see if I can find a hole deep enough to bathe in," she said, fiddling with a chokecherry branch as she turned to Yakima. "You don't have an extra pair of trousers and a shirt, do you? They'd be considerably better for riding than this thin dress."

Yakima dropped the saddle at the base of a cottonwood and turned to her. She was so sweaty and dusty that the dress clung to every curve, tight as a second skin. Her full breasts were clearly delineated beneath her soaked chemise and the threadbare cotton of the dress.

Catching himself staring, Yakima flushed and raised his gaze to Faith's. Her cheeks dimpled as she sucked her bottom lip. "Um . . . should I repeat the question?"

"Huh?"

Faith chuckled. "I asked if you had an extra pair of trousers and a shirt."

"In the pack," Yakima said, glancing at the burlap sack he used for a possibles bag, looped over his saddle horn. "Got an extra pair of longjohns in there, too. It's warm now, but it's gonna get cold tonight. You'll want to put them on in a few hours."

"Thanks." Faith sauntered over to the burlap sack and began rummaging inside.

Yakima led Wolf to the edge of the creek. As the horse drew water, Yakima rubbed his sweat-lathered coat down with a thick patch of burlap. He couldn't help keeping an eye skinned on Faith while he worked. Ironic, how he'd swamped a whorehouse for nine months and never got his ashes hauled once.

Thornton had rules against his hired hands—especially half-breeds—trifling with the girls.

When Faith had found a pair of patched denims, a red

flannel shirt, and faded red longjohns, she tossed a blanket over her shoulder and strolled into the trees near Yakima.

"Thanks for the duds," she said, setting the load down in the grass and reaching behind her back as if to unbutton her dress. "The denims'll pad my bottom a little better than that dress, and I don't mind telling you, your horse has a hard back."

Yakima scrubbed sweat from the black's right forelock. He'd taken his eyes off Faith, but now he looked back at her. She was, indeed, unbuttoning her dress. He could tell by the way it loosened in front, billowing away from parts of her breasts while clinging to other parts.

"If we had another horse, another saddle . . ." He let his voice trail off. Faith peeled her dress off her shoulders, down her arms. Yakima turned back to his work. "The riding would be easier, but once we hit the plains."

Faith cut him off. "Yakima, you could take me into the mountains. I know a banker at Gold Cache who's offered to lend me the money to start my own place—"

Working on the horse's right hip, he glanced at her. She'd turned partially away from him. She was naked, the dress and chemise bunched around her ankles. As she stooped to retrieve the blanket, her breasts swayed out from her chest.

"A banker?" Yakima said.

"He was passing through Thornton's on the stage a few months back. I reckon I encouraged him to stay a whole week." She chuckled as she turned to Yakima, draping the blanket around her shoulders but letting the ends dangle from her shoulders, in no hurry to cover her breasts.

Yakima turned away and sidestepped to the horse's head, ran the burlap down Wolf's broad snout. "That high up, it'll snow before we get there. Besides, Wolf couldn't carry us both that far."

"We could buy a horse from a prospector. I've got some money saved up."

"We wouldn't make it, Faith."

"We could have fun, you and me, Yakima. You know we could."

Yakima glanced over his left shoulder. She stood only a few feet from him, the blanket draped loosely over her shoulders. She cupped her breasts with the ends of the blanket, hiding only the nipples. The orbs swelled alluringly. Her legs were bare from her thighs down, her feet fine and delicate in the tough brown grass.

"I reckon we could at that—till we froze to death." Yakima tossed the burlap down and led Wolf into the deeper grass where the creek curved back toward the bank.

"Typical man," Faith called behind him. "Don't know a good thing when you see it."

"I see it," Yakima said, not torturing himself with another look at her, keeping his eyes straight ahead. "I just don't wanna die for it."

"Come for a swim?"

Yakima stopped, turned halfway around. He slitted one eye. She stood staring at him wistfully, one foot atop the other, the blanket draped over one arm.

Her breasts, bronzed by the westering sun, stood proudly out from her chest, nipples jutting. Her long blond hair framed them like sun-gilded corn silk.

"I ain't taking you to Gold Cache."

"Maybe I can change your mind." Her cheeks dimpled as she smiled. "But I ain't attaching any strings to it." She wagged a bent knee at him and, throwing her hair out from her shoulders, jogged off through the trees.

Yakima stared after her, scowling. His loins were heavy. Damn her, to do this to him. To make him want her. Ah, hell, he'd wanted her for a long time. But all that exposed skin had made him *need* her. She was a fine-looking woman. A little skinny, but nicely rounded in the breasts and hips. Now that he'd been invited, his surging blood wouldn't let him turn her down.

But he'd be damned if he'd take her to Gold Cache. Shit, neither one of them would make it alive, and he wasn't a pimp. He'd been many things since his mother had died. There weren't many things he hadn't done, but he'd never pimped, and he didn't aim to ever do it.

He snorted as he hobbled the horse. What do you know? There was even a job too low for him.

When he'd gathered some deadfall branches and built a low fire, he filled his teakettle with water from the creek. Tea had been Ralph's drink—he claimed it lightened the limbs and buoyed the spirit, and Yakima had found it to be true.

He'd just about talked himself out of going after Faith— what woman didn't attach strings to a free poke?—when her voice rose from upstream, a gentle, glassy keen above the rustling weeds and cottonwood leaves.

"Yaaa-kima?"

A siren cry if he'd ever heard one.

He broke a few of the thicker branches onto the fire and blew on the fledgling flame. She called him again, louder this time. He rose, wiped his hands on his buckskins, and began making his way upstream through the columnar shadows of the cottonwoods.

"Here!" Faith cried.

He turned his head to see her lolling on the other side of the creek, inside a sunny horseshoe where the water appeared to be about four feet or more. Faith lay with her back to the six-foot earthen bank behind her, hands grasping old tree roots protruding from the clay above her head.

Her breasts rode up out of the water. She smiled and kicked a foot.

"It's cold but very refreshing!"

Yakima's heart wrenched as he watched the girl frolic on the other side of the creek, bouncing up and down in the water, shaking her wet hair around her head.

He kicked off his boots and was out of his clothes in less than a minute. He stepped off the bank and began striding across the stream with long, fluid steps, his legs pushing at the steady current, arms swinging stiffly at his sides, as if to pull the water back behind him.

The cold air numbed him, rose gooseflesh across his shoulders, but did nothing to taint his desire.

As he moved purposefully toward her, splashing water up around his thighs, Faith held herself still by the tree roots behind and above her. She stared at him, her eyes sweeping across his body, her cheeks flushed, eyes bright, full lips slightly parted.

He didn't slow his pace until he was inches away from her. Then he stopped, the water rising to just beneath his buttocks, and crouched down. He grabbed her shoulders, drew her to him, and closed his mouth over hers.

She opened her lips for him, and their tongues tangled for nearly a minute before Faith placed her hands on his chest and pushed him back.

She ran her eyes across his chest, ran her hands over the hublike knobs of his shoulders, down his bulging, vein-corded arms. For a moment, he thought she was reconsidering her offer, but then she dropped lower in the water and pressed her back to the bank. Placing her hands on his buttocks, she drew him toward her and wrapped her legs around his thighs.

After a few minutes, she cried out softly and groaned, digging her fingers into his biceps and throwing her head back, arching her spine. She quivered for a few seconds, then, breathing hard, lifted her head. Her eyes were soft and heavy-lidded as they met his.

She didn't say anything, just stared at him obliquely, breasts rising and falling sharply, as she clung to his arms and kept her legs wrapped tightly around his thighs.

After a time, she shivered and pressed her face to his chest. "Cold . . ."

He lifted her, turned, and carried her back across the creek. He aimed for a patch of bright sunshine between cottonwoods, then climbed the bank, and lowered her gently into the grass. He shook out his own long hair, then lay down beside her, pressed his back to the grass, felt the sunshine begin to penetrate the cold.

Soon, when the sunlight was a second warm skin covering his body, she rose up on an elbow, stared down at him, ran her hand along his hard jaw, swept her thumb across his lips. She didn't say anything, just stared into his eyes before lowering her lips to his, kissing him tenderly.

She pulled away, continued staring down at him, a pensive smile pulling at her mouth. "Where do you come from, Yakima?"

He jerked a shoulder, ran his left hand down the graceful curve of her slender back. "Here and there."

"I mean, in the beginning. Where were you born, to who?"

"My ma was an Indian, a Yakima, from the west coast. My old man was a fur trapper. Henry was his name. Zachariah Henry. One-quarter Cheyenne. Don't recollect where he came from. Maybe Ma never said."

He stopped, saw that she was waiting for more.

He jerked his shoulder again, uncomfortable at talking about himself. And then, too, there was so much he didn't know. "Pa took her away from her people, and they traveled around the mountains, living in cabins and running trotlines. I was born sometime in there somewhere. Heard they did a little prospecting, but I must have been too young to remember. Pa taught me a few Cheyenne ways, some of the tongue. He died, got sick or something, and then Ma got sick and sent me to a Catholic orphanage in Denver City. I never heard from her after that, so I just assumed she was dead."

He rested his head back on his bent arm and stared at the sky. The discomfort of talking was tempered by a flood of sensory impressions, wisps of colored smoke, from his past.

"I remember rain in the mountains and the smell of wet deerskins. One time we had to tunnel out of our cabin, the snow was so deep. I remember a big bald eagle. Pa and Ma, they must have had one for a pet or something, maybe it was injured. I can remember its eyes and how its feathers felt when I petted it, and the choking, croaking noise it sometimes made."

He traced a high, puffy cloud with his eyes, frowning as he tried to gather larger pieces of his patchwork past, always so frustrating, because they never came together to form a whole image.

"Ma had a little half-moon birthmark under her left eye. Pa had a thick, curly gray beard. When he died, she went away for a spell, left me alone. Then she returned with her hair cut off, arms and hands hacked up. We wandered for a couple years after that. Sometimes she cooked and cleaned for farmers or for businesspeople in towns, and we'd live in the barn. Sometimes we'd just live in a creek bottom somewhere—through the warm months, anyway—and we'd trap rabbits to eat."

He remembered certain dogs and horses and trees and creeks and fishing holes. He remembered a banker's large white house with trim at the roof's peaks that resembled the icing on a cake. And there was a black woman, a maid, whom he and his mother had once been friends with.

He remembered the angry looks and harsh words directed at an Indian woman and her half-breed son, and being run out of places or threatened with beatings—which was why they steered wide of large settlements. But he didn't go on about any of that, because none of it really made any sense to him and he wasn't sure how much was real and how much he'd made up simply because he'd yearned to have a history. No use yakking about it to Faith.

He looked up at her. She was running the back of her left index finger back and forth along his belt line, a somber expression on her face.

"What about you, Faith? Where did you come from?"

She smiled and stared at her finger. "Oh, I don't even remember, and that's just fine with me." She placed a hand on either side of his face, kissed him tenderly. While they kissed, she ran her hand down to his crotch, squeezed and caressed until he was ready for her once more.

As she straddled him, her shadow fell across Yakima's face, making it impossible for him to see the sun flashing off a spyglass directed at them from a hill on the other side of the stream.

Chapter 11

Two feet from the crest of the knoll, Alvin Pauk looked at his partner, Leo Salon, staring through a spyglass toward the opposite side of the creek. Salon was grinning beneath the flat brim of his black hat, which he wore cavalry style, tipped over his left eye.

Salon chuckled.

"What the hell's so funny?" asked Pauk, keeping his head behind a sage clump beside Salon. "What the hell's goin' on?"

Salon continued staring through the spyglass, showing crooked teeth as he laughed. "Christ, those two are goin' at it like a coupla minks!"

"Huh? What do you mean they're goin' at it? Let me see."

"I don't think so, my friend," Salon said, shaking his head slightly as he kept the spyglass snugged to his right eye. "You ain't old enough to see such carryin's-on as that."

"Goddamn it!" Pauk reached up and snagged the glass from Salon's gloved hands. "I'm only a year younger than you."

Salon—who was dressed much like Pauk, in a gaudy gambler's suit complete with a frilly vest, claw-hammer frock coat, and polished black stockman's boots with cow dung forever ingrained in the stitching—poked his shabby bowler hat off his forehead and aimed the spyglass between the sage clump and a rock the size and shape of a shoe box.

He adjusted the focus until the Indian and the girl appeared on the creek's far bank, framed by willows and partially hidden in the tall, tan grass. The girl straddled the Indian, knees clutching his sides, her back to the creek, her long, wheat-colored hair bouncing on her shoulders. The savage's brown hands gripped her narrow waist, just above her hips.

Salon and Pauk, down-at-the-heel drovers-turned-gamblers, had spied the pair two hours ago, threading a broad canyon. The idea had come to Salon instantly: They'd steal the pair's fine black mustang and sell the horse in Gold Cache for a gambling stake. Salon and Pauk, who'd learned to play poker in bunkhouses across the frontier, owned the affliction common among bunkhouse sharpies—they overestimated their gambling prowess to such a severe degree that they saw gambling as their way out of the bunkhouse forever.

They also didn't see that stealing a horse from an Indian and a girl could be considered a crime, only a stunt that no one but the Indian and the girl could begrudge them.

"Christalmighty," Pauk wheezed, his heart hammering as he stared at the thrashing weeds on the other side of the creek.

Beside him, propped on an elbow and keeping his head well below the knoll's crest, Salon laughed. "Just like a coupla minks. Didn't I tell ya?"

"You know what I think, Alvin?" Pauk swallowed, then parted his lips to breathe through his mouth. "That's a fine-lookin' woman down there. Yessir. I think we oughta go down there and join the fun."

Salon grabbed the spyglass away from Pauk, his single black brow ridged. "After the savage has had her?" He gave a disapproving chuff and looped the spyglass around his neck, tucking it inside his threadbare wine-colored vest. "Besides, now's our chance to grab the horse."

He scuttled down the knoll, but stopped when he saw Pauk still staring over the crest. "Come on!"

Pauk looked at Salon over his left shoulder. His thin blond mustache was damp with sweat. "I ain't had me a woman in a good month or more, Leo."

"Well, you can't have that one. She's done been soiled by the Injun. Besides, we'd have to kill him to get her, and a shot in Ute country is bound to bring trouble." Salon tugged on Pauk's brown boot. "Now, come on. That horse'll bring a good three, four hundred dollars up at Gold Cache, enough to stake us for the winter."

"Ah, shit!" Pauk spat under his breath, crabbing straight down the back of the knoll. "I reckon there'll be more women up at Gold Cache."

Salon stood and turned downstream. "I hear the whores up in Gold Cache are some o' the finest you'll see this side of New Orleans. The bordellos have real carpet on their floors and everything."

"Well, I ain't tinhorn enough to believe such blather as that," Pauk said, stumbling after his partner, shoving shadbark out of his way with both hands, "but I reckon they *might* be as purty as that one there, anyways."

When the pair had walked fifty yards, tracing a bend in the stream, they stopped at the creek's edge. Salon looked upstream and into the willows. The Indian and the girl were out of sight, which meant that Salon and Pauk would be out of sight as well.

"Come on," Salon said, stepping through the cattails and into the creek, planting his boots firmly on rocks rising above the water's frothy surface. "Easy now, don't make any noise. Injuns got ears like bats."

Both men were across the shallow stream in three awkward leaps, Pauk slipping once and sending up a splash. On the far bank, they pushed through the wheatgrass under the cottonwoods.

Salon stopped suddenly. Fifteen yards before him, the horse stood eyeing them warily, a tuft of green grass in its jaws, twitching its ears.

"Damn, that's a fine-lookin' beast," said Pauk. "Look at that big broad chest and them pasterns. Legs straight as ladders!"

"We'll admire him later," Salon said, moving toward the black. "Easy now, horse. Easy, boy . . ."

Spent, Faith slumped down atop Yakima.

She flattened her breasts against his chest and buried her face in his neck. He ran his hands through her hair, down her back. His heavy breathing kept time with hers.

"I don't want to go anywhere," Faith muttered, her lips warm and wet against his ear. "I want to stay here forever."

"I can't recommend it." Yakima ran his hands up her back, the skin smooth as porcelain beneath his fingers. "In a few hours, we'd be getting right chilly."

"You'll move the fire over here."

Staring dreamily at the cobalt sky, he remembered the fire he'd built downstream. He took a deep breath and was about to suggest they drink a cup of tea, then saddle up and ride for another hour, when a shrill whinny rose on the breeze.

Wolf.

Yakima gave Faith a brusque shove, rolling her into the grass, then leapt to his feet. He grabbed the Winchester and, crouching and whipping his gaze from right to left, rammed a fresh shell into the rifle's breech.

"What was that?" Faith said behind him.

As if in reply, the horse whinnied again. Then he snorted, and they heard the loud thuds of hooves hitting the ground hard.

"Stay here!"

Taking no time to dress, Yakima lunged forward, breaking into a run upstream, crashing barefoot through the tall grass, leaping logs and fallen branches. He ran around a mossy boulder and jumped a freshet. Ahead, his fire smoldered, burned down to white ashes. He flew past it and into the brush where he'd hobbled Wolf.

No sign of the horse but trampled weeds.

He'd begun following a trail of bent brush downstream, when another shrill whinny rose. He stopped, dropped to a crouch, and swung the rifle around.

Fifty yards ahead and to the right, two riders trotted out from a crease between two hogbacks, the tails of their claw-hammer coats blowing in the breeze. One of the men was leading Wolf by his bridle reins. Wolf fought the lead, jerking his head back and lifting his tail as he reared.

Yakima spat a curse and bolted between two cotton-woods. As he ran out from the grove and into the sunlight, he snapped the rifle to his shoulder.

His right foot clipped a deadfall, and he fell hard. Ignoring the burn of his scraped elbows and knees, he heaved himself back to his feet and snapped another look at the horse thieves.

While one rode southwest with Wolf, booting his own horse into a halting gallop toward a bend in the stream, the other—stocky, blond, sunburned—raised a rifle to his shoulder. Smoke puffed around the barrel. The crack followed, the bullet plunking into the branch Yakima had tripped over.

Yakima threw himself to the left as the rifle boomed again, another slug tearing up sod where he'd just been standing. Rolling off his shoulder and rising to one knee, Yakima raised his own rifle.

The blond shooter had turned to follow his partner and Wolf. Frightened by the gunfire, the horse was no longer fighting the lead with as much vehemence as before, but trotting along behind, tail raised, shaking his head.

Yakima stared down his Yellowboy's barrel and fingered the trigger. He cursed and lowered the rifle. If he took a shot, he might hit his own horse.

He stared after the two riders splashing across the creek and heading for the game trail on the other side. They would no doubt follow the trail downstream.

Yakima took his rifle in one hand and sprinted across the flat ground rising toward the western hogbacks, which were beginning to glow copper in the waning light. Reaching the base of the closest bluff, he bounded straight up the side, pursing his lips as he dug his bare heels into the short brown weeds, avoiding patches of prickly pear and Spanish bayonet.

He crested the butte in five swift strides, paused for a few seconds to catch his breath, then ran west along the ridge. Spying a game trail, he plunged into the crease on the other side, bulled through the thick shrubs at the bottom, and traced a slanting course up the face of the far butte. Seconds later, he was at the crest, his lungs on fire, chest heaving, a copper taste in his throat.

From below rose the thuds of galloping hooves. He lifted his head to see the two horse thieves splitting ass along the creek, Wolf loping behind them and shaking his head stubbornly. The men were hunkered low in their saddles, casting wary looks over their shoulders.

Yakima started to raise the rifle to his shoulder, but stopped. They were too far away.

Taking the rifle again in one hand, he ran along the butte crest, paralleling the riders. Where the slope gentled, he ran down and crossed the canyon bottom toward the creek, aiming for a beaver dam and keeping his head low so they couldn't see him over the cattails.

He was nearly even with the two riders when he pushed through the thick brush and leapt onto the tightly woven branches of the beaver dam. The rush of the water over the dam covered his footsteps. Midway across the dam, he stopped, planted his feet in the ankle-deep rushing water, curling his toes over a couple of solid branches, and raised the rifle to his shoulder.

The men were straight across the creek, moving to his right at a fast clip, heads and shoulders bouncing above the swaying weed tips.

Yakima planted a quick bead on the gent with the blond hair peeking below his frayed bowler. As he pulled the trigger, the man swung his head around to look behind. The slug sliced over his right ear and plunked into the chalky bluff beyond, puffing dust.

The man ducked and turned his gaze toward Yakima, eyes wide, mouth forming a large, dark oval. As he and his partner continued downstream, Yakima quickly levered the Yellowboy and snapped off another shot. The report hadn't stopped echoing before the branch under his right foot gave way.

He lost his footing, threw his arms up, tossing the rifle over his head, and tumbled into the stream.

The cold water was like an electric charge through his

bones. He ground his feet into the stream's stony bottom, and lifted his head and chest above the water. Clearing his eyes and blowing, he staggered around in the hip-deep stream, getting his bearings in time to see the two horse thieves gallop around a southwestern bend.

As the riders disappeared through a notch in the hogbacks, Wolf, fiddle-footing and chomping his bit several paces behind, looked back over his right shoulder.

For an instant, the horse's dark, beseeching gaze met Yakima's.

Then the fold swallowed him, and Yakima stood in the stream, hearing only the dwindling hoofbeats, the thieves' muffled laughter, and the breeze rustling the weeds around him.

Yakima slapped the water and cursed, then stood staring at the notch in the hills as if he could will his horse back. He imagined his hands around the necks of the men who'd taken him . . . squeezing . . .

Finally, he turned toward the dam. His right foot came down on his rifle. He stooped to retrieve it from the stream bottom, then scrambled up onto the beaver dam and back through the weeds and over the bluffs toward Faith.

Chapter 12

It was almost dark when Wit Bardoul and Roy Brindley walked their horses into the yard of Thornton's roadhouse. Bardoul, smoking a cigarette stub, stopped his horse in the middle of the yard, raking his gaze over the nearly dark roadhouse, only a couple of windows lit, two saddle horses hanging their heads at the hitchrack.

"Looks like business has slowed down," he remarked without turning to Brindley on his left.

Brindley spat over his horse's shoulder. "Nothin' like a crazy half-breed shootin' up the place to sour trade."

"Nothin' like losin' your best whore, too," Bardoul snorted, shoving his sombrero back on his salt-and-pepper curls and swinging down from the Appaloosa's saddle. He tossed his reins to Brindley, then beat dust from his shotgun chaps and buckskins and started toward the roadhouse. "Tend the hosses. I'll go see if Thornton's still kickin'."

As Bardoul mounted the creaky porch steps, Brindley muttered behind him, at a volume not meant to be heard, "Tend your own damn horse, ya kill-crazy coot."

Bardoul stopped atop the porch and turned. "What's that, Roy? You say somethin'?"

Brindley was leading both horses toward the barn. He

glanced over his left shoulder and quickened his pace. It was too dark for Bardoul to see his expression. "Uh . . . nothin', Mr. Bardoul. I was just askin' these hosses why they couldn't unleather themselves." He chuckled nervously and turned toward the barn, where a light shone in the lean-to room off the east side.

Bardoul doffed his sombrero and beat it against the roadhouse wall as he stepped through the batwings. He paused inside the door, looked around.

The big redheaded bartender, Avery Sykes, was trimming his nails with a skinning knife. Two saddle tramps stood at the bar, drinking beers in stony silence. One of the whores sat at a table near the piano, laying out solitaire by the light of a bracket lamp hanging on a nearby joist.

Sykes and the saddle tramps regarded Bardoul expectantly. The bounty hunter crossed to the bar, asked for whiskey, and didn't bother to drop any coins when Sykes had set the bottle on the mahogany.

The bartender looked at him from beneath his bushy red eyebrows, thick mustache lifted so that the waxed ends nearly touched his nose.

"Do I still have an employer?"

Sykes set the bottle on the bar, tossed the cork down beside it. "Rage is a healing elixir. By the time you bring those heads back, he'll be good as new."

Bardoul grabbed the bottle by the neck, took a pull. "The patient in his room?"

"Where else?"

Holding the bottle by the neck, Bardoul sauntered past the two saddle tramps nursing their beers and regarding him warily. As he headed for the stairs, the whore, who'd stopped playing solitaire when he'd entered the saloon, cleared her throat and said, "You didn't see Nettie and Claire along the road, did you, Mr. Bardoul?"

Halfway up the stairs, Bardoul turned toward the girl and, winking, lifted the bottle to her. "Sure did. They said to say hi!"

The girl's face blanched.

Bardoul sipped the whiskey and continued up the stairs. When he got to the top of the staircase, he started whistling softly and didn't stop till he stood before Thornton's door. He knocked with the knuckles of his left hand.

Thornton's gravelly voice, thick with drink, answered: "Who is it?"

"Santy Claus."

"Get in here, Bardoul!"

The bounty hunter threw open the door and stood in the doorway, stovepipe boots spread wide, whiskey bottle in one hand, the other hand resting on the horn handle of his big bowie knife. His bushy tobacco-and-whiskey-stained beard spread with a grin, lifting the birthmark beside his nose.

On the bed before Bardoul, Thornton lay naked except for the bandage around his waist, the sheets and quilts twisted about his hairy, potbellied frame. A pan of water was wedged between his legs. On his right lay one of the remaining whores—a plump youngster with pear-shaped breasts and short brown hair. Eve, Bardoul thought she was called.

She reclined on one elbow, regarding the bounty hunter with little interest as, with her left hand, she slowly mopped Thornton's chest with a wet cloth. Her brown eyes reflected the wan light of the two lamps atop the cluttered dresser and the flames snapping in the charcoal brazier.

Bardoul stepped forward and tipped the bottle back, taking a long pull. Lowering it, he raked his lusty gaze over the whore—from her breasts brushing Thornton's side to her full hips and creamy thighs to her pink feet lying one atop the other beside Thornton's hairy calves. "Heard you're havin' whore trouble. But not at the moment, I see."

Thornton lifted his head slightly from his pillow. "Did Brindley kill those other two bitches?"

"No. I did."

"You bring the heads?"

Bardoul smiled sheepishly. "We had to . . . uh . . . get outta there fast."

Thornton chuffed knowingly.

Bardoul kept his eyes on the whore. She stopped swabbing Thornton's chest for a moment, one eye half closing. Then she dropped the cloth in the basin, squeezed out the water, and went to work on Thornton's neck.

"I reckon Brindley told you I'm offering a thousand for one more—and the rock worshiper."

"A thousand dollars. That ain't a whole lotta dinero for two."

"Five hundred now, five hundred when you've delivered the heads."

"Like I said . . ."

"Take it or leave it, Bardoul. I am in no mood to be *diddled*. If you don't want the job, I'll send someone else." Thornton tilted his head so the whore could scrub under his left ear. "You aren't the only headhunter around."

"But I'm the most reliable." Bardoul tipped back the bottle, gulping, whiskey streaming down both sides of his mouth and running down his beard. Then he sauntered across the room, dragged an overstuffed leather chair over to Thornton's bed, and sat down heavily, resting the whiskey on his right knee. "But I reckon a thousand's a respectable number, if you throw in a few other enticements."

"Such as?"

"I'm gonna need a coupla boys to tend horses and help track. Not that I can't track a tick through a pine forest, but that savage might be tougher than your run-o'-the-mill white-eyes, and my own eyes ain't as good as they once was. Three sets are better than one. That Brindley and your other hostler will do, though I will not share one cent of the bounty with them."

The girl wrung out the cloth in the pan, then dabbed gently around Thornton's bandaged wound. The roadhouse manager winced and slapped her hand away, his eyes on Bardoul. "Pour me a drink."

Bardoul set his own whiskey at his feet, then reached over and filled a glass on Thornton's bedside table from a flat brandy bottle. He gave the glass to Thornton, then picked up his bottle, lifting it in salute.

"I want plenty of grub and whiskey, and I want free drinks and"—he shuttled his flat gaze to the whore, who was now cleaning Thornton's right thigh—"free women and free room and board."

Thornton scowled. "For how long?"

"What sounds fair?"

"Three months."

"Make it six and you got a deal. Starting tonight."

Thornton looked at the whore crouched over his waist, her nipples dragging along his thigh. "She makin' you think manly thoughts, is she? She ain't doin' nothin' for me, not with this damn hole in my side. Eve, you'll go with—"

"I done had Eve last time," Bardoul said. "I don't think I've had the one downstairs, though."

"Who's downstairs?" Thornton asked the whore.

"Kansas Jen."

"Well, then," Bardoul said, standing and taking another

pull from the half-empty bottle. "I reckon we got us a deal, Thornton."

"Don't go ridin' off with your tail in the air," Thornton warned, extending his whiskey glass at the bounty hunter, poking his index finger out. "You seen what he did here the other night. The son of a bitch has invisible wings, and he's damn good with a knife."

"I used to hunt bounties down in Apacheria," Bardoul said, moving toward the door, pivoting drunkenly at the waist. "Two dollars a head. Nothin' harder to catch or kill than an Apache." He turned back toward Thornton. "This Yakima breed—he won't be no trouble at all."

Bardoul's brows suddenly furrowed. "You sure you want me to kill that whore—Faith? Sure you don't want me to bring her back alive? You and her—weren't you . . . ?"

Thornton stared at him, a thoughtful cast to his gaze. He rested his head back against the pillow. Eve, who had moved down to the bottom of the bed and was gently washing his feet, looked up at her boss.

"Kill her," Thornton said, staring at the ceiling. "Kill 'em both and be done with it."

Bardoul nodded and raised the bottle, saluting again. "Have a good rest of the evenin'." He opened the door, went out, drew the door closed behind him, and began whistling again as he meandered back the way he'd come.

Halfway down the stairs, he stopped whistling and peered into the saloon's main hall. The saddle tramps were still standing before the bar, but one had the whore wrapped around his waist, rising up on her bare toes, nibbling his chin and giggling.

"I told you, Jen," the saddle tramp said—a tall lad with sandy hair combed back from a widow's peak, "I ain't got no money."

"I told *you*," the whore said, pulling his head down,

kissing his cheek, "I'd see about giving you a little discount this evenin'."

Beyond them, near the door, Brindley and the other hostler, Higgins, were playing two-handed poker, a bottle and two shot glasses before them. Bardoul continued down the stairs. "Brindley, you and your pal are pullin' foot with me at first light. I suggest you start puttin' up trail supplies now, and pick out two of Thornton's best horses for ridin' and one for packin'."

At the bottom of the stairs, he turned toward the bar. "And don't forget the whiskey."

Brindley scowled over his cards, eyes pinched to slits. "Thornton say so?"

"You got it."

Bardoul walked up to the tall saddle tramp and placed his hand on the girl's arm. She had long, curly brown hair, and while her legs and arms were willowy and her breasts were only a little larger than coffee mugs, she had a fine, round ass. "Come on, Jen. This is your lucky night!"

Kansas Jen looked at him, her eyes dark, forehead wrinkled. "No . . . I . . . I'm Bobby's girl tonight."

"The hell you are. Bobby don't have nothin' but cockleburs and horseshit in his pockets, anyway."

Bobby pulled the girl away from Bardoul and stepped out from the bar. "You heard her. She's mine tonight, bounty man."

"Sorry, but I got dibs."

"No, you don't," Jen said, pulling her dress strap over her shoulder and stepping behind Bobby. "You don't got dibs on me. You're mean . . . an' . . . an' dirty . . . and you're"—her voice cracked and tears rolled down her cheeks—"a cold-blooded *killer*!"

Bardoul threw his head back and laughed. Then his face

went slack, and he glared at the girl peeking out from behind Bobby's right shoulder. "Ain't nice—insultin' a man for the way he makes a livin'."

As Bardoul sprang forward, the girl screamed. The bounty hunter swung his whiskey bottle up soundly between Bobby's chap-covered legs, smacking his crotch with a solid thump. Bobby sucked a hard breath and bent forward, covering his crotch with both arms.

At the same time, Bardoul slammed his right knee into Bobby's face.

"Uhhhh-ah!" Bobby screamed, half straightening and staggering off down the bar, the girl giving another shriek and running out from behind him. Bobby left one hand on his crotch while lifting the other to his nose, blood spurting between his fingers, painting his face.

Bobby's partner snarled at Bardoul, "You mangy son of a—"

He began sliding his Schofield from its worn leather holster, but stopped when he saw the long barrel of Bardoul's .45 an inch from his belly button. He removed his hand from the Schofield's grip and, face blanching, raised his hands to his shoulders.

Bardoul looked at Bobby. The young saddle tramp was down on his knees, cursing, holding his legs close together, and pressing his hand over his gushing nose. The fight seemed to be out of him, so Bardoul holstered the Remy and grabbed the girl's arm. He crouched, slung her over his shoulder like a potato sack, and turned toward the stairs.

"Come on, Jen." Bardoul whooped as the girl kicked and punched his back. "We're gonna have us a high old time, you an' me!"

Chapter 13

Jogging bare-assed naked through the wheat- and needle-grass, hurdling horehound, silverthorn, and rock as he headed back toward his and Faith's camp along the creek, Yakima crested a rise and stopped.

His heart pounded from exertion. His body was slick with sweat. Over and over in his mind he saw Wolf—his magnificent black mustang—looking back as the two thieves led him off through the river bluffs. Fear and beseeching had been in Wolf's eyes.

The stallion and Yakima had rarely been apart.

Bending forward to catch his wind, Yakima spied movement in the direction of the creek. Faith ran toward him.

He waited while she mounted the knoll, only practically conscious of his nakedness, not embarrassed by it. He felt foolish for letting two men sneak into his camp and steal his horse while he'd been in the throes of carnal passion. Outraged at himself was a better word. But his nakedness was a minor thing, only something to be amended so he could take off after the thieves and get his horse back.

Faith stopped before him, clad in his old denims, plaid shirt, and moccasins. The slim leather belt was too long for her, and she'd tied it around her waist, the end dangling. In her arms she carried Yakima's longjohns, buckskin pants, wool shirt, boots, and hat.

She, too, was out of breath. "Did they get away?"

Yakima laid the rifle in the grass, grabbed his underwear, and quickly stepped into the bottoms. "Heading upstream. I'm going after them."

"On foot?"

"Don't have much choice."

"It'll be dark soon. Best wait till morning."

"I might be able to catch 'em if I head cross-country. I know the trail they're on. It wraps around through the buttes for several miles." He shrugged into his shirt, then sat down to pull his boots on. "You stay here. Keep the fire small, and keep my pistol handy."

"I wish you'd wait till morning."

"If it rained tonight, or if a wind came up, I'd lose their trail. They're not getting away with Wolf." Yakima stuffed his shirttail in his pants, then stooped to pick up his rifle. He had no spare shells, but he figured there would be eight or nine shots in the Yellowboy's breech.

"You'll be okay," he told Faith as she eyed him warily, her blond hair blowing around in the wind. "I'll be back before daylight. If not, follow the trail south. Sooner or later you'll find a freighter or someone who'll take you out of the foothills to Denver."

He turned and began jogging back into the bluffs. After a few yards, he turned back to her. She stood atop the knoll, watching him, one foot cocked, her arms hanging straight down at her sides.

"You'll be all right," Yakima told her again.

He turned and quickened his pace into the thickening late-afternoon shadows. When he glanced back once more, she was walking toward the creek, holding her hair in both hands above her head.

Faith wasn't sure how long she'd been sitting near the fire, her back to a tree, blankets drawn up to her neck, when she was thrust suddenly from a light sleep.

She blinked and looked around. She'd heard something.

Before her, the fire had burned down to a dull orange glow. She remembered Yakima's pistol, and picked it up. With her other hand, she pushed herself to her feet.

Westward, a foot crunched dew-damp grass.

A constriction formed in Faith's throat, and her heart pounded. She looked around. What should she do? Hide or call out for the newcomer to identify himself?

Labored breaths sounded as the footsteps drew near.

Holding the pistol in both hands, a thumb on the hammer, she backed slowly toward the creek.

She was several feet beyond the fire when a voice rose, low but clear. "It's Yakima."

Her muscles relaxing, she lowered the pistol and drew a deep, relieved breath. She tossed several logs on the fire and set the half-full coffeepot, in which she'd brewed green tea, on the glowing coals. A shadow moved in the cottonwoods, and then Yakima stepped into the fire's wan glow, his chest rising and falling sharply, his shirt pasted to him with sweat.

"Thank God," Faith said, wrapping her arms around his neck and pressing her face to his hot, damp chest. He smelled like sage and the night wind. He'd come back for her. Knowing how much the black stallion meant to him, she had begun to think he wouldn't. "Any sign of Wolf?"

Yakima nodded and moved off toward the creek. He disappeared into the darkness, but his voice rose clearly above the creek's tinny murmur. "I went to where the trails fork, one going to Jamestown, the other to Gold Cache. They're headin' for Gold Cache."

Water splashed.

Faith remained by the fire, a blanket wrapped about her, for the night was sharply cool. The sound of Yakima washing in the cold water made her shudder.

Shortly, Yakima strode back into the firelight, his face and hair wet, breath puffing about his shoulders. Crouching over the fire, he filled a tin cup with tea from the pot.

He sipped the hot brew and looked over his shoulder at Faith, a tired smile carving deep lines in his face. "I reckon you're going to Gold Cache, after all."

"We're gonna walk?"

Hunkered before the fire, he sipped the smoking tea. "Walk till we find horses or run into a freight outfit. If we offer cash, someone might give us a ride." He took another sip, and his voice was flat and hard. "Less'n we can catch up to those horse thieves and Wolf before we get to Gold Cache."

He straightened, threw his tea dregs into the weeds, dropped the cup by the fire, and collapsed on his saddle blanket. Resting his head against his saddle, he drew another blanket over his chest and heaved a vast sigh. "Best get some sleep. It's a long walk, most of it uphill."

Faith tossed another log on the fire, gathered the rest of her blankets about her and lay down beside Yakima. She turned, snuggled her face against his chest. "Why did you come back? You'd gained several miles on 'em."

Yakima lay his arm across his forehead. "Couldn't leave my pistol and saddle, could I?"

She lifted her head, regarded him with stitched brows.

He chuckled.

Faith ground a fist into his ribs, rested her head on his chest again, and in a few minutes they were both asleep.

They were on the trail at first light, after a quick breakfast of tea, jerky, and wild berries, and after Yakima hid his tack under rocks and fashioned a sling with which to carry his war bag over his shoulder.

He'd made the sling from the four-point capote he'd carried his bedroll in. He and Faith would need the heavy coat, which he'd sewn from wool trading blankets and deerskins, when they entered the high country.

He'd hidden his boots with his tack as well, donning deerskin, fur-lined moccasin boots, which were better for walking than the stiff cowhide boots.

Capote sack over one shoulder, his Yellowboy slung over the other, he strode out ahead of Faith, setting a moderately fast pace. She kept up well. He often glanced behind to see her taking long strides on the trail behind him, looking like a small, fine-boned man in Yakima's spare trail clothes, rolled cuffs jouncing about her laced moccasins, leather hat shielding her head from the climbing sun. She'd stuffed her hair beneath the hat. The end of the too long belt flapped about her hip.

Late in the morning they came to where the trail forked. Taking the right fork, toward Gold Cache, they were soon following the rutted freight trail along the north bank of the St. Vrain River, snaking their way ever higher toward the Continental Divide.

Rugged granite peaks shouldered on both sides of the canyon, and the quickly dropping river shot through its narrow, rocky bed, frothy as beer foam and raising a steady mist and roar.

They met several prospectors heading out of the mountains for the winter—bearded, owl-eyed gents trailing mules or donkeys, a few driving light farm wagons filled with supplies. One man walked, pushing a two-wheeled cart, a German shepherd trailing with half a dead raccoon in its jaws.

Only one outfit passed them heading for Gold Cache. The two wagons were overloaded, however, and Yakima didn't bother asking for a ride. One of the drivers—a walleyed hombre in a wolf coat and knee-high boots—gave Faith the thrice-over in her men's baggy clothes, then winked and threw his head back, laughing lustily.

After meeting others, Yakima decided that it would be best if they stayed off the trail from then on. No use begging more trouble than they already had.

He didn't have to ask the men they met if they'd seen two men leading a black mustang. He knew Wolf's shoe prints as well as his own, and they were clearly marked in the trail beneath his moccasins.

After the sun sank behind the pine-carpeted western slopes, they camped in a gorge along the St. Vrain, well off the freight trail, and hid their fire among sheltering rocks. They fried the trout Yakima impaled with a makeshift spear, slept soundly, and were on the road again before the sun had lifted from behind the granite knobs.

At eleven o'clock that morning, yells and shouted epithets rose from the base of the hill they'd just climbed, well away from the river. They heard the sharp cracks of a blacksnake, followed by the indignant brays of mules.

"Another wagon train," Yakima said without turning around. Unused to foot travel, Faith was having a tougher time today, and she was limping from blisters on both feet. "Best you ride now, if they're a fit bunch."

"I reckon I'm just slowing you down."

"No point in torturing yourself if you don't have to." He

turned now to peer back down the switchbacking trail. No sign of the freighters yet, but by the sounds of the mules and the blacksnakes and the heated shouts, they'd be along soon.

Twenty minutes later, they were walking along a relatively flat stretch of trail when Yakima turned to see two mules rise over a hill brow, heads bobbing as they leaned into the collars, manes ruffling.

Yakima took Faith's arm, and together they climbed the rocks north of the trail. They were hunkered among in the boulders, thirty feet above the trail and looking down, as the three wagons approached—big Pittsburgs with heavy brakes for mountain grades, and log chains from axles to doubletrees for sharp cornering. Dirty white tarpaulins were stretched taut over their boxes. Dust rose, brassy in the midday light, and the mules' hooves clomped heavily, the wheels screeching like angry hawks.

As the wagons passed, Yakima and Faith tracked them, watching. When the last wagon was ten yards beyond, Faith began to rise. Yakima grabbed her arm, pulled her back down beside him.

"That gent in the second wagon. Bad hombre. Jumped me in an alley down in Alamosa after I beat him and three Texas high rollers at stud." Yakima shook his head, eyes on the rear wagon lumbering into the distance. "You won't be ridin' with them."

Faith looked at him, a faint smile pulling at her lips.

When the dust had settled over the trail and the breezy mountain silence had once again fallen over the canyon, Yakima hefted his war bag and rifle. "We'd best get a move on."

They continued walking but rested several times, Faith bathing her blistered feet in the stream. She kept up a good face and a joking tone, but she was sunburned and tired. Yakima knew she couldn't put in another day.

An hour after their last stop, after they'd turned away from the St. Vrain, the orange ball of the falling sun was split by a thumb of jagged basalt. Shadows tilted from rocks, and draws were filled with purple velvet.

Yakima and Faith ambled down a hill and into a clearing, low ridges on both sides of the trail. A leaning wooden sign announced DEVIL'S GULCH in faded red letters, beneath which STABLES, FOOD, SLEEP had been printed in black. Beyond, clay-colored boulders and pines surrounded an L-shaped, two-story roadhouse of square, chinked pine logs.

A barn and corrals spread out on the left side of the trail. The three wagons they'd seen earlier were parked in the yard, and the drivers were unhitching the mules. There was another, lighter wagon parked before the corrals, and a big black man—bare-chested and wearing a red bandanna around his neck and a black sombrero on his head—was wrestling a hub off the rear axle.

Yakima walked Faith up the steps of the roadhouse's front porch and through the front door. Inside, a long counter ran along the left wall. Cured meat hung from the rafters. Several tables and a smoky stove stood among cracker barrels and displays of mining supplies.

An old, silver-haired couple, their humble but civilized attire streaked with trail dust, sat at one of the tables, drinking coffee. A beefy, sandy-haired lad, similarly dressed in a bowler and a wool suit coat, sat to the right of the old woman, forking large bites of apricot pie into his mouth.

"Miss, you're welcome. But no Injuns."

The voice came from the back of the room, where a fat man with wavy red hair and a shaggy red beard stood, a broom in his hand.

He glanced at a plaque behind the bar, above the mirror, bearing the painted words: NO INDIANS IN RODEHOUSE. At the right end of the plaque was a figure drawing of a broad-nosed, red face capped by a gaudy headdress. A white cross was marked over it.

Faith turned to Yakima, then to the big redhead at the back of the room. She opened her mouth to speak, but Yakima stopped her with a hand on her elbow.

"Easy. No trouble," he said softly. "You stay in here, get a room. I'll go outside, see about getting some horses."

Faith frowned up at him. "But—"

"No buts. And no trouble." Yakima cast her a firm glance, then turned, went back outside and down the porch steps, and crossed the yard at an angle, stepping around the big, sweat-lathered mules the freighters were leading to the barn.

A man with a wooden stump where his left leg should have been sat on a barrel to the right of the barn, whittling an ironwood stick with a barlow knife. He was sixty or so, his face resembling a raisin set back behind a shaggy red beard and framed by woolly red hair streaked with silver. No doubt the father of the younger, bigger redhead inside the roadhouse. His sharp blue eyes regarded Yakima cunningly. A pair of handmade crutches leaned against the barrel.

When Yakima was twelve feet from the one-legged gent, one of the mule skinners stopped to Yakima's right, a wheel hub in his thick hands. It was one of the men Yakima had whipped at stud poker in Alamosa. The man regarded Yakima through slitted eyes, then licked his plump, chapped lips and tilted his head to one side.

"Where I seen you before, breed?"

Yakima looked at him dully. "Alamosa. Last winter."

The man, whose name started with a "D"—Driesen or Drexler?—stared at Yakima for a good ten seconds. Yakima held the gaze, his own eyes bored. The mule skinner blinked first, then continued toting the wheel hub toward the portable blacksmith forge east of the barn.

As he walked away, he drew the looks of his two stocky comrades and nodded his head toward Yakima. Grumbling, the skinners continued putting up their mules and tack.

Yakima turned to the one-legged gent grinning at him dubiously. "Got any horses for sale?"

The old man hiked a shoulder. "Depends on how much money you got."

"Forty-five dollars."

The old gent cackled. "I don't stable nags here, breed!"

"Rent me one, then. I'll have him back in a week."

"Don't rent out horses. In these parts, it's hard to get 'em back."

Yakima glanced at the four horses milling in the nearest corral. Good horseflesh, all. He saw a long-legged paint that could no doubt eat up the trail to Gold Cache in two, maybe two and a half days. With such a horse, he might be able to overtake the men who'd stolen Wolf before they got to the mining camp and possibly sold him.

Yakima turned his gaze to a stone well with a shake roof and a wooden bucket in a patch of red willows west of the roadhouse. "Mind if I wash, fill my canteen yonder?"

The grin in place, the old man jerked his knife toward a stock tank where one of the mule skinners was letting a mule draw from the hay- and seed-flecked water. "That should do ye."

"It's all yours, breed," the skinner laughed, pulling the mule away from the tank. "Sunshine here's had his fill, but he left plenty!"

Chuckling with the other two skinners, the man led the mule on into the barn.

Yakima moved toward the tank. Doing so, he saw the big black man looking at him, expressionless, as he slid a new wheel onto the farm wagon's axle, his huge ebony arms expanding and contracting as he worked. Yakima dropped his gear beside the tank, rolled up his shirtsleeves, crouched over the tank, and cupped the brackish water to his face, scrubbing away the dust and the sweat.

When he lifted his head, he saw a thin shadow slide across the ground to his left, heard a low rasp of something flying through the air over his head. He tensed, but before he could turn around or raise his arms, the lariat loop dropped over his head and shoulders.

The rope drew taut, grinding into his upper arms, and he was jerked off his feet. His back hit the ground, the air leaving his lungs with a grunt.

He looked up to see the three mule skinners circle him slowly, grinning down at him. One held an ax handle, another a shovel.

The man he'd beaten at cards held the lariat in one hand while brandishing a bullwhip in the other. He was laughing.

Chapter 14

"Boys," said the man wielding the bullwhip, "what do you say we have a little fun with this breed who stole seventy-three dollars off'n me down Alamosa way?"

Yakima sat up. He didn't struggle against the rope around his arms.

"Stole?" He spat dust from his lips, kept his voice jovial as he smiled up at the mule skinners. "I don't recollect *stealin'* anything off you, friend. I do recall you getting sore because I *beat* you square and plumb."

"That's your story, breed. Everyone knows an Injun can't win at cards less'n he cheats!" The man whose name Yakima couldn't quite remember stepped back and cracked the bullwhip's popper a foot from Yakima's left ear.

Yakima blinked. His smile grew taut while his tone remained jovial. "I also recall you jumpin' me with two other friends in an alley. Say, how're those ribs of yours? They heal all right?"

The other two mule skinners, wielding their ax handle and shovel respectively, chuckled as they traced a slow circle around him. The man with the bullwhip flushed and shot a dark glance to each of his partners.

"It was dark that night," he grumbled. "And I'd had more

than my share of busthead. Now"—he leaned forward and
cracked the bullwhip just to the right of Yakima's right ear—
"I'm feelin' just fine."

The man swung the bullwhip back behind him, laughing,
then slung it over his head.

Yakima raised a brow and edged his voice with menace.
"One more time, and you're gonna wear that blacksnake
around your neck."

"Think so?"

"Get him, Dietrich," said the man with the ax handle.
"This breed here needs a tattoo on his ass." To Yakima, he
said, "Son, don't you know how to talk to your betters?"

"Sure, I do," Yakima said, his eyes crinkling at the corners as he shuttled a glance to the man.

He was a squat little ranny in a green canvas coat and
high-top, lace-up boots. He had a shaggy, tobacco-stained
beard but no mustache. Tapping the ax handle in the palm of
his left hand, he continued sidestepping around Yakima,
breathing hard and grinning beneath the brim of his black
sombrero.

"I just don't see anyone better than me in this yard,"
Yakima added, erasing the half smile from his own face.

He hadn't yet finished the sentence before Dietrich
whipped the blacksnake toward him. Yakima had had blacksnakes whipped at him before. Calmly, he watched the popper spin through the air, growing larger and larger as it
approached his shoulder.

At the last second, Yakima threw out his arm, forcing up
the rope around his chest. He closed his hand around the
whip, about a foot up from the popper, quashing the crack.
The pain was sharp, like a knife slice across his palm, but he
did not react. Instead, he jerked the whip's rawhide handle
from Dietrich's grasp.

"*Jay-sus!*" Dietrich barked, stumbling forward, grabbing his wrist and looking down at his wrenched right hand as if making sure it was still there.

At the same time, Yakima spied movement in the corner of his right eye. He half turned, saw the ax handle careening toward his head. He ducked, heard the handle's whistle through the air as well as the squat man's surprised grunt.

Ripping the lariat noose over his head, Yakima leapt to his feet, then jumped two feet off the ground. He twisted, set one moccasin down while the other spun high and connected soundly with the squat man's mouth.

Planting both feet in the dirt, he whipped his head around, arms straight out from his shoulders.

Dietrich bounded toward him, swinging his left fist. Yakima ducked, saw the third man swinging the shovel, and pivoted toward him.

He broke the shovel's swing with his right forearm, then jabbed the man's face twice with his fists, feeling the nose flatten beneath his knuckles. Screaming, the man dropped his shovel as he staggered back and fell to his knees, blood spurting against his face, seeping through his fingers.

He hadn't yet hit the ground when Yakima ducked another swing from Dietrich, then leapt onto the toes of his left foot and brought the heel of the other straight up and sideways.

The mocassin smashed into Dietrich's left cheek. Dietrich's feet left the yard, and he hit the ground hard on his right shoulder.

Screaming and cursing, his face pinched with red fury, Dietrich scrambled onto his hands and knees and began crawling toward his wagon. An old Springfield rifle hung on the wagon box, above a toolbox and a water barrel.

"Goddamn lousy son of a bitch of a bastard *rock wor-shiper!*"

Yakima spied the bullwhip on the ground in front of his right moccasin. He picked it up casually, then reached for his Yellowboy.

Shifting the rifle to his left hand, the bullwhip to his right, he stepped toward Dietrich and flung the whip. As the black rawhide dropped toward the man, Yakima eased the handle back. The end of the whip wound twice around Dietrich's neck, squeezing like a boa constrictor.

The mule skinner's cheek bunched, and he flung his hands to his neck. "Gughhhahh!"

Yakima pulled the whip back, jerking Dietrich off his knees. He landed in the dust on his back, clawing at the whip, his eyes slitted as he strangled, grinding his heels in the sand.

Yakima dropped the whip. Dietrich got his hands under the braided leather wrapped around his neck, started working it up over his face. He had it to his forehead when Yakima, who'd sauntered up to him, Yellowboy hanging low in his right hand, thrust the end of the barrel into Dietrich's mouth.

Dietrich's eyes snapped wide.

He gagged.

His hands rose to the barrel, then lowered as Yakima jammed the barrel farther down his throat. Dietrich rose up on his heels, keeping the back of his head against the ground, arching his back.

Holding the Yellowboy firm, Yakima glanced around. Dietrich's amigos were down—one on all fours spitting teeth, the other holding a handkerchief to his bloody nose and shaking his head like a horse that had gotten into the locoweed. Already the man's eyes were swelling shut.

The old one-legged gent remained on his keg, grinning and staring at Yakima as if he couldn't wait to see what would happen next. On the porch stood the younger red-head, holding a double-barreled greener across his chest and regarding Yakima skeptically. Faith stood at the other end of the porch, hands on the railing, looking worried.

Yakima dropped his gaze to Dietrich and slackened the barrel slightly. The man's back sank to the ground as he sucked a pinched breath.

"I see you again," Yakima said tautly, "I'll kill you. Savvy?"

Dietrich stared up the Yellowboy's barrel at Yakima, then bobbed his head quickly.

Yakima removed the barrel from the man's mouth, spittle stringing off the foresight. He held the rifle low as he strode to the roadhouse, stopped at the base of the porch steps. He looked up at the chubby redhead standing there, shotgun still crossed in his arms. The redhead's eyes had acquired a wary cast.

Yakima nodded toward Faith. "That young lady will be staying here tonight. Give her a good bed, plenty of grub." He looked around at the mule skinners, all three looking like they'd just been dropped off the back of a fast-moving wagon.

Yakima turned back to the beefy redhead. "I'll be holding you responsible for her safety."

The redhead slid his eyes to Faith, glanced at Yakima, his nostrils flaring slightly, then turned and ambled back into the roadhouse, brushing past the old woman and the sandy-haired lad peering owl-eyed around the doorframe.

Yakima began walking back to where he'd left his pack and canteen. Faith's voice stopped him. He turned around as she moved down the steps and paused before him. She slid a lock of hair away from her eyes, tipped back the brim of her man's leather hat.

"The old couple inside have offered me a ride tomorrow."

"That's good. They look like decent folks." He smiled thinly. "I'll be seein' you in Gold Cache, then."

He turned.

"Wait." She didn't say anything for a moment, her eyes searching his. "Did you get a horse?"

"Not yet. But, like I said, I'll see you in Gold Cache."

Yakima looked around. The one-legged oldster regarded him and Faith with mute interest. Finally, Yakima looked at Faith once more, pinched his hat brim at her. "Safe travel."

Her eyes crinkled slightly. "You, too."

Yakima turned and headed back to the stock trough. Dietrich and the other two mule skinners had gathered there, splashing water on their faces, grumbling under their breath. The man who'd been wielding the shovel looked up at Yakima, wincing and showing broken teeth and bloody gums, then quickly lowered his face back down to the water.

Yakima picked up his pack and canteen, strapping both around his neck and heading east around the corrals.

He passed the Negro smithy, still working on the wagon's rear wheel. The man didn't look up as Yakima passed him and turned around the corrals, heading for a rocky knob south and east, about a hundred yards from the roadhouse and from which a single pine tree grew crooked, as though perpetually bent by the wind.

True night. Darkness had closed down tight as a drumhead.

Yakima had feasted on the trout he'd caught in the creek that angled through the willows at the base of the southern ridge. He sat atop the rocky knoll, under the wind-twisted pine. The fire snapped and popped, the flames tearing on the night wind that smelled of cold earth and snow.

Winter was on the way. Maybe only a few miles farther up the trail. The wind was especially cold tonight. His four-point capote was barely keeping it out.

Faith.

He took a deep drag from his cigarette, held it down deep in his lungs, let it go. The wind tore the smoke from his lips. Sipping tea from his tin cup, he saw in his mind's eye an image of her sitting naked in the stream, feet and pink-nippled breasts protruding above the water's rippling surface, her hands clutching the roots above her head.

He'd see her again in Gold Cache, say his final good-bye.

What else could he do? It wasn't like they had a future together. A half-breed and a whore. Still, he felt as though a dull knife were prodding him down deep in his belly.

He turned his head slightly. The lights of the roadhouse shone in the darkness, the hulking wagons silhouetted against it. She was probably asleep now, in a bed with a corn-shuck mattress and a flour-sack pillow. She would wake well rested and light out early with the old folks and the boy.

The freighters would leave her alone. They were no doubt in too much pain to try anything with a woman tonight. Still, Yakima held his gaze on the flickering lights. He'd keep an eye on the place, his ears pricked for trouble. She'd be safe as long he was on the scout.

At the same time, on the roadhouse's second floor, Faith opened her eyes. She'd only been dozing on the creaky cot. The old woman lay nearby, snoring softly, while the men snored loudly on the other side of a makeshift rope-and-trade-blanket curtain.

Faith rose onto her elbows, swept the sack curtain away from the window, and peered into the southern darkness.

There on the rocky knoll, the flames of Yakima's fire guttered—a ragged, wind-torn glow in the darkness. The bent pine was silhouetted against the stars.

Faith looked out the window for a long time.

A chill touched her, and she shuddered. Drawing her blankets up to her chin, she lay back against the pillow and closed her eyes.

It took her a half hour to fall asleep.

Chapter 15

Yakima woke when his inner alarm clock rang around four thirty, the black sky still star-dusted, the air nippy, dew dappling the sage and cedars.

He drank water from his canteen—cold as snow water—and kicked dirt into his fire pit. Shouldering his gear, he peered at the dark roadhouse hunkered against the low bluffs in the north, then walked down the knoll, angling across the sage meadow to the corrals and the barn.

He crouched through corral slats and slowly pulled one of the two rear barn doors open, the warm hay smell and ammonia instantly filling his nostrils. When the opening was two feet wide, he stepped inside and to the right, so the backlight wouldn't silhouette him.

Ears pricked, he listened.

Snores rumbled softly somewhere off to his left. That would be the Negro smithy, asleep in his quarters.

Yakima stepped forward, set his gear gently in a hay cart, and fumbled around in the barn's heavy, musty shadows until his eyes adjusted enough that he found a tack room. A minute later he stepped through the back door with a saddle and blanket on his shoulder, a bridle looped over the saddle horn. He moved deliberately, trying to make as little noise as possible while thoroughly enjoying the deep, rhythmic snores.

Setting the saddle and blanket on the top corral slat just outside the barn doors, he grabbed the bridle and slowly approached the seven horses snorting and fiddle-footing at the back of the corral, six clumped around a tall, sharp-eyed stallion. The stallion would have been the perfect choice for a long, hard run, but the wild-eyed horse would probably put up a fuss and wake the big smithy as well as everyone in the roadhouse.

Yakima singled out a brown and white paint mare with three white stockings. She was ewe-necked and more than a little sickle-hocked, but the broad chest and muscular hips bespoke endurance. He clucked to the horse, ran his hands gently across her withers and down her neck, then calmly slipped the bridle over her ears, the bit into her mouth, and led her toward the barn.

He kept an eye on the stallion, relieved that the big horse seemed satisfied to bob his head and show his teeth back where the others were gathered around him like children around their mother.

Yakima looped the paint's bridle reins around one of the corral's peeled-log poles, set the blanket on her back, the saddle on top of it. He cinched the latigo and froze, his head against the paint's ribs, ears pricked at the barn.

The snores had stopped.

A deep voice thick with sleep said, "Don't forget this."

Yakima turned sharply. The big mahogany figure filled the doorway. He tossed Yakima's Yellowboy to him. Yakima caught the rifle with his right hand, then canted his head, wary.

"I'm takin' this here mare," Yakima said.

"I didn't think you were saddling her 'cause you thought she'd look purty all leathered up."

The big man's chest heaved and there was a grating sound that could only have been a chuckle. He flung an arm forward. Yakima's pack and canteen landed in the dust before his moccasins.

The wheezing chuckle again. "You don't remember me, do you, Yakima Henry?"

Yakima looked at him. The big man stepped into the violet darkness. "We came up the Texas trail together some six, seven years ago."

Yakima squinted and then a taut grin spread across his lips. "Well, I'll be damned. Jeff Ironsides."

"I shod the horses and fed the waddies. You peeled potatoes for me, time or two." Ironsides nodded at the saddle horse. "Picked you out a fine one. Not so purty, but a stayer."

"I'll bring her back."

"Figured you would."

Yakima reached into his right front pocket. "I'll pay you a silver cartwheel in advance—"

"I ain't takin' your money, Yakima. Chances are the crippled old bastard who runs the place won't even notice she's gone. Just bring her back in one piece, and that's all I got to say on the subject."

As Ironsides opened the gate, Yakima swung into the leather and hung his canteen and war bag over the saddle horn, his rifle down his back. He gigged the horse through the gate, pinched his hat brim at the big, bullet-headed black man. "Much obliged."

As Yakima turned the horse toward the yard, Ironsides called softly, "Like I said, she's a stayer, but she needs water often and she don't see in the dark as good as some."

Yakima threw up an arm in acknowledgment, then

walked the horse through the yard, keeping an eye on the cabin in which a single rear window glowed. Faith was probably still asleep. A pang of guilt and regret for leaving her shot through him, but this was best for them both.

When he was past the last of the outbuildings, he gigged the paint into a trot. The horse clung to the trail nicely, seemed eager to run, so Yakima gave her her head, and the hooves drummed along the right track of the two-track trail.

Faith dreamed that Thornton was grabbing her by her right arm. With his free hand he held a knife before her face, tilting the point toward her right eye, ordering her to hold still.

Teeth gritted, eyes flashing like daggers, he leaned toward her and shouted, "It'll only hurt worse if you fight me, whore!"

"No!" Faith cried, trying to jerk her arm from the roadhouse owner's grip.

She snapped her eyes open.

An old woman, gray hair wrapped in a tight bun, crouched over Faith's cot. The woman's eyes were wide as she held her left hand up, palm out, barely visible in the early-morning darkness. Her other hand was splayed across her bosom.

Her voice came gently. "I'm not going to hurt you, child. Just wanted to wake you. Ed said we'd be needing to pull out in twenty minutes or so."

On her elbows, Faith heaved a sigh and flushed with embarrassment. It was the old woman who'd offered her a ride. Faith's heart slowed.

"Thank you, Mrs. Schaeffer. I'll be ready."

The woman offered a kind smile, then straightened and

disappeared through the blanket partition. Faith turned to the window, swept the curtain aside.

Dawn had painted a pale pink glow behind the bluffs and mountains in the east. The rise on which Yakima had camped was a black smudge, the single gnarled tree pointing like a crooked finger. No fire or any other sign of a camp. Yakima had likely cleared out well before dawn.

Faith wondered if he'd walked or if he'd somehow secured a horse.

A vague, lonely ache plagued her as she washed, dressed, gathered her gear, and went downstairs. The one-legged man was frying flapjacks, bacon, and eggs at the big iron range, and the man's son was filling coffee cups. The Schaeffers and the three freighters sat at two wooden tables arranged side by side near the stairs, a lamp burning on each table, another on the bar. The smoky room was rife with the smells of the food, boiled coffee, and tobacco.

As Faith strode to the Schaeffers' table, the freighters turned their heads toward her, then turned away, snickering. Mr. Schaeffer and the younger Schaeffer, whose name was Jules, stood up politely, shyly averting their gazes.

"Good mornin', ma'am," said the elder Schaeffer in his resonant preacher's tenor. He was tall, bald, and hawknosed, with a pious, taciturn demeanor. "I hope you slept well?"

"Just fine, thank you."

Chuckling broke out among the freighters. Faith turned her head. They glanced at her, then glanced away, like lewd schoolboys.

"Don't mind them, ma'am," said Mr. Schaeffer over his cup of steaming coffee. "They just don't know any better."

"Sure we do, Grandpa," squealed one of the freighters, his lips swollen and blue. "Sure we do!"

All three laughed, and the one who'd tried to whip Yakima splashed clear corn liquor into their coffee cups.

The Schaeffers ignored them, and so did Faith, who was glad when the food came so she could distract herself from the freighters and the nebulous ache in the pit of her stomach.

She felt much lighter when the freighters, having wolfed their food and coffee and filled the room with cigarette smoke, shuffled out to their wagons. Soon after, Mr. Schaeffer and Jules left to hitch their own two mules to their old Conestoga, and in a short while the Schaeffers and Faith were jolting along the trail that angled deeper and higher into the mountains.

Snow-mantled peaks rose before them. Along the sunwashed trail, yellow aspen leaves fluttered in the cool breeze. Riding in the back of the cramped, rattling wagon with Jules, Faith pulled her blanket tighter around her shoulders.

She and Jules were on their third game of checkers, though he was so shy he had yet to say anything except, "Miss Faith, could I interest you in checkers to while away the time?"

Now Faith slid a black checker forward, jumping one of Jules's red ones. Mrs. Schaeffer, riding on the seat with the preacher, turned her head to the side to speak through the front opening of the canvas cover. "Miss Faith, I've been wondering what could bring such a pretty girl to such a remote place as Gold Cache? Oh, don't tell me if you harbor reservations. I'm just being nosy, of course!"

Faith tensed slightly, smiled to cover it. "My father has a shop there. A clothing shop. I'm gonna work for him."

"I see." Mrs. Schaeffer turned forward to watch the trail.

Jules made a move. Faith countered it. In the corner of her left eye, she saw Mrs. Schaeffer turn toward her again. Again she tensed.

"Why on earth, dear, were you traveling with that Indian, if I might again be so forward? Couldn't your father provide accommodations?"

Faith turned to the woman, slid a lock of hair back from her face. She smiled and kept her tone light. "Yakima saved my life, Mrs. Schaeffer."

The old woman turned to her husband, slumped in the driver's seat. They shared a conspiratorial glance, then faced forward again, and that was the last of the conversation until the preacher turned the wagon off the road and announced, "Water break and a blow. Steep hill ahead."

While Mr. Schaeffer tended the mules and Jules gathered wood for a coffee fire, Faith and Mrs. Schaeffer walked down to a creek running along the base of a steep, low bank and shrouded in pines. Faith bathed her face in the water, drank, then, smoothing her damp hair back from her face, walked back to where smoke curled near the wagon.

Jules knelt beside the fledgling fire, blowing on the tinder he'd piled in the middle of an old rock ring. Mr. Schaeffer was draping a feed sack over the off mule's snout.

Faith moved to the fire ring and reached for the blackened coffeepot standing between two mossy pine branches. "I'll fetch water."

"You don't have to do that, ma'am," Jules said. "I can get it."

"Gotta earn my keep," Faith said.

She'd begun turning away but stopped abruptly when a branch snapped in the woods ahead of the wagon. She turned to see the three freighters step through the trees, moving slowly, their faces tense, rifles in their hands.

"Everybody just stay right where you are," said the man called Dietrich. He slid his dark gaze to Faith. "'Ceptin' you, miss. You can come right on over here."

Faith heard a sharp intake of breath behind her. She

didn't turn around as Mrs. Schaeffer exclaimed in a hushed tone, "Oh, for the love of God!"

"What's the meaning of this?" said Mr. Schaeffer, standing up by the head of the off mule.

"That girl there—that Injun-lovin' whore—we're gonna take her off your hands," said the freighter whose name Faith had learned was Grayson.

"Whore, sure enough," said Dietrich, staring at Faith, his eyes bright with lust. "Whore from Thornton's roadhouse. I remembered where I seen her before just a couple hours ago. Me an' the boys ain't had us a woman fer a long time!"

"Get over here, missy!" said the third freighter, with the smashed lips. His name was Clem something. "We ain't got all day. Git over here *now*!"

"This is wrong," said Mrs. Schaeffer, coming up behind Faith. "You can't take this poor girl against her will. I . . . we won't allow it."

All three men were walking toward Faith and Mrs. Schaeffer. Mrs. Schaeffer put her hand on Faith's arm. Out of the corner of her right eye, Faith saw Jules still squatting by the fire, looking at the three approaching freighters. He sat so still that Faith thought he must be holding his breath.

"Listen, gentlemen," said the tall preacher, who'd taken off his shabby suit coat and wore only his vest over a plain white shirt, the sleeves rolled up his forearms, "certainly you won't commit such an atrocity against God, yourselves, and all that's holy on His green Earth?"

Dietrich stopped suddenly, swung the rifle toward the preacher. "No!" Faith shouted as the rifle boomed, blowing up gravel at the preacher's thick-soled shoe.

The man jumped back as Jules cried, "*Pa!*"

Both mules jerked their heads up, braying, cracked corn spilling from their feed sacks.

"Get the message, Preacher?" said Dietrich, chuckling as he rammed a fresh shell into his rifle breech, the spent shell arcing over his right shoulder to chink in the grass behind him. He aimed the rifle at Mrs. Schaeffer, who moaned softly and shifted her weight from one foot to the other. "Or how 'bout I shoot the old woman?"

"No!" Faith said, stepping forward. "I'll come."

She strode over to the freighters, her heart pounding, and turned to regard the Schaeffers. Mr. Schaeffer stood with his hands raised, palms out, at his shoulders. Mrs. Schaeffer clasped her hands to her throat.

Jules stood before the fire ring, holding the coffeepot down low at his side, lower jaw hanging, blond hair sliding in the breeze.

"A . . . doxie?" said Mrs. Schaeffer, squinting her eyes at Faith. She turned to Mr. Schaeffer. "Perhaps this is none of our affair, Reverend."

Schaeffer nodded grimly, his flat eyes moving down Faith's body and up again, as if seeing her for the first time. "I believe you're right, Mrs. Schaeffer." His eyes met Faith's. "We'll pray for your eternal soul, miss."

"Thanks," Faith said as Dietrich grabbed her arm and began pulling her back through the trees.

As the other two freighters, laughing, fell into step behind her and Dietrich, Faith turned to see all three Schaeffers staring dully after her. Tears dribbled down her cheeks, and her chest heaved, but she did not cry aloud.

"Yakima," she said under her breath, tightening her jaws, trying to keep her lips from quivering, "where the hell are you when a girl needs you, you half-breed bastard?"

Chapter 16

The freighters' massive wagons were parked along the trail, under a line of black cottonwoods shaking their silver leaves in the breeze. The man called Dietrich grabbed Faith around her waist—she winced at the sudden pain of his brusque grasp—and lifted her over the right front wheel and into the lead wagon's driver's box.

"Time you rode in style, purty lady!"

The freighter called Grayson laughed as he crawled into the driver's box of the second wagon. "Bullshit, Dietrich. You just want your ashes hauled."

"Not a bad idea," allowed Dietrich, climbing over Faith's legs. "But she ain't gettin' none of *my* stuff before she's cooked and washed the dishes!" He guffawed, sat down, and removed the reins from the brake handle. "No, sir. No matter how hard she begs me fer it!"

He threw his head back, laughing as he released the brake and cracked the blacksnake over the mules' backs. As the lumbering beasts moved out, leaning into their collars, Faith grabbed the seat to keep from being thrown onto the trail.

She'd been a whore long enough, been around dangerous men long enough, that her fear of them didn't last long before it turned to a deep, simmering rage. Some girls couldn't think when enraged, but Faith could. Since the first night Preacher Saudoff had visited her bedroom, when she was twelve years old, back on the farm near the Chugwater Buttes, her indignation and outrage quickly burned down to rational, cunning plans for survival.

Now that cunning led her to glance to her left, at the rifle that Dietrich had stowed beneath the seat. There was a holstered pistol there as well, but she knew for certain the rifle was loaded. So when the time came, she would appropriate the rifle, make sure a shell was levered into the breech, and shoot him.

Then she'd shoot the other two quickly, before they realized what was happening.

After that?

She would unharness one of the mules and ride bareback to Gold Cache.

Her heart thudded at the prospect, and in spite of the cool breeze funneling around a narrowing of the canyon dead ahead, sweat formed on her brow and above her lip, made her hand slick as it clutched the thin brass rail along the right side of the seat.

"How much you think you're worth?"

Faith turned to Dietrich, who was grinning around a fat stogie in his teeth. His low hairline and broad, pitted nose gave him an apelike appearance. When she didn't say anything, he glanced at her, his bushy brows forming a V over the bridge of his nose, then returned his gaze to the trail beyond the mules' bobbing heads.

"In Gold Cache. How much you think you're worth up there? Assumin', of course, word about you and that savage hasn't made it that far . . ."

"In the pimping business now?" Faith sneered, chuckling

and smoothing her baggy denims across her thighs. "Well, I don't know. I still have my looks, don't I?"

Dietrich looked her over, grinning, his eyes taking in her legs, the trim waist, and the full bust tenting the flannel shirt, then traveling back to her heart-shaped face beneath the brim of her man's leather hat. "I reckon you do at that, girl. I heard tell you were somethin' special. How much did Thornton pay for you?"

"He never told me. Why don't you be your own man, set your own price?"

"Well, if I'm going to do that, I reckon I'm gonna have to do some investigatin' on my own." Drool dribbled from around his cigar, down his chin, and onto the floor of the driver's box. "And I don't mind tellin' you," he added, running his lusty, bright gaze down her figure once more, "I can't wait to get me a piece of that!"

Just what Faith had in mind. Men were never more vulnerable than when their peckers were doing their thinking. Inflame their peckers, shrink their brains. But there was no point in being overly eager and arousing the dullard's suspicions.

"And you call Yakima a savage," she said, peering over the mules.

Dietrich laughed and cracked the blacksnake over the team, the wagon climbing a hill and bringing a flame-shaped, snow-dusted peak into view. The peak shouldered above several others. In the clear air, it looked close enough to reach out and grab.

If Faith could spring herself from the freighters in a couple of hours and climb aboard a mule, she might be able to make Gold Cache in two or three days.

And while Gold Cache would be a far cry from starting life all over again, she could at least start fresh—putting a down payment on her own saloon and brothel with a loan and with the money she'd saved at Thornton's.

Her fate would be in her own hands at last.

Faith discovered a hitch in her plan not long after she'd decided to shoot the freighters with Dietrich's rifle. If she shot the men while they were driving, or anywhere near the mules, the mules would bolt, probably wrecking the wagons, laming or killing themselves, and leaving her afoot. She had to wait until Dietrich and the other men were away from the wagons, probably during a break or early that night, to carry out her plan.

She resigned herself to sitting quietly while the mules labored along the trail winding through one canyon after another, the blacksnakes cracking like pistol fire, the smell of the animals and the sweaty men assaulting her nostrils.

"Here," Dietrich said during a short break for the mules, handing her his canteen, from which he'd just taken a long drink.

She looked at the lip no doubt infested with his filth, inwardly recoiled, and shook her head. He laughed, took another drink from the flask, then put it away and shook the ribbons over the mules' dusty, sweaty backs.

When they stopped again, at the top of another long, steep hill, Dietrich again offered her the canteen after he'd taken a drink. She curled her nose, revolted, but her throat was so dry that she took the flask and tipped it back, letting the brackish water roll over her tongue and down her throat.

Dietrich snorted and grabbed the canteen out of her hands. "That's enough, stupid bitch. We won't meet up with a creek again for a couple hours."

Faith wiped her mouth with the back of her hand. "You're a real gentleman, Dietrich."

By the time they pulled off the road early that evening, the sun angling low behind the flame-shaped, snow-mantled peak in the west, Faith's back and bottom ached from the hard plank seat. Her eyes and nose were caked with dust. She felt so fatigued by the long wagon ride that she was no longer sure she could put her plan into operation.

She chased the doubt from her mind. She had to do it. Otherwise, these men would be taking their pleasure. The thought nearly made her gag. She'd slept with some unappealing hombres before, but never with men as apelike as these.

"Go over and sit down under that tree yonder," Dietrich said, hauling her brusquely off the wagon. "You wander off, I'll chase you down and tie you. Understand?"

"Don't worry," Faith said, as the freighters set to work unhitching the teams. "I'm too tired to do anything but eat and sleep."

"You rest up," Dietrich yelled as he crouched to free the doubletree, adding with a laugh, "'cause you and me got business later."

"Have you ever had a woman you didn't force?"

Dietrich's head shot up, his face red, tiny eyes pinched angrily. "What was that?"

"Nothing," Faith said, grabbing a blanket from under the wagon's dusty tarp. "Since I'll be entertaining tonight, I reckon I best go freshen up in the creek."

"Yeah, you do that. And watch your mouth. No one likes a mouthy whore."

While Dietrich and the other two freighters cursed the harness buckles, stays, and sweat-shrunk collars, Faith drew the blanket around her shoulders. The lower the sun sank, the colder the canyon grew. She walked around behind the wagon, heading for the tree and the narrow creek murmuring along a basalt bluff on the other side.

Ten feet from the wagon, she glanced behind her. A rifle was mounted on the side of the wagon, above a grease box and an iron-banded water barrel. It looked old and rusty, no doubt a spare, but it wouldn't be hanging there if it didn't work.

Faith's heart quickened.

She slid her gaze to the head of the wagon, where Dietrich was milling among the mules, grousing and cursing and trying to keep them calm while he removed the harness straps and collars. Looking at the two wagons behind, she saw that the other two freighters were similarly occupied. None of them were looking toward her.

Slowly but purposefully, she moseyed over to the wagon, her gaze jackrabbiting between Dietrich and the other two men. She dried her sweaty hands on her jeans, then, with another quick look around, reached out and placed her hands around the rifle's weathered wood.

Biting her lower lip, she lifted the rifle from the two rusty steel hooks it hung on and quickly stuck it inside her blanket.

With one hand, she held the rifle straight down before her. With her free hand, she held the blanket closed at her chest.

Dietrich's angry voice rose suddenly, and Faith froze in her tracks. "Goddamn it, Rafe, will you get up here and help with this damn buckle you *adjusted* yesterday? I can't pop it loose fer *nothin'*!"

Heart pounding painfully against her ribs, Faith continued into the brush and strolled slowly, nonchalantly, toward the creek. On the far side of the tree, she opened the old Springfield's breech, saw a brass shell in the chamber, and closed it, easing the hammer down to the firing pin.

She heaved a deep sigh. "Maybe there is a god after all."

She looked back toward the wagons. Dietrich and Grayson were leading their teams off while the third man, Clem Schultz, was still fooling with his.

Faith hoped none of the men would miss the rifle.

She laid the Springfield in the brush beside the rock, brushed dry leaves and pinecones over it, then stood and walked to the creek. She knelt down, removed the blanket, unbuttoned her shirt, and began cupping the cold water to her face and neck. She stole occasional looks downstream, over a jumble of rocks and driftwood, where Grayson and Schultz watered the mules while Dietrich strung a picket line through several stout aspens.

She'd kill all three when they came over to set up camp. She'd center the rifle on Dietrich's chest, then on the closest man after that, and then the third man. If all went as planned, they'd be dead within seconds. None wore sidearms, and she couldn't give them time to go for their long guns.

She could handle a rifle. She'd handled them before. In fact, the preacher she'd lived with had had a Springfield just like this one . . .

When she finished washing, she decided to gather firewood. That way, when she moved to the boulder for the rifle, she wouldn't arouse the men's suspicions.

She'd gathered a sizable pile of driftwood and deadfall when all three men filed toward a tree under which was a barren patch of ground and a rock ring blackened from many fires.

"Well, lookee here," said Dietrich, a brown-paper cigarette dangling from between his lips, sweat streaking the dirt and grit on his burned cheekbones and low cap of tight, curly black hair. He tossed his hat on the ground. "The bitch can do *real* work, after all."

"I'll be damned," said Schultz, tossing a bundle of blankets and a burlap food sack on the ground near the fire ring. "How 'bout we see if you can light a fire, too, missy. It's gettin' right chilly." He hugged himself, running his hands up and down his arms.

"Then you can git to work on whippin' us up some grub," said Grayson, throwing down his own gear, dropping beside it, and resting his back against a small aspen. "My backbone and my stomach are gettin' way too friendly."

"Sure," Faith said, trying to keep her voice from trembling. She wheeled and strode toward the boulder, turning her head to keep an eye on the men behind her. "Let me just fetch one more stick of wood . . ."

"And when you've done the dishes," Dietrich said, on his knees and rummaging around in a war bag, "you can strip yourself naked and climb into my hot roll." He chuffed and popped the cork on a bottle. "You an' me—we're gonna give a whole new meanin' to 'hot roll'!"

The other two laughed.

Faith stooped down behind the boulder, picked up the rifle, thumbed back the hammer, and holding it straight out before her, moved back toward the three men gathered on the far side of the fire ring.

"Hey!" shouted Schultz. "She's got the goddamn Springfield!"

The other two turned to her sharply, Dietrich lowering the bottle so quickly that whiskey washed over his lips and down his chest.

"Yeah, I got a rifle," Faith said, squeezing the weathered forestock and planting the front sight on the pale strip of skin beneath Dietrich's black hairline.

"Goddamn it, bitch!" the freighter shouted, his face going white. "Put that rifle down *now*!"

At the same time, Schultz cried, "Miss, don't do this!"

Faith smiled as she steadied the rifle and drew her index finger back on the trigger. The hammer dropped with a metallic click.

Faith squinted, steeling herself for the explosion and kick. It didn't come. There was only the click.

Before her, leaning back on his haunches, frozen with his arms up to shield his face, Dietrich blinked.

Then he smiled. After another second, his lips stretched a smile. "That's the problem with that old rifle. It misfires every fourth or fifth shot!"

Faith's heart turned a somersault.

Fear and fury churning within, she fumbled with the Springfield's trigger-guard cocking lever. At the same time, Dietrich gained his feet and rushed toward her. She screamed, abandoned the idea of cocking the rifle, and clutching the forestock, swung it toward Dietrich.

He laughed, grabbed the gun by the barrel, and jerked it out of her hands.

The freighter tossed the Springfield out behind him. As he continued moving toward Faith, she screamed, *"Pig!"* and swung her clenched right fist against his cheekbone.

The blow gave him momentary pause. He brushed his left hand across the two-inch cut, glanced at the blood smeared on his fingers, then turned his gaze, sparkling with fury and animal lust, on Faith.

"Tried to kill me, huh?" He backhanded her. As she spun, he grabbed her hair and fumbled with his fly buttons. "I'm gonna show you what I do to whores that try to blow out my lamp!"

Chapter 17

Faith dropped to her left knee, then catapulted back to her feet. Jerking her hair free of Dietrich's grasp, she ran toward the creek shimmering in the near-darkness at the base of the stone bluff.

"Get back here, whore!" the freighter shouted.

"Want me to plug her from here?" asked Grayson, his voice just audible above Faith's heavy breathing and footfalls. "I got a bead on her."

"No," Dietrich said tightly, his breath labored. "She's mine."

"That girl's nothin' but trouble," exclaimed Schultz. "I say we slit her damn throat when . . ."

Faith didn't hear the rest. As she plunged straight into the stream, the splashing water drowned the men's angry exclamations. She swung her arms and lifted her knees as high as she could, the frigid water piercing her like sharp knives. She turned to look back.

Dietrich ran behind her, pumping his arms and legs, his ugly face set with grim fury.

Faith made for the opposite bank.

She had no idea where she was headed. If she climbed to the top of the stone bluff—assuming she could make it—

would Dietrich give up on her, decide she wasn't worth trifling with?

Halfway across the narrow stream, she turned her head. She was gaining some distance from Dietrich, a bulky shadow behind her. He was slipping on the rocks at the creek's bottom, throwing his arms out for balance. Her chest welling hopefully, she lunged toward the far shore.

She would run to that crevice in the bluff, climb up through the trough to the top.

When she was nearly out of the stream, her left foot slipped off a rock, twisting her ankle. She groaned as the pain shot up her lower leg, and before she realized it, she was down on both knees at the edge of the creek, turning onto her butt and grabbing her calf.

"No!" she cried, her voice edged with rage, the cold water biting her deep. She turned to Dietrich stepping high in the knee-deep water. "Goddamn you!"

"Goddamn me?" Dietrich bellowed, grabbing her collar and hauling her onto the bank. "Goddamn *you*!"

Faith kicked and screamed as he dragged her across the sand and rocks and high, brown grass and shrubs. She grunted and clawed at his hands, cursing him.

He threw her into the tall grass and spindly willows at the base of the bluff, smacked her hard across her face. Kneeling down, he jerked one knee away from the other, then crawled up between her legs and leaned forward to unbutton her men's denim trousers.

"Goddamn you to hell, Dietrich!" she cried, kicking at him futilely, her strength all but gone, a sharp pain spike grinding into her ankle. "I'll *kill* you!"

Dietrich laughed and jerked her pants halfway down her thighs.

She leaned back and closed her eyes. There was no point

in resisting anymore. His slaps had addled her, and her head swam. She wanted only to fall back into a warm, dark place and sleep.

A rifle cracked in the direction of the camp. As the report echoed, a man shouted.

Faith opened her eyes as Dietrich snapped his head back and twisted around to look beyond the creek. With an incredulous grunt, he stood.

Another rifle cracked, then two more shots echoed around the canyon. Dietrich stood and ran back through the brush, grunting and reaching for the big knife sheathed on his left hip.

The shots had been like a cold slap of water. Faith gained her knees and pulled her jeans up to her waist, quickly buttoning the fly. She rose onto her right foot and hobbled after Dietrich.

Just beyond the brush, she stopped. Dietrich stood at the edge of the water, facing away from Faith. The freighter crouched, his knife glinting in his right hand.

Beyond him, a broad-shouldered man ran toward him, long hair bouncing on his shoulders, a rifle held across his chest. Water splashed up around Yakima's buckskinned thighs. He was across the creek in seconds.

Stopping suddenly before Dietrich, he jerked his arms and shoulders forward, thrusting his hips and belly back, as the freighter slashed with the knife at Yakima's chest. Yakima lunged forward, slammed his rifle stock against Dietrich's left cheek.

The man staggered.

Yakima lunged at him again, drove the rifle's butt into Dietrich's stomach.

As the freighter expelled air with a loud whoosh, knees buckling, Yakima set his rifle atop a flat rock. He grabbed a handful of Dietrich's curly black hair and, teeth gritted and flashing in the failing light, half dragged the freighter into the creek.

Holding the man's hair with one hand, Yakima rammed the toe of his right boot moccasin into his gut. Dietrich went down with a shrill cry, arms flailing, fighting to regain his feet.

Stepping toward him with balled fists, Yakima kicked the man onto his back, then pressed his left knee against the man's chest, up close to his neck, pushing his head under the water.

Dietrich's arms flailed at Yakima's thigh, and he kicked frantically, splashing water and blowing bubbles. Faith watched in horror as Yakima held the man's head beneath the water until, gradually, Dietrich stopped thrashing and lay motionless beneath Yakima's knee.

Yakima thumped his knee once more upon the man's chest, then stood and turned to where Faith knelt at the edge of the brush, tears dribbling down her cheeks.

Yakima's broad chest rose and fell heavily, but his voice was calm. "You all right?"

Barely able to hold her head up, Faith nodded. "Where . . . where did you come from?"

Yakima turned back to Dietrich. The freighter's arms and legs bobbed in the current, his lifeless body skidding slowly along the rocks, turning downstream.

Yakima stepped onto the shore, stooped down beside Faith, snaked his arms beneath her, and drew her up to his chest. His arms felt strong beneath her legs and back, and she relaxed as he retrieved his rifle, holding it in his left hand under Faith's knees as he backstepped into the stream, heading for the other side.

"Can't let you outta my sight for a minute."

Faith let her head loll against his chest and sighed. "You came back for me?"

"I reckon."

"I'm glad."

Faith drowsed against Yakima's chest as he carried her to the other side of the creek. As he walked across the freighters' encampment she opened her eyes and looked around.

Schultz lay on his belly near the fire ring, cheek to the ground, arms resting straight down at his sides. Blood seeped into the dirt and pine needles around him. Grayson lay on his back at the edge of the camp, one ankle on a log, his eyes staring glassily up at the pine bough over his head as he clutched his rifle, breech open, across his bloody chest.

As Yakima continued across the camp, heading toward the trail nearly hidden by the fading light, Faith closed her eyes and fell into a warm, dark pit of slumber.

She was only vaguely aware of hearing Yakima's sharp breaths, as if he were carrying her uphill. Just as vaguely, she felt the warmth of a fire, smelled the pine smoke and tea, heard the pops and cracks of the flames.

Then deep sleep again overtook her.

She had no idea how much time had passed before she again heard resin sizzling in flames. There was a slight crunching sound and several snorts. Smelling charred meat along with the pine smoke and tea, she opened her eyes.

Yakima squatted on the other side of a low fire, watching a haunch of venison roast on an iron spit as he held a smoking tin cup in both of his gloved hands, one of which also held a cigarette. Over Faith's right shoulder a paint horse and a dark-brown mule cropped the tough blond grass growing along the base of a gray boulder.

They seemed to be on the shoulder of a hill stippled with sparse pines and sheltered with large scarps and boulders. Beyond the horse and the mule, the hill dropped off to a deep valley, beyond which were distant, toothy mountains, their peaks hidden by clouds.

"Think you've slept long enough, or you wanna keep sawing wood till noon?"

She turned to see Yakima regarding her over the fire. "Where are we?"

He sipped his tea, then set his cup down and reached for a leather pad.

"About five miles from where I found you. North of the trail. Three men behind us—I spied 'em with a glass I found in the freighters' wagons. Decided to take a shortcut."

"Men? Who?"

Yakima shook his head. "They were a ways off, but I think two were Thornton's hostlers. Couldn't place the third man."

Faith blinked to clear the sleep fog and rose up on her elbows. A half dozen blankets and fur robes covered her, pressing her down. The blankets must also be from the freighters' wagons.

Yakima walked over and extended a steaming cup to her. "It's been on the fire a while, so it's a mite charred."

Rising to a sitting position, Faith took the cup. The wind blew the steam from its rim. She shivered as the chill found her—a deeper cold, more penetrating than before.

"We must've climbed a good ways," she said. "Cold up here."

"It's gonna get colder. I was fixin' to make for that pass yonder"—Yakima jerked his head toward a gap between two mountains in the west, the peaks of which were lost in the clouds—"but we got a storm comin' from the north. We'll have to hole up till it's over."

Faith glanced over the steaming cup at him. He'd hunkered back down on his haunches, absorbing the fire's warmth and drawing on his cigarette.

She looked around. Aside from the sparse trees and the granite knobs, they were dangerously exposed up here. "Hole up where?"

"Found a little hollow with a small cave, a little ways down the other side of this mountain. Plenty of protection in there—as long as the bobcat who calls it home don't come back—and shelter for the mare and my new mule."

Faith glanced at the mule again, cropping grass nearby. It was outfitted with a makeshift pack of swelling burlap bags and rope and had a rope halter fitted across its ears and snout. The bags appeared full.

"What about the other mules?" Faith asked.

"Turned 'em loose. Some other freighter will be glad to get 'em. Glad to get Dietrich's goods, too. What I didn't take, that is."

Sipping her tea, Faith looked at the blanket coat, red-and-white-striped muffler, rabbit hat, and heavy deerskin mittens piled beside her. There was also a pair of fur-lined boots.

"For me?"

"You're gonna need 'em soon." Yakima used his knife to hack off a chunk of the charred, sizzling meat. He plopped the meat on a tin pan, then brought the pan over to Faith. "Fresh venison. You're gonna need this, too, when the *real* cold hits. Eat up. There's a whole deer."

When Faith had taken a few bites, washing it down with the strong, hot tea, she looked at Yakima doing the same on the other side of the fire.

"So, you shot a deer this morning, cooked breakfast,

and found a place for us to wait out the storm." It wasn't a question.

Yakima stretched a grin and lifted a chunk of bloody tenderloin, the juices dripping to his plate. "What else was I supposed to do while you sawed logs."

Chewing, Faith gave him a sidelong glance. "You'd make a right fine husband, Yakima Henry."

"I wouldn't go that far."

By the time they'd finished eating, a fine, granular snow was whipping down at a slant. Yakima removed the meat from the spit, wrapped what was left of the quarter in burlap, and tied the bundle to the mule.

He kicked out the fire, then helped Faith onto the mule. She'd put on the blanket coat, rabbit hat, and mittens, and was knotting the muffler under her chin.

"You think the storm's going to be bad?" she called to Yakima, who was mounting his saddled paint.

"Hard to say," he yelled back, "but the fall storms can howl pretty loud up here."

"What about Thornton's men?"

Yakima glanced at the sky. "Maybe the storm will give 'em second thoughts."

He turned the paint westward, pulling the mule along by a lead rope. They moved between scarps, then over the lip of the mountain and down a steep grade through pines and cedars.

They followed the shoulder of the mountain into a steep-walled box canyon. Yakima led the mule between towering granite knobs and into an alcove of sorts, with a stone overhang. Beneath the overhang, the limestone had been eroded away from the mountain wall, creating a low-ceilinged, shallow cave.

The wind was picking up, howling over the peaks and

roaring in the pine tops. The slashing snow felt like steel pellets against their faces.

Yakima helped Faith down from the mule and gave her a food sack.

"Go on inside. I've put in a good store of firewood." He tossed her a box of matches. "Start a fire and put some tea on. We're gonna need all the heat we can get—inside and out."

Yakima unleathered and hobbled the horse and the mule in the alcove just outside the cave, throwing blankets over their backs. When he'd finished hauling the sacks of food and supplies into the cave, the snow was beginning to stick on the ground and glue itself to the windward sides of the granite knobs. The lead-colored clouds hung low, and soon it was nearly a whiteout.

The fire warmed the cave, and the snow that leaked into the notch melted within a few minutes of falling.

Yakima and Faith hunkered down by the fire, Faith buried in blankets and robes and warming her hands on a hot cup of tea. Yakima sat cross-legged beside her, sharpening his knife on a whetstone. A tin cup steamed near his moccasins.

"What about Wolf?" Faith said, turning toward him after staring thoughtfully into the fire for a long time.

Yakima lifted the knife from the stone and stared at the wet, glistening blade. "Those bastards'll sell him in Gold Cache. I'll find him."

Faith's eyes shone with tears. "I'm sorry, Yakima."

"Wasn't your fault they stole my horse."

"I'm sorry for everything. How many men have you killed now because of me—a worthless whore?"

Yakima turned to her. "Hey, now . . ."

"I mean it. I am worthless. I cause trouble everywhere I go. If I make it to Gold Cache, I'll just cause more trouble there." Tears dribbled down her cheeks. "I wouldn't blame you if you just left me here."

"Can't do that. Wolves would get ya," Yakima said, trying to make a joke.

She sniffed and wiped a tear from her cheek with the back of her hand. She kept her eyes on him. "Why did you come back?"

Yakima's face warmed. He looked at the whetstone, then the knife. He raised his eyes to hers. "I was worried about you."

More tears welled out from her blue eyes, shining in the firelight. In a small, pinched voice, she said, "No one's ever worried about me before."

He set the knife and the whetstone down and leaned toward her, wrapping his arms around her and kissing her. He pulled away, but she dug her fingers into his upper arms and moved against him.

In minutes, they'd wrestled out of their clothes, and Yakima had joined her under the blankets and furs. He kissed her passionately as he lowered himself between her spread legs, and she reached down and gently guided him inside.

"I'm not going back to whoring," she said absently, when they'd finished making love and lay tangled together, Faith sprawled atop him beneath the robes, her head on his chest. She stretched her arm out with his, running her fingers along his bicep and the corded muscles of his forearm. Her body felt warm, her breasts soft, her nipples like small buds against his belly.

"What're you gonna do?"

"Ain't sure, but not that. Don't think I'd have the stomach for it anymore."

He ran his hand through her long, silky hair.

She rose up suddenly and stared into his eyes. "I've been thinking about this for a long time, and I just decided. I'll buy a saloon, and you can help me run it. I thought about opening a brothel and running it without doing any entertaining myself, but Gold Cache already has one whorehouse. I know the madame, and she wouldn't like the competition, anyway. But she wouldn't be as piss-burned if I just opened a tavern."

"And ran it with an Injun?" Yakima said. "A half-breed?"

"It'd work in a wide-open town like Gold Cache. Hell, those miners don't care who's serving their beer as long as it's good and the whiskey isn't watered down or laced with gunpowder. When we start making money, we can hire entertainers, like opera singers and play actors and the like."

Yakima wrapped his thick arms around her and stared back at her.

She pinched his thumb. "What do you say? We partners, or what?"

Yakima chuckled, smoothed her hair away from her face and kissed her softly. "I reckon I'd better stick around, make sure you stay out of trouble."

"I'll make it worth your while." Her eyes sparkled devilishly, and she lowered her head to his chest, kissing him every inch or so as she moved down to his belly and beyond.

As her lips closed over him, his body tensed.

He sighed and pressed his hands flat against the ground.

Chapter 18

"We gotta stop!" Brindley shouted above the wind as he drew up to the bounty hunter's right stirrup. "Can't go on any further. Snow's getting too deep!"

Wit Bardoul ran a deerskin-gloved hand down his face, dislodging the thick snow from his brows and eyelashes, and drew back on the big Appaloosa's reins. He'd wrapped a muffler over his head under his sombrero and tied it beneath his chin. Still, his cold ears felt as though someone had stabbed each with a fork.

"We gotta stop and build a fire," said Higgins, checking down his dapple gray on the other side of Brindley, barely discernible behind the slanting veil of wind-whipped snow. "I'm froze clean through, Bardoul!"

"Shut up, both of ye, and stop your goddamn whining before I send you back to Thornton belly down across your saddles!"

Bardoul looked at the trail disappearing into the dense pine woods before him. He hated to admit it, but the tinhorns were right. The trace would no doubt be impassable in just a couple of hours. If that long.

The storm had roared down out of the northwest—a real high-country ass-kicker. The sun would probably come out tomorrow, making the sky as clear as a preacher's conscience, but the ravines and canyons would be socked in for a good long time.

Bardoul pounded his saddle horn and cursed. Just a few hours ago, before the snow had started covering the trail, they'd had that damn Injun and Thornton's whore in their sights!

The bounty hunter booted his horse ahead and turned him right, into the ravine's mouth. The ravine was sheltered from the brunt of the wind, and the wagon trail following the ravine's right shoulder hadn't yet been erased by the snow. Following the trace while hunkering deep in his coat, Bardoul looked behind him.

The hostlers followed, their horses stumbling and shying at the gusting wind, manes buffeting. The mounts' brown eyes were wild and fearful. Brindley and Higgins were gray shadows hunkered atop the frightened mounts strung out in a shaggy line behind the bounty hunter, the wet snow sticking to their coats, hats, and saddles.

Bardoul turned forward to follow the trail with his eyes. Last time he'd been through this country, on the trail of those owlhoots who'd intended to hide in the mountains after robbing a string of stagecoaches in Kansas, he'd stumbled on a cabin at the far end of this ravine.

At least, he thought it was this ravine. When you'd been up and down as many ravines as Wit Bardoul had, they tended to run together.

He followed the canyon for a good quarter mile before, rounding a bend, he blew a long sigh. Where the ravine widened into a valley fifty yards before him, two lighted windows shone through the gauzy air, and the smell of woodsmoke tickled Bardoul's nostrils. Sure enough. The cabin—just a little log box with a sod roof and a lean-to shed and corral off its east wall.

"Hey, look!" Roy Brindley shouted behind Bardoul. "A cabin!"

Bardoul snickered and glanced at Brindley over his shoulder. Brindley's railroad cap was tied down with a heavy red muffler covering his ears and knotted beneath his chin. "Roy, you're just about as smart as they come in these parts, ain't you?"

Ignoring the bounty hunter, Brindley glanced over his right shoulder at Ace Higgins, riding with his head down, one hand holding his blanket coat closed. "Hey, Ace! Take a look! We done found a cabin!"

"*We* done found a cabin," Bardoul growled, turning his Appy toward the cabin and giving an involuntary shiver, the prospect of a warm fire pointing up how cold and wet he was. And, hell, wasn't that venison riding piggyback on the wood-smoke?

Bardoul's stomach growled. At the same time, a door latch clicked loudly and hinges squawked. A short man, a fur coat hanging off his stooped shoulders, stepped onto the narrow porch holding a double-barreled shotgun. Gray hair swirled around the bald top of his head.

His voice sounded hoarse and angry. "Who's there?"

"We're friendly, old-timer," Bardoul said, drawing his horse to a halt before the stoop. "Got caught in the storm. Can we hole up here for the night?"

The old man—he didn't appear to weigh much over a hundred pounds—cast his close-set, mean eyes about the other two men flanking the bounty hunter. "What's your business in these parts?"

"Don't worry, we ain't after your claim. We're trackin' a

half-breed who kidnapped a girl from Thornton's road-house."

The old man held his rifle across his sparrow's chest, considering the information. Finally, he spat downwind. "I don't run a hotel, but I reckon it wouldn't be Christian to turn men out in a storm. Put your horses up in the corral, and you can spread your hot rolls on my floor." He said this last as he stepped inside, punctuating the sentence by slamming the door.

Left of Bardoul, Ace Higgins chuckled at their good fortune. To Bardoul's right, Brindley tipped his chin back and drew a deep breath. "Somethin' sure smells good!"

"Well, why don't we put our horses away before we freeze to death?" Bardoul glowered at Brindley. "Less'n you wanna spend the night here smellin' the smoke."

When they'd turned their horses into the corral with two mares and a mule taking shelter beneath the lean-to roof, they slogged through the deepening snow to the cabin's front door.

Bardoul knocked, tripped the latch, opened the door a foot, and peeked inside, tentative. You couldn't be too careful around these isolated prospectors. Some would as soon shoot you as serve you a handful of dried beans, and steal your hardware and horses. This wasn't exactly the most prosperous country for rock farmers.

Seeing the old man sitting at a table to the right in the dim, earthen-floored room, his shotgun leaning against the table's far end, Bardoul pushed the door wide and stepped inside, Brindley and Higgins following, stamping their feet and breathing hard, teeth chattering.

Bardoul dropped his tack in the nearest corner and raked the room with his eyes—instantly taking in the sparse, mean furnishings including a table, a couple of chairs, burning lamps and candles, and a sheet-iron stove. Over a rack in the fire-place, an iron kettle bubbled and steamed, sending the smell of venison stew across the room.

A slender, full-figured girl stood at a small table in the kitchen area of the cabin, rolling dough and giving the new-comers the twice-over. She was neither pretty nor ugly, but had the tired look of a girl who worked too hard and would rather have been anywhere but where she was.

After a single sweep of the cabin, Bardoul thought there was only the old man and the girl here, but then he saw the figure slumped in a rocking chair on the other side of the fireplace, cloaked in shadows. By the size, it had to be a man, but the person was so covered in blankets and quilts, with a night sock pulled over its forehead, that the bounty hunter couldn't tell for sure.

The girl's Southern accent brought Bardoul's gaze back to the kitchen. "Supper's gonna be a while. Take off those wet clothes and sit up by the fire. Don't expect me to dish up your plates. When the food's ready, you'll fill your own."

"Obliged, miss," Bardoul said, Brindley and Higgins of-fering their own thanks as they dropped their tack and began struggling out of their coats.

"Hang your duds on that line back there," the girl said, turning her head so that her stringy chestnut hair danced away from her neck as she continued working the dough. "Back there by Karl. Don't mind him. He won't bother you if you don't bother him."

Bardoul, Brindley, and Higgins cast their gazes at the blanketed figure in the shadows beyond the fireplace. The chair moved a little, as did the figure, in a jittery, jerking way, as though the person were vaguely agitated.

"We ain't here to bother no one, ma'am," said Brindley,

chuckling uncomfortably. "We're just here to get warm. And if you got extra vittles, we'd be obliged."

"I told you supper ain't ready yet," the girl snapped, rising onto the balls of her feet to give the dough a good working with the heels of her hands.

Bardoul removed his coat and hung it on the line, eyeing the figure in the rocking chair warily, seeing little more than what he'd seen from the door. When his coat was secure and Brindley and Higgins were hanging up their own, Bardoul turned to the old man, who was laying out a solitaire game at the table, the shotgun still close by his side.

"You folks mind if I break open a bottle to help kill the chill?"

The girl said nothing, only continued working the bread dough, but the old man snapped his head up eagerly, blue eyes flashing. "Whiskey?"

"*Good* whiskey."

"Only if you'll share."

"Wouldn't have it any other way, Mr. . . ."

"Gillespie. Mike Gillespie. That's my daughter, Helen. The one in the chair—what's left of him after the mule kicked him last month—is her husband, Karl."

As Bardoul retrieved his bottle from his saddlebags, Gillespie plucked four stone mugs off a shelf above the range. He hobbled back to the table and set the mugs down before his card game. Bardoul popped the cork on the bottle and began splashing whiskey into each cup, introducing himself and the two Thornton hostlers.

Gillespie sat back down in his chair, lifted the cup to his lips, and sniffed. "Smells all right." He took a sip and smacked his lips. "Tastes all right, too. I been outta hooch 'cause with my bum leg I can't make it down to Thornton's my ownself, and ol' Karl there is . . . as you can see . . . about as handy as a goddamn cigar store Injun."

Helen turned sharply from the table where she was shaping the dough into buns. "Papa, you git your consarned mouth off Karl. He can hear you, and when he gits better, he's gonna give you a floggin' like you never had since the Yankees whupped your behind and sent you runnin' for Dalton!"

Gillespie's face shot toward her as if pulled by a string, and he slammed both fists on the table as if ready to leap from his chair. "Heed your mouth, girl, or so help me Christ, I'll come over there, and—!"

"And *what*?" she yelled, grabbing a knife from among several others in a stone crock on her worktable. She held the knife out before her, showing the blade to the old man, slitting her hazel eyes devilishly over the curved tip.

Bardoul had hauled a chair over to the fire, and he stood behind it now, watching the old man and the girl with sheepish fascination. Brindley and Higgins stood behind him, having finished hanging up their coats, and he could hear them breathing back there in the shadows, both no doubt wearing expressions similar to his own—that of a child who'd just stepped into the schoolhouse late and been caught by the teacher.

Helen let a silence draw tight as fence wire as she stared over the knife at the old man, who just sat there, glaring back at her, fists on the table near his game, saying nothing.

Finally satisfied she'd gotten her message across, Helen dropped the knife back into the crock with the others, then picked up the Dutch oven containing the baking powder biscuits and, not so much as glancing at the old man, Bardoul, or the others, brought it over to the fireplace.

Bardoul pulled his chair back out of her way, and when she'd hung the Dutch oven on the rod beside the stewpot and returned to her worktable, Bardoul and the others sat down in front of the fire.

They didn't say anything. They sat and drank and stared at the flames, hearing the Dutch oven creak and the stew kettle bubble and hiss as the gravy dribbled out from beneath the lid to fall on the glowing coals below.

The smell of the charred gravy made Bardoul's stomach chug hungrily.

In the shadows to the right of Brindley, Karl just sat and fidgeted, occasionally lifting a big hand to his face and running it across his mouth or bristled cheek before returning it to his lap and muttering incoherently.

At the table, the old man sipped his whiskey and played solitaire in moody silence.

The silence continued through the meal, all of them except Karl squeezed in around the table. The only sounds were the snap and pop of the fire, the wind howling outside, snow pelting the cabin like sand, Karl muttering frenetically, the tink and scrape of forks, and the click of the stone mugs being set down on the table. Ace Higgins groaned softly with every bite.

Helen brought Karl a plate and stayed with him, feeding him several mouthfuls, getting him started, then leaving him to feed himself while she returned to the table and filled a plate of her own.

"Y'all can wash your own dishes," she said when everyone was finished and she'd scraped her chair back from the table. "The pump and the washtub is right over yonder, plain as day." She dropped her own dishes into the corrugated tin tub hanging from the pump spout, then turned to Bardoul. "And you, Mr. Bardoul, can help me fetch wood from the lean-to. The way this storm is shapin' up, we're gonna need plenty less'n we all wanna freeze by mornin'."

"It'd be a privilege, Miss Helen."

She strode across the cabin to retrieve Karl's half-finished plate. Heading back toward the kitchen, staring straight ahead, she said, "You can split while I drag out the driest logs from down inside the stack."

While the other men carried their plates to the washtub, Bardoul grabbed his coat off the line and shrugged into it. The woman grabbed a coat off a hook by the door, stepped into a pair of fur-lined boots, and pulled on a wolf cap with earflaps, leaving the flaps to hang loose along her cheeks.

She opened the door and went out, Bardoul following and pulling the door closed behind him.

It was dark now, and the snow was drifting up against the cabin, a good three inches frosting the porch. The chill wind sucked the breath from Bardoul's lungs as, shrugging down deep in his coat and pulling his damp, shrunken gloves on with his teeth, he followed Helen off the east end of the stoop and ducked through the corral's unpeeled pine poles.

The wood was stacked against the cabin wall at the far end of the deep lean-to, past where the horses stood, facing the cabin, their hindquarters spotted with snow. As Bardoul grabbed the wood-splitter from the chopping block, Helen said, "Forget that. I've got enough wood split."

He looked at her as she stood facing him. "Huh?"

"Pull your pecker out."

Bardoul blinked as he stared at her. Then he laughed. "Say again?"

"Pull your pecker out. I'm gonna show you what a great lay I am."

"Ma'am, I don't know what the hell you're talking about, but . . ."

The bounty hunter let his voice trail off as Helen climbed into a niche in the woodpile, squirming around to get comfortable, and began hiking up her dress.

Chapter 19

Wit Bardoul stared at the young woman, dumbfounded, as she hiked up her dress, wincing and sighing with the effort, then peeled her men's longjohns down to her ankles.

"Not bad, huh?" she said saucily, holding the skirt up with one hand and regarding the bounty hunter proudly.

Involuntarily, Bardoul's loins responded, in spite of the wind funneling under the lean-to roof and dancing stray snowflakes about his ankles. In spite of the piercing cold and the cabin behind the girl—the cabin in which her husband and father were housed not twenty feet away.

"What the hell you got in mind, woman?"

"What the hell you think I got in mind, you dumb bastard?" Helen laughed caustically and dropped her eyes to the bounty hunter's crotch. "Pull your pecker out and give it to me."

"What about Karl and your old man?"

"Karl's limp as a coat hanger." Her voice suddenly turned snidely suspicious as, still holding up the dress to reveal her furred love box, she turned her head to one side. "And what are you insinuating about me and my old man?"

"Nothin'. They're right in there!"

"The walls are thick and Pa's hard o' hearin', anyway. Now, you wanna do it or don't you? Make up your mind."

She jerked her legs up and down, groaning impatiently. "We don't have all night."

Bardoul looked around. Only the horses and the mule were watching them. The animals provided nearly as much heat as a woodstove, but the wind funneled in behind them.

Still, Bardoul cursed and unbuckled his cartridge belt. As he let the belt drop to the ground, he began unbuttoning his pants, cursing. Someday his pecker was going to be the death of him.

It surely was . . .

Helen gathered her dress up higher, spreading it out beneath her, padding her bottom against the logs.

"Goddamn it," Bardoul said as he lowered his buckskin breeches and balbriggans, "you're one horny wench, aren't ye?"

She laughed wickedly and spread her legs, adjusting her butt again on the split logs as Bardoul shoved toward her.

"Wait a second," Helen said, placing both hands on his chest, holding him back. "You gotta promise me somethin'."

"Shit!"

"You gotta promise on your way back from huntin' that breed, that you'll pick me up and take me to Denver."

When he only stared at her, one eye slitted, she said, "I'm goin' plumb loco, and I can't bear another winter in this cabin with them two. Especially now that Karl's gone."

"You want me take you to *Denver*? What the hell you gonna do *there*?"

"Anything I have to." Helen drew Bardoul toward him and kissed him hungrily, then pulled back and regarded him with lustful eyes.

She made her voice small and breathy as she wrapped her naked legs around him, pulling his erect shaft against her crotch. "I don't have any extra money, but I'll fuck you good every night we're on the trail. I *will* make it worth your while, Wit. You understand?"

"Christ," Bardoul laughed, and worked his shaft inside her. "You sure as shit better, you crazy bitch."

She groaned and beat her heels against Bardoul's butt as he plunged against her. Her moaning grew so loud, frightening the horses, that Bardoul finally clamped a hand over her mouth as he finished the job, dislodging several logs in the process, one landing on his right foot and tempering his final pleasure.

When they were finished, they got their clothes in order, silently gathered wood in their arms, and headed back to the cabin's front door. Helen fumbled the door open, and Bardoul followed her inside, kicking the door closed and looking around.

Old Gillespie and Ace Higgins sat at the table playing checkers while Brindley scrubbed a pan with a wire brush in the washtub. "Hey, Wit," he said, jerking his head back to indicate the old man, "Mr. Gillespie says he seen the half-breed and the whore heading northwest not more than two hours before we showed up, just before the snow started fallin' in earnest."

Shifting the wood in his arms, feeling a log slip, Bardoul turned to Gillespie, who puffed his pipe as he double-jumped Higgins.

"King me," the old man said to Higgins. He glanced at Bardoul. "They're probably takin' the old Basque trail into Gold Cache. Only place they could be headin' out here."

"What trail?"

"The trace the old Basques made, herdin' sheep between meadows. One runs along the ridges yonder clear to Gold Cache Gulch."

"You know where they might hole up tonight?"

"There's a coupla sheltered hollows up in the rocks yonder, atop the mountain just behind us. Gonna be deep snow in the mornin', though." Gillespie shook his head. "You can pick up the trail there. Tough goin' to get up there, but once you're up there, the snow won't be as deep where the wind clears it."

Bardoul shuffled over to the fireplace and dropped his unwieldy load atop the other wood stacked on the hearth's right side. He glanced into the shadows at Karl. The man was sitting in the rocker, scratching his cheek, staring at the ceiling, and muttering incoherently, deep in tortured thought.

Bardoul turned to Helen. She returned his glance, the corners of her mouth quirking up as she prodded the log she'd laid in the fire with an iron poker.

Stone-faced, Bardoul looked quickly past her at Gillespie, who was again jumping Higgins's checkers. "Can you draw us a map of that Basque trail?"

"Boy, you're lucky we ain't playin' for money!" Gillespie laughed as Higgins kinged him while cursing under his breath.

The old man turned to Bardoul. "Yeah, I'll draw ye a map. First thing in the mornin'. Say, who is that half-breed, anyways? When I seen 'em hightailin' through the canyon here, the woman looked willing enough to me."

Bardoul had pulled an old, yellowed wanted flyer from his coat pocket. Now he tossed the flyer and a pencil on the table before Gillespie. "Draw that map now," the bounty hunter ordered. "We're pullin' foot first thing in the mornin'."

Gillespie snapped his head up at Bardoul, brows furrowed curiously. He hiked a shoulder, smoothed out the flyer, and picked up the pencil.

When the old man was finished drawing the trail and the main landmarks surrounding it, Bardoul grabbed the paper off the table and stuffed it into his shirt pocket. He grabbed the bottle off the table, ran a sleeve across his beard, and plopped onto one of the three cots in the room.

"That's where Karl sleeps," Helen said.

"I'm taking it," Bardoul said, tipping back the whiskey. When he'd lowered the bottle he curled his upper lip at Helen standing tensely by the fire. "I had a long day—and a hard night. I'm tired."

Helen glared at him, her nostrils flared. She glanced at Karl, who was still pondering the rafters, then turned and stalked into the kitchen.

The old man turned in his chair to regard her curiously, then swung his gaze back to Bardoul. All three of the men at the table—Higgins, Brindley, and Gillespie—were staring at him. Brindley's eyes were bright from the hooch.

Bardoul grinned devilishly, took another long pull, then corked the bottle and kicked his boots off.

Bardoul woke at the first wash of dawn in the eastern windows. As he blinked the sleep from his eyes, he heard the thuds of a poker punching logs. He looked over at the fireplace and saw Helen squatting, a blanket about her shoulders, blowing and prodding the glowing coals back to life.

Bardoul's cot creaked as he swung his stocking feet to the floor. Helen turned her head to him quickly. She glanced around the room, where the other four men still lay slumped on cots or, in Brindley's and Higgins's case, on the floor, their snores resounding.

She rose and walked over to Bardoul, let the blanket sag off her shoulders, revealing her breasts in the milky light washing through the frosted window behind Bardoul's cot.

"You don't forget me, hear?" she said.

Bardoul turned to look out the window. The lilac sky was clear as a bell, the last stars still twinkling above the snow-mantled ridges looming over the cabin. The yard was white as a bridal gown.

"Did I promise you somethin', Helen?" Bardoul said, reaching into his shirt pocket for his makings sack. He looked up at her, one cheek rising with a lopsided grin. "I'm sorry. I don't remember promisin' you a damn thing."

As she glared down at him, her jaw hardening, Bardoul dug into his makings sack, producing a small wad of papers. He peeled one paper from the wad, shoved the others back into the sack. "Besides, I'll have my hands full when I'm headin' back to Thornton's. No time to fool with a woman."

Bardoul sprinkled tobacco onto the wheat paper troughed between the first two fingers of his left hand. The woman stared down at him. He could hear her breathing—deep, exasperated breaths.

Suddenly she slapped the makings out of his grasp. She cocked her arm to slap him with the back of her hand, but before she could bring the hand forward, old Gillespie called, "Helen?"

She lowered the hand quickly, wheeled to her right. She swallowed, took a short, sharp breath. "I'm just gettin' the fire goin' now," she said, her voice husky with forced calm. "Coffee'll be a couple minutes."

Helen glanced at Bardoul once more, rage in her eyes, then, holding the blanket tightly about her shoulders, stalked back to the fire and picked up the poker. When she'd busied herself with the fire, adding kindling, Bardoul chuckled to himself. Women had to be the most gullible damn creatures on God's green earth. He picked up his makings, shook out fresh tobacco, and rolled a smoke.

He lit his cigarette and stomped into his boots, then gave both Brindley and Higgins a good kick to rouse them from their blanket rolls. Lazily, still chuckling to himself, he shrugged into his coat.

When he and his two compatriots had gone out and saddled their horses, they led the mounts through the knee-high drifts to the hitchrack before the stoop, tied them, and went back inside, where the fire popped, warming the cabin. Last night's stew was bubbling over the fire while Gillespie dressed and Helen helped Karl back to his rocking chair.

The woman didn't say a single word to anyone all through breakfast. The way she glowered at Bardoul over her stew bowl, he thought for sure she'd try to stick a knife in his back—or maybe she'd poisoned his stew . . .

He was relieved, after breakfast, to swing up onto his Appaloosa's back and head off through the new-fallen snow while old Gillespie stared after him and his companions, pensively puffing his pipe.

Bardoul, Brindley, and Higgins followed Gillespie's directions northward through the canyon as the sun climbed, making the snow sparkle like jewels and causing their eyes to ache as though pierced by a million tiny javelins.

Higgins chuckled. "You son of a bitch, Bardoul—you went and got your ashes hauled!"

The bounty hunter glanced cautiously behind. The cabin and corral had disappeared behind a bend in the canyon wall. "Say what?"

"Say *what*?" Brindley laughed, riding drag. "Don't you think we done heard you and the woman going at it last night in the woodpile?" He laughed louder. "Shit, you're just lucky her husband's loco and her old man's deaf as a fence post!"

"Goddamn it!" Bardoul threw his head back, guffawing. "I had a feelin' you could hear us out there!"

He hipped around in his saddle toward Brindley. "Did you hear how I made that bitch scream?"

"Shit," Brindley said under his railroad cap and muffler. "For a while there, I thought you was carvin' her up with a bowie knife!"

Higgins reached over and slapped Bardoul's shoulder. "We thought you was practicin' up for Thornton's runaway whore!"

Cackling like drunken soldiers, the trio climbed the sloping hills toward the rocky crags and the pine-studded ridge before them.

As the sunlight penetrated the cave's opening and set the fire's smoke to glowing like golden vapor, Yakima slid the blankets and furs down to reveal Faith's soft right breast, then knelt down and kissed the nipple.

Sound asleep since they'd finished making love the night before, Faith stirred, the corners of her full mouth lifting. She groaned and stretched luxuriously, opening her eyes halfway. "Is it morning already?"

"Already?" Yakima stood and looked around. "The sun's full up."

Faith looked beyond the smoking fire, on which the teapot gurgled and beans bubbled in a tin kettle. The sky was blue, the sun bright on the new-fallen snow. The paint mare and the mule stood nearby, eating from the grain sacks Yakima had draped over their ears.

"Pretty out there," Faith said, yawning. "But it looks cold."

"It's not bad. The sun'll warm it up fast."

He turned away from her, and she grabbed his wrist, drew him down toward her. "Stay with me, Yakima."

He leaned down, smoothed the mussed hair back from her cheek, and kissed her gently. "No time. Thornton's men, remember?"

"I bet the storm discouraged them." She entwined her hands behind his neck, kissing him. "They've hightailed it out of the mountains."

"Not likely." Yakima returned another kiss and leaned back on his heels. "Come on. Shake a leg."

"Let me doze a little while longer," Faith said, breathing deeply, turning her head to one side and closing her eyes.

Yakima stared down at her. She was a beautiful woman, especially beautiful in the mornings. Warm and soft, childlike. It used to be that he'd thought women were here only to satisfy men's natural cravings, like food and drink. He no longer felt that way about this beautiful woman lying before him. He'd been looking askance at the notion for some time, but he knew now with certainty that he'd fallen in love with her.

The notion filled him with both tenderness and dread. For what could be the fate of two such disparate lovers as him and Faith?

"Come on," he said, grabbing her left ankle through the blankets and furs and shaking it gently. "Time to pull our picket pins. I've warmed your clothes by the fire. They're good and toasty."

"Yakima, don't be such a drill sergeant," she pouted, keeping her eyes closed.

"Come on," he said, shaking both her ankles this time.

"Oh!" she cried, flinging the blankets back to reveal her long, pale body with the full, pink-tipped orbs. "The tea smells good, anyway, and I could eat a horse!"

"Can't spare a horse, but the beans are ready."

"Yakima?"

She knelt upon the blankets, holding her men's long underwear in one hand out before her, and regarding him with gravity. Her blond hair hung over her left shoulder, curling down the side of her left breast. She seemed to be trying to peer through some screen obscuring her view of him.

"You'll stay with me, won't you? In Gold Cache? We'll be partners?"

He hesitated for only a second, reaching for the teapot. "I reckon I don't have anywhere else to go," he said, splashing the steaming tea into her cup. He wanted to stay with her, but of course it wasn't possible. He couldn't find the words to tell her. Hell, maybe she already knew and was only clinging to the dream for lack of anything else to hold her.

She threw her arms around his neck, pressed her breasts to his sheepskin coat. "It won't matter who we are in Gold Cache. It's the good thing, maybe the *only* good thing about gold camps. Nobody cares who you are or where you came from—or who you're in love with."

He turned to her, the teapot in his right hand. He smiled and ran his hand through her hair, sifting it through his fingers until his hand reached the small of her back. He splayed his fingers against her warm, smooth skin just above her bottom, and pressed her toward him gently. His heart swelled, but he kept his voice lightly cajoling.

"Drink your tea and eat your beans. If we're gonna get to Gold Cache and start our own business, we best fork leather soon."

She held the balbriggans against her breasts. "What are we going to do about Thornton's men?"

Yakima set the teapot on the fire, dropped the leather pad, and rose. "Kill 'em."

He picked up a saddle and walked out of the cave, heading toward his horse.

Chapter 20

In the brothel that she owned and operated in Gold Cache, Crazy Kate Sweney ran a brush through her long black hair and stared at her own pensive expression in the gilt-framed mirror before her.

She was seated in her own inner sanctum tucked away in the brothel's bowels and decorated in the latest French fashions, with reds and purples and so many lighted candles lined up on the imported furniture that her Mexican patrons often mistook the room for a Catholic shrine.

A fire snapped in the hearth. Beyond the curtained windows thick with frost and pocked with snow from last night's storm, ore wagons squawked and clattered. Men cursed the weather. Somewhere, a dog barked, and she could hear the regular scrapes of a snow shovel as Max Lerner, Crazy Kate's bartender, cleared the brothel's front porch.

There would likely be a surge in business today, the coldest of the season so far. The prospectors and miners would be attracted to Kate's warm rooms and warm girls, as most were housed in drafty cabins little better appointed than chicken coops.

Crazy Kate stared into her own eyes in the mirror, the dream she'd just awakened from remaining with her like a cloying odor from the Chinese shacks just down the gulch. As if to rid her mind of the dream, she set down the tortoiseshell comb, picked up the long black cheroot smoldering in the ashtray before her, and took a deep drag.

Behind her, a man's groan came from her broad four-poster bed. The springs squawked. She took another deep drag from the cheroot as a figure rose from the bed behind her.

"What the hell—it's morning already?"

Crazy Kate didn't say anything. She picked up her brandy glass in the same hand in which she held the cheroot and sipped the pungent brew. Only in a mining camp would such coffin varnish pass for French brandy.

From the bed, Sebastian Kirk cleared his throat. "Kate?"

"What?" she said, impatient and annoyed, half turning her head toward him.

Kate hated it when he stayed the entire night in her room. She preferred sleeping alone. But what could she do? Sebastian had staked her to this claim, and she still owed money on the note. She either paid with her body or paid with money, and the only thing Crazy Kate hated worse than satisfying men as old as herself was parting with cash.

"I asked you a question," the man said, his voice thick with sleep and bourbon from the night before.

"Yes, it's morning. Can't you see the light in the window?"

"I haven't opened my eyes yet."

"Well, open 'em, for chrissakes! And get dressed and get outta here. I'm gonna have a busy day. I can't sit around here all morning, entertaining your fool questions!"

Kate turned back to her own haggard face in the mirror—a face that, in spite of her own best efforts, showed every seam and wrinkle of her thirty-seven years. She'd been called Crazy Kate since her early twenties, for the simple fact that her bright green eyes set deep in her long, dark face—a witch's face, sure enough—made her look loco and lusty in a devious, compelling sort of way. There was the matter of her clairvoyance and ability to read palms and cipher the tarot cards and read skull bumps, but it was her face first and foremost that had earned her the unflattering though commercially colorful handle. She'd long ago stopped taking offense. The handle was good for business. She was the kind of crazy, exotic-looking woman who could earn a living only by whoring in mining camps, and that was what she'd done for the past twenty years.

Behind her, the bed squawked and jostled, the big bear spread rustling. Kate continued staring into her eyes as, in the periphery of her vision, Sebastian Kirk rose naked from the bed.

A tall, bald man with broad shoulders once muscular but now reminding Kate of an underfed mule's pronounced ribs, and a heavy, sagging gut, he ambled over to her. He bent down behind her, his eyes meeting hers as he ran his hands up her sheer, flesh-colored wrapper and cupped her large, pear-shaped breasts in his hands, hefting them as though testing the ripeness of fruit.

"What's with the harsh tone, my pet? Didn't you sleep well?" He nuzzled her neck. He'd once been a pugilist, and he still had a boxer's grip and brusque love habits.

Kate took another sip of the brandy. She had to admit that the man's presence, even his rough touch, was a comfort on this frozen morning after another one of her oddly portentous dreams.

"I should have gotten up when I first awakened," Crazy Kate said in her husky smoker's drawl. "A strange feeling came over me. It wouldn't have happened if I'd gotten up and had my usual drink and smoke instead of lying there."

Still holding her heavy breasts in his hands, Sebastian nuzzled the other side of her neck, gently nibbling her skin.

Kate chuckled and turned her head away. "Sebastian, that tickles."

"Last night, it got you rather worked up, if you remember."

Kate turned back to her own eyes in the mirror, her dark face growing serious, pensive. "I saw a woman on a black horse riding into the gulch."

Sebastian chuckled again and straightened, removing his hands from Kate's breasts. "A good-looking woman? You know what the Irishmen say—you can't have enough pretty girls in Gold Cache."

Kate took that as a slight against her doves. It wasn't easy getting clean, comely girls this high in the mountains. "But the Irishmen aren't exactly blooded studs, are they?"

Sebastian sighed. He himself was Irish, though he'd nearly lost his accent. "I reckon I'll be getting these old bones off to the mine." He was the superintendent of the fledgling Gold Cache Mining & Smelting Company, which employed forty-seven men. "I can tell you're in no mood for teasing."

"I didn't see the woman's face," Kate said, crossing her legs as Sebastian wandered around the room, gathering his strewn clothes. He appeared paler than usual in the snow-bright light pushing through the frosted windows. "Just the horse. It was tall and black."

"Sounds like a harmless enough dream. A dream as non-sensical as any other."

"It does at that," Kate said, taking a drag from the cheroot and blowing smoke at the mirror. She leaned forward, rested her face in her hand. "But why, then, do I have this feeling of dread down deep in my gut?"

"Perhaps in your sordid past, you've crossed paths with a

black stallion and treated him horribly," said Sebastian, accentuating his Irish accent while stepping into his serge suit slacks, breathing hard, his pale face reddening with the effort. He looked at her, a mischievous smile touching his lips. "As you're wont to do, Pet."

"Fuck you, Sebastian."

"See?" he chuckled, flapping his shirt out before him.

"Why do I tell you anything?"

"Because you haven't anyone else in the camp to tell." He leaned down and kissed the back of Crazy Kate's head, then sat on the bed to pull his socks on.

Kate finished the cheroot, mashed it out, then picked up her brandy glass and strode to the window. Holding the glass in one hand, she stretched her other arm high above her head. In the little stone tavern across the street, still cloaked in the shadow of the high, pine-clad mountain behind it, someone played a banjo. The sound was oddly out of sync with the cold, snowy morning and the skeins of smoke ribboning from the stovepipes lining Gold Cache's short main street.

"Come on, boys," Kate said, turning her head to gaze south, toward the mine, where the night shift should be ending, spilling a good dozen or so work-weary miners into Gold Cache's business district. "Bring those Irish and Russian and Norski peckers over here. I'll need money for another freight run . . ." Kate let her voice trail off. Her eyes narrowed as they followed a figure along the street. Figures, rather.

"Sebastian?" Her voice sounded thin and fragile.

The mine superintendent was tying his right brogan. Startled by Kate's voice, he looked up at her, frowning. "Pet?"

"Come here."

Tucking his white shirttail into his slacks, Sebastian came

over and stood beside her. She tapped the glass with her left index finger. "Look."

On the snow-covered street already gouged with the tracks of men, wagons, and horses, two men rode toward the brothel from the south, tracing the corner around the German's wood-framed canvas hophouse, the north side of which had collapsed under the weight of last night's snow. One of the riders approaching the hophouse was tall, with longish brown hair, and clad in a red-plaid mackinaw and a black, flat-brimmed hat. The other was short and blond. He wore a coat of wolf hair and deerskin, the fur collar raised. Tied to his head with a green muffler was a brown bowler hat with a frayed brim.

The stocky blond man rode a dun with three white stockings. At the end of his long lead rope, fighting the hackamore, rolling its eyes, and raising its tail defiantly, pranced a tall black stallion.

There was a trill in Crazy Kate's voice. "The horse from my dream."

Sebastian stared out the window. He continued tucking his shirttail into his pants. Wonder mixed with the humor in his gravelly voice. "Just a coincidence, Kate."

Kate stared out the window so intently that she didn't notice that Sebastian turned away to tie the black four-in-hand necktie in front of her dresser mirror.

On the street before the collapsed hophouse, the two riders reined their horses to a halt. They seemed to be speaking to the two Germans in buffalo coats and cloth caps who were shoveling snow off the collapsed hophouse roof. One of the Germans turned and pointed north along the street, beyond the hotel. The man with the brown hair and the black, flat-brimmed hat smiled, pinched his hat brim, and reined his claybank into the street.

As the shorter man kneed his dun ahead, jerking on the stallion's lead rope, Kate wheeled to Sebastian. "I have to find out who they are. Will you come with me?"

Sebastian straightened and absently ran his hand over the tufts of wiry silver hair framing his pale, bald pate. "Now, Kate, don't you think—?" He saw the fierce look in her ethereal green eyes, and his face fell. "Why not?"

Kate threw back her brandy, set the glass on the bedside table, and grabbed a long flannel wrapper off a wall hook near the door. She stepped into a pair of high-topped rabbit slippers—she shouldn't be seen in the saloon in such shabby attire, but she didn't have time to doll herself up—and opened the door.

She was still knotting the robe's belt around her thick waist when, half a minute later, she descended the brothel's broad mahogany staircase, the burgundy carpet rendering her hurried steps nearly soundless. Behind her, Sebastian Kirk wheezed, trying to keep up as he secured the bows of his silver spectacles behind his ears.

Since it wasn't yet ten o'clock, the saloon and gambling parlor entertained only two customers—soiled, unshaven men who had the look of market hunters about them. They played a desultory card game in the middle of the broad room, yawning and smoking over their poker hands. The barman, Max Lerner, was polishing the backbar's grand mirror while humming to himself. Two whores, Emily and Maxine, stood near the bottom of the stairs, all fluffed out and painted up for a working day and staring up at Crazy Kate expectantly.

"Not now, girls," Kate said. She had no time to be barraged with the whores' endless troubles.

Maxine said, "Kate—"

"It'll have to wait."

"Kate," Emily blurted, flushed, her eyes bright with worry as she held her steepled hands to her lips, "Doc says I got one up the chute!"

Kate stopped at the bottom of the stairs. "Not again!"

"I'm sorry, Kate. I was tryin' to be careful. Honest!"

Kate expelled a sharp sigh as Sebastian stopped two steps above her. Kate looked at Emily. "How far along?"

"Doc says two months."

Kate looked at the other whore, Maxine. "Fetch my kit to Emily's room. We'll meet there in a few minutes to remedy the problem."

Kate rolled her eyes at Sebastian, who shrugged, then continued striding toward the double front doors flanked by two big, sunlit windows.

"Kate," Emily called behind her. "I think I'd like to keep this one!"

Without turning around or slowing her stride, Kate lifted her head and shouted, "You ain't keepin' *nothin'*!"

Kate opened the left door and stepped onto the shoveled stoop, raising a hand to shield her eyes against the sunlight careening off the snow like ricocheting bullets. She looked around.

A few paces to her right, the two newcomers were walking their horses southward on the right side of the street, avoiding a couple of oncoming drays hauling firewood. The stocky blond man riding behind the dark-haired hombre was having trouble with the black stallion, which snorted and tipped his head up, tail cocked, obviously enraged.

"Goddamn it!" the blond man said as he gave the rope a fierce tug.

At the same time, the black lowered his head and rammed the rump of the dun. The dun started, giving a shrill whinny, and buck-kicked.

Because he'd been pulling the rope, which had slackened suddenly when the black lowered his head and drove forward, the blond was caught off guard. He gave a cry as he flew forward, reaching for but missing his saddle horn, and was emptied ass over teakettle down the dun's right shoulder.

He hit the snow on his back, feet pointing toward the street's right side. One of the firewood drays missed his legs by only six inches or so. The dark-haired gent half turned his own mount and chuckled.

"That goddamn son of a bitch!" bellowed the thrown rider as he gained his knees.

He was still holding the black's lead. The stallion reared and shied, trying to jerk the rope from the blond man's fist.

Covered with snow, the blond man held tight to the rope. He glared at his chuckling partner, then turned to the stallion, which stood sideways in the street, nickering and twitching his ears with satisfaction, tail arched.

"I'm so goddamn tired of this consarned beast"—the blond man lifted the skirt of his wolf coat and pulled his pistol from its holster—"I'm gonna do what I been wantin' to do ever since we got him!"

As he thumbed the pistol's hammer back, the dark-haired man rode up and kicked the pistol out of the blond man's fist. The pistol hit the snow and skidded against the snowbank fronting the opposite boardwalk.

"Goddamn you, Leo!" the blond man screeched, holding his right fist to his belly and glaring up at his partner. He still held the black's lead in his left hand.

The dark man leaned down, gritting his teeth. "That horse is worth five hundred dollars if he's worth a cent, you copperriveted fool!"

The blond man pointed his injured hand at the horse, which was eyeing him with challenge. "But he—"

"We didn't come all this way to sell him just so's you could shoot him, Alvin!"

Holding her robe tight about her shoulders, Crazy Kate, flanked by Sebastian Kirk, had made her way southward down the boardwalk. She now stood parallel to the two strangers, regarding the horse with fascination.

Before either could say another word, Kate said, "You men say that horse is for sale?"

They both looked at her skeptically. A cunning light grew in Salon's brown eyes, slitted against the sun's glare. "Yes, ma'am, he shore is." Salon grabbed the rope from Pauk's hand and led the angrily snorting black to the boardwalk.

The banjo had ceased playing in the beer parlor on the other side of the street. Two men in canvas coats stood under the tavern's brush awning, one holding a banjo, both staring at Kate, the horse, and the two strangers.

Crazy Kate stared at the horse. The horse drew up before her and shook his head. Then his eyes met hers, and they stood staring at each other, their breath puffing around their faces as the horse pushed his regal head forward, working his nose.

"If you ever seen a better horse than this one here, ma'am," Salon said, "then you sure got a leg up on me!"

"Where did you get him?" Kate said.

"Bought him off a half-breed," Salon told her. He glanced at Pauk, who'd heaved himself up and was walking toward his six-shooter half buried in the snow along the street. "Didn't we, Alvin?" He turned back to Kate and Sebastian. "Back along the trail somewheres."

"What was a half-breed doing with a horse like this?" Sebastian said, stepping forward to run a careful hand along the black's sleek neck.

"We didn't converse about it, 'ceptin' he assured us it weren't stolen. He probably needed money to provide for the blond gal he was ridin' with." Salon had spoken to Sebastian. Now he turned his eager eyes to Crazy Kate. "If you got five hundred dollars, ma'am, he's yours. Hell, you rent him to stud three times in a month for more—!"

Kate cut him off, snapping her keen green eyes from the horse to Salon. "Did you say 'blond woman'?"

Salon looked at her dubiously, frowning. He shrugged a shoulder. "So I did." He paused. "The point is, a horse like this one here is a damn good investment."

"Why are you selling him?" Sebastian asked.

Kate was only half listening. She stared at the horse, remembering her dream about the black stallion and the blond woman.

What did it mean? What did this horse and the blonde have to do with her?

"Well," Salon said with a sheepish grin, "me and Alvin here ain't exactly horse men. We're gamblers. We prefer to spend our time in gambling parlors and leave the horses to the stableboys, if you get my drift."

"I'll take him," Kate said, still staring at the horse but snapping out of her reverie. Something in the back of her mind was telling her that in order to find out what the dream meant, she had to have the horse.

Salon grinned.

Kate turned to Sebastian. "Give the man five hundred dollars. Add it to my note." She looked at Salon. Pauk now stood beside Salon's dun, staring at the woman, his lower jaw slack.

"Stable him at the Occidental, over yonder," Kate said,

jerking her head to indicate the big barn half a block up on the other side of the street. "If you boys want gambling and the best women in the Rockies, you'll find 'em both at Crazy Kate's." She turned and, as if in a dream, moved back toward the brothel, hearing her voice say automatically, "Don't make yourselves strangers now, hear . . . ?"

Chapter 21

.

Yakima crouched atop a rocky scarp and used the freighters' German-made glasses to scout his and Faith's back trail.

A high hill strewn with black boulders rose on his left, about fifty yards away. To the right, the land dropped gradually to a distant, pine-choked ravine.

Straight south lay a lake in a broad hollow, unseen from this distance. Yakima and Faith had stopped for lunch by that frozen lake. He'd glassed their back trail thoroughly from a hill on the other side of the lake and had seen no sign of the three men he'd thought were trailing them.

He saw nothing now, either, except drifting snow and purple shadows bleeding out from the trees and boulders, brown weed tips protruding above the scalloped snow covering the ground where the wind hadn't swept it clear.

There weren't many places to hide up here among the ridges, where trees grew mainly in the ravines and valley bottoms. If the pursuers were still stalking him, he'd no doubt have spotted them by now, especially through the good German field glasses. It wasn't likely—Thornton had probably put a high price on his and Faith's heads—but maybe he really had lost them.

His heart feeling lighter, Yakima straightened, turned,

and hopscotched the boulders to the brow of the ridge behind him. He'd crested the hill and was descending the other side, leaping from one rock to the next, when he stopped suddenly, dropping to his haunches atop a flat rock and raising his rifle to his chest.

Below, the tea fire he'd built at the base of the hill bent and tore in the wind. Faith was perched on the same rock she'd been sitting on when he'd climbed the hill to glass their back trail.

On the other side of the fire from her, five riders approached her from across a snow-dusted, weed-tufted hill dome. They were not the ones Yakima had spied following them before.

The first of the riders strung out in a shaggy line was only ten or so yards from the fire. So intently were they staring at Faith, lascivious grins on their faces, that they hadn't seen Yakima yet, perched halfway up the hill. Faith sat holding one of the freighters' rifles across her denim-clad knees, her back stiff, blond hair whipping in the wind.

"Hello, there, ma'am," hailed the lead rider. He wore a rabbit hat with ear flaps, and a long, ratty buffalo coat. Long brown chin whiskers brushed the medallion hanging around his neck by a rawhide thong.

Faith jerked a tense look up the hill behind her. She turned back toward the strangers, then jerked her gaze up the hill again, her eyes finding Yakima perched on the boulder. The strangers followed her gaze, all stiffening slightly as they stopped their horses five yards beyond the coffee fire.

Yakima loudly levered a shell into his Winchester's breech and straightened, holding the rifle low across his thighs. "Help you, boys?"

The leader glanced at the others riding behind him. Their horses stood hang-headed. They'd been riding hard. Fleeing the law? They had the scruffy, tattered look of renegades, their weapons prominently displayed. One wore his Navy Colts in crisscrossing shoulder rigs on the outside of his buffalo coat.

Turning back to Yakima, the leader grinned. "We saw the lady out here alone and was gonna offer our assistance." A couple of the others chuckled. "Pretty high up in the mountains for a lady to be out here alone."

Yakima smiled solemnly as he ran his eyes over the other riders—one was an older, gray-bearded gent who used to ride for a ranch east of Thornton's—then back to the leader. "It would be."

No one said anything for a time. The riders stared at Yakima, who stared back. Faith turned her head between them, her eyes wary.

The wind blew the snow around under the crystal blue sky. Gray mountain jays fluttered among the rocks behind Yakima. The gray-bearded man's sorrel suddenly shook its head, its bit chains jangling.

The lead rider dropped his gaze to Faith. "Miss, you'd be better off with us than that savage up there. We got us a shack not far from here."

Because of the fire and the breeze rustling around him, Yakima couldn't hear her reply, only saw her head shake slightly.

The others glanced at the lead rider, who shrugged a shoulder. "Have it your way. It's gonna get mighty cold tonight."

With that, he pinched his hat at Faith, reined his horse away from the fire, and touched his spurs to its flanks. In a minute, all five were drifting over the crest of the northwestern hill and into the woods on the other side.

Faith stood and turned to Yakima as he continued striding

down the hill to her. Her chest rose and fell sharply. "Well, that was a little rattling."

"You all right?"

"Getting to be so a woman can't trust anyone in these parts." She looked off across the fire. "Think they'll be back?"

"I wouldn't bet against it." Yakima reached down, removed the teapot from the fire, and kicked snow over the flames.

They traveled just below the ridgelines, sometimes climbing above timberline, then plunging through snow-socked valleys before climbing to another pass, until the sun had fallen and an impenetrable chill had descended from the starry, black sky.

Yakima built a fire in the hollow of a large, uprooted spruce, the tree's massive, curling, snowcapped roots forming a wall to one side, blocking the wind and the view of the fire from down the sloping ravine.

That was the direction from which trouble would come, if it came. Yakima was relatively certain it would come. At least, you always had to assume so.

While the horses pawed for grass beneath the deep snow, Faith made coffee and roasted the rabbits Yakima had snared.

That night, he sat atop the spruce trunk, above the fire, holding a steaming cup of tea and whiskey in one hand as he stared down the ravine, his right hand holding his rifle around the brass receiver. The whiskey was more booty from the freight wagons. Yakima's legs were curled beneath him, Indian style. The ravine was a trough, with towering spruces and tamaracks studding its slopes under a cold, black velvet ceiling dusted with stars.

Behind him, the small fire popped and the teapot wheezed.

"Yakima?"

He turned to Faith, who sat huddled beside the fire, a blanket draped over her coat, a tin coffee cup steaming between her mittened hands. "Shh."

She whispered, "Yakima?"

"What?"

"How much farther to Gold Cache?"

"Not far." He kept his ears pricked to the night and replied, "We should be there tomorrow, late."

Silence. An owl hooted and a tuft of snow, warmed by the fire's updraft, fell in a clump up ravine of the camp.

"Yakima?" Faith whispered again.

He lowered his cup from his lips. "What?"

"How long are we gonna have to whisper?"

"As long as *we* keep talking."

"You think they're really that randy for me?"

In spite of himself he turned full around and cracked a smile. "If they have blood in their veins."

She chuckled without mirth and sipped her toddy. After a while, her whispers rose to him again above the cracks and pops of the fire. "We'll have us a fine place in Gold Cache, Yakima. The banker I know told me anytime I wanted to go into business on my own—if I ever got away from Thornton, that was—he'd back me any way he could. I've got a recipe for beer an old German gave me. He said—"

"Quiet!" Yakima rasped, staring intently down ravine. He'd heard something. The soft snap of a twig beneath snow.

Bracing himself with one hand, he swung down from the spruce trunk, dropping soundlessly onto the cleared ground, and hunkered beside Faith.

Her wide eyes regarded him worriedly. He squeezed her arm. "Just like we said."

She swallowed, nodding.

Grabbing her Winchester carbine, she stood and crept off into the brush on the other side of the fire, into the snag of another downed tree. Listening to the faint rustle and snaps of the brittle twigs as she burrowed deep under the prone trunk, Yakima squatted beside the spruce and pressed his back to the roots rising a good eight feet above his head.

He glanced across the fire. He and Faith had piled their blankets and robes over a couple of long wood chunks, then scattered their spare clothes beside the mound. It looked like two people "bundling" together against the cold, enjoying each other's warmth.

He hoped the renegades would think so. If that was who'd made the sound he'd heard.

He'd waited ten minutes, breathing through his parted lips, when his horse nickered softly up ravine.

He squeezed the Henry in his gloved hands and stared into the woods beyond the fire, not wanting the flames to ruin his night vision.

After another couple of tense minutes, boots crunched snow along the wooded slope to his right. More crunches and weed snaps rose from down ravine. Very faintly, he felt the roots behind him vibrate, as though someone had stepped onto the fallen trunk.

A shadow moved to his right. The man came down the slope and sidled up to a fir about ten yards from the fire. The fire shone red on the high cheekbones above his scruffy gray beard and reflected off the brass housing of the Winchester in his hands.

Footsteps grew behind Yakima, faintly crunching snow.

There was a phlegmy sniff, as of a man with a head cold. The roots jostled faintly against Yakima's back, and bark scraped under boot heels straight above his head.

He could hear breathing up there, see the vapor puffing in the air above the roots.

On the slope, beside the fir, the other man waited, his forehead shaded by his hat brim. The hat was canted down toward the mound of blankets and quilts.

In another few seconds, they would realize it was a trap.

Yakima stepped out away from the roots. He pivoted, saw the man looming over him, a rifle in his hands. He reached up with one hand, grabbed the man's cartridge belt, and pulled.

The man gave a startled cry as he flew forward over the tangled roots, snapping off several as he plummeted into the camp and landed facefirst in the cook fire. The teapot clattered on the rocks. Steam from the spilled tea sizzled. The man screamed and rolled out of the fire ring, his arms and legs flailing as the flames chewed at his fur coat and buckskins.

Fluidly, Yakima raised the Yellowboy to his shoulder, drawing a quick bead on the man who'd been standing by the fir. The man had just snugged the Spencer to his shoulder when Yakima's Winchester boomed.

The Spencer coughed at the same time Yakima's bullet plunged through the man's deerskin coat, throwing him straight back against the fir with a strangled scream.

Though Yakima couldn't hear much but the screams of the man fighting the flames from his clothes by the fire, he knew the third man was bolting toward him along the spruce's prone trunk.

With few movements, Yakima slipped around the opposite side of the root ball, leapt atop the bole, and hunkered on his haunches.

The third man now stood where Yakima had been a moment ago, yelling, "Where'd you go, ya goddamn savage?"

A voice rose from the black slope to Yakima's left. "On the tree, Bill!"

The voice hadn't died before Yakima fired twice through the spruce's roots, drilling one neat hole through Bill's startled face, then one through his right ear as he turned away, falling.

Rifles snapped on the slope, blue-red flames stabbing toward the camp. One bullet plunked into the spruce just below Yakima's fur-lined moccasins. Another cracked a stubby branch to his right.

Yakima ejected a smoking shell, the brass casing clattering on a rock below the tree, and raised the Yellowboy to his shoulder as he seated a fresh cartridge. He could see no movement amid the velvet black of the wooded slope, but he keyed on one of the two gun flashes and fired.

A half second later, both rifles flashed again, the reports following as both slugs whistled just shy of Yakima's head.

Squatting on the spruce trunk, Yakima cut loose with the Yellowboy until five more casings littered the snow beneath the tree, sizzling softly. By his third shot, the small fusillade from the slope had died, and now in the quiet night—the burning man's cries had died to a low, intermittent keening as the flames engulfed him—he heard crunching snow, thrashing brush, and the rasps of labored breathing.

The two shooters were fleeing up the slope.

Yakima leapt into the snow beneath the spruce, instinctively zigzagged to the base of the slope, and bolted up

through the woods, lifting his feet high above the snow and
the brambles grabbing at his moccasins.

Ahead and to the left, a shadow moved.

Yakima stopped, raised the Yellowboy, and cocked it. The
shadow was gone. Yakima aimed a little ahead of where he'd
last seen the shadow, between the black columns of the
birches and firs, and fired.

"Eeenggg!" the man cried. There was the crunch of a
body dropping into the snow.

Yakima couldn't see the wounded man. It had been a lucky
shot, but he'd take them any way he could get them. If these
two got away, they might try to avenge their companions.

He ran forward, hearing the other man's strained breaths
ahead and to the right. Seeing the dark shape on the snow
before him, between two pines and tangled in brambles,
Yakima crouched over the man.

He lay facedown, trying to push himself up on his hands
and knees. Yakima couldn't tell where he was shot, but he
could smell the warm, metallic odor of the blood in the
cold air.

Yakima looked around, then leaped atop the man's back,
forcing him down to the ground with a low groan, and
rammed the brass-shod butt of the Yellowboy hard against
the back of his head.

The skull cracked. The man loosed a long sigh and lay still.

Crouching atop the dead man, Yakima cast another quick
glance around. He saw nothing but the inky black tree
columns and nebulous bramble thickets, but he heard the
other man fleeing up the slope to his right. He was probably
about fifty yards away.

Yakima wanted to let him go, to return to the camp and
Faith. But bushwhackers, like wild dogs, had to be turned
under.

Yakima leapt into the snow and continued running uphill, taking long, fluid strides as he angled to the right. He dodged around pines and firs, leapt deadfalls, swerved around snow-flocked boulders.

He saw the short figure beside the lightning-topped birch just in time. As the rifle flashed, Yakima threw himself behind a spruce.

The bushwhacker's shot shattered the night.

Yakima rolled off his right shoulder on the other side of the spruce and came up firing the Yellowboy from his right hip.

Boom-rasp! Boom-rasp! Boom!

Silence. Slowly, Yakima ejected the hot shell and slid another into the chamber.

The acrid odor of cordite wafted around his face. He stared through the smoke.

The short figure had fused with the taller tree and dropped to its knees, head hanging. A rifle lay several feet away.

Slowly, Yakima approached, stopping three feet in front of the slumped figure.

The man lifted his head, the flaps of the rabbit hat hanging straight down on either side of his face. His long chin whiskers wisped around in the breeze. Blood oozed out one corner of his mouth, glistening in the starlight reflecting off the snow.

The man's face bunched with pain. "Who . . . are you, breed?"

Yakima stared down at him, his chest rising and falling heavily, the medallion winking in the night's ambient light. Yakima raised the Yellowboy to the man's forehead. The man stared up at him fearfully.

"Go to hell wondering, hombre."

The rifle barked. The man fell straight back in the snow, kicking.

Yakima turned and started jogging back down the hill toward the camp.

Chapter 22

The gunshot flatted out across the lonely, star-capped ridges, echoing faintly and setting several coyotes to howling.

Ace Higgins turned to Bardoul and Brindley, standing along the ridge of the low hill beside him, their breath wreathing in the chill night. "Came from straight north," Higgins said, pointing over a jog of pine-covered rimrocks limned by starlight.

No one said anything. They stood staring across the snow-basted bluffs, shivering at the slight breeze sliding icy hands beneath their coat collars and tied-down hats. In the hollow down the hill behind them, their campfire made a small orange smudge in the aspen copse.

"We can't be that far off the trail," said Brindley as the howling of the coyotes faded.

"Well, how the hell would we know without a map?" Bardoul said, ramming the back of his fist against Brindley's shoulder. Brindley staggered sideways, grabbing his upper arm and casting the bounty hunter an injured look.

Earlier that day, Brindley had hunkered down beside their coffee fire to study the map. He'd turned his head away for a time, peering into the distance. When he'd turned back to the map, he saw that he'd let the paper hang too close to the flames. It had caught fire, and by the time he'd stamped it out, the map was little more than brittle ashes flung about on the wind.

"I done told ya I was sorry, Bardoul!" Brindley could barely see through his swollen right eye, which Bardoul had blackened when he saw what remained of the map Gillespie had drawn of the old Basque shepherds' trail. "You could do with a little forgiveness, you know that? It was an honest mistake. Don't tell me you haven't made 'em before!"

Bardoul stepped toward him, raising his fist and gritting his teeth. Three shots echoed quickly, one after another. Bardoul jerked his head northward once more, letting his clenched fist sag to his side.

Again, they all stood listening as another shot flatted out across the glowing night.

After nearly five more minutes of hearing only the coyotes and the breeze combing the new-fallen snow, Higgins turned to Bardoul. "It ain't necessarily the breed and the woman. Could be a mountain man or a prospector."

Bardoul ran his gloved hand across his runny nose. "This late at night?"

"Maybe someone's huntin' a bobcat," offered Brindley meekly. "Or, shit, maybe—"

"Shut up!" Bardoul turned to him sharply and flung an arm toward the camp. "Saddle the horses. We're headin' north."

Higgins stared at him. "Tonight? *In the dark?*"

"We done lost enough time chasin' shadows because of this goddamned lead-headed tinhorn here," Bardoul said, glancing at Brindley, who leapt back like a frightened doe, raising his hands defensively. "We're gonna make up that time tonight, so get movin'!"

He jerked forward, threatening. Higgins and Brindley

jumped up and, tramped toward the campfire like scolded schoolboys.

Bardoul turned northward and stared. "It's you, ain't it, breed? You half-wild savage, you." He sucked at the chaw in his lip and spat, then licked the remains from his beard. "Yeah, it's you."

Bardoul turned and followed Brindley and Higgins into the aspens.

When Yakima had jogged back down to the camp, where the burning bushwhacker was still burning, he found Faith safe in her hiding place beneath the deadfall. He doused the burning man with snow, then dragged him and the other two dead men a good fifty yards down ravine from the camp and rolled their bodies into a brush-choked gully.

Food for the carrion eaters.

He and Faith had a cup of tea, then rolled into their blankets and robes, their limbs entangled, and slept till dawn.

They made good time the next day, until around noon when the mule threw a shoe. Yakima built a fire and brewed tea. Faith sat on a rock and sipped the tea as Yakima removed the mule's other three shoes. The beast could go without shoes in this snowy terrain at what seemed to be the top of the world, blue-green pine forests rolling away in all directions, relieved only by occasional rocky scarps and frozen lakes appearing like rare pearls studding a lush green carpet.

There was another short delay while they waited for a snow squall to blow through. When the storm had drifted southeast, leaving another foot of powder on top of the already deep snow and a good twenty-degree drop in temperature, they moved on toward the distant conifer-stippled saddle. On the other side of the saddle lay Gold Cache, only fifteen or so miles as the crow flies but another seven or eight hours away via snaking valleys, stream fords, and canyons.

Yakima figured that Thornton's men had lost their trail. Still, he kept a keen eye skinned.

It was during a habitual sweep of their back trail, as they traversed a deep, pine-studded ravine, that he spied two men jogging through the trees they'd just left. The men were heavily bundled and carrying rifles, and they were obviously trying to gain position on Yakima and Faith.

Yakima reined his horse to a sudden halt, turning the paint sideways as he stared at the edge of the clearing. The men had disappeared behind tree boles.

"What is it?" Faith asked, riding the mule behind him.

Yakima reached behind and grabbed the reins from her hands. "Hold on!"

He heeled the mare into a lunging gallop, jerking the balky mule along behind. They'd galloped twenty yards through the deep, scalloped snow before two shots resounded, one after the other. Yakima glanced over his left shoulder.

Smoke puffed amid the trees. There were three more erratic shots, but the shooters were too far away now to have much chance of hitting two fast-moving targets.

The thought had no sooner passed through Yakima's mind than something tore into his upper left arm. The bullet had come from ahead and to the right. Yakima cursed and sagged back in the saddle, gritting his teeth as cold fire engulfed him.

Faith jerked her head toward him. *"Yakima!"*

"Go!" With his right hand, he tossed her the reins. When she'd caught them, Yakima reached for his rifle.

Before he could slide the Yellowboy from the boot, another bullet spanged off a rock two feet before the paint's left front hoof, and the report echoed sharply off a snow-blanketed scarp towering over the ravine's right, pine-studded wall.

The horse screamed and reared. Yakima was holding the reins in his left hand as he'd reached for the rifle with his right, and he didn't grab the horn in time to brace himself. Before he knew it, he was falling off the horse's left hip, hitting the snow and rolling downslope.

"Yakima!" Faith cried as his horse raced past her. She was turning the fiddle-footing mule toward him, her face etched with terror.

Yakima looked ahead. A sombrero-hatted man in a heavy buffalo coat squatted atop a rock-studded hillock, aiming a rifle at Yakima. The rifle stabbed smoke and fire, and the bullet tore up a gout of snow and sod a foot from Yakima's left knee, the heavy-caliber slug sounding like a cannon blast as it echoed off the scarp.

Behind came the sound of men running through the snow, breathing hard, their heavy clothes rustling.

Yakima glanced at Faith, swinging his right arm wildly. *"Goooo!"*

Sitting on his butt, he clawed his Colt .44 from the holster beneath his capote and cocked it, then kicked himself around. The two men were heading for him, trudging through the knee-deep snow, holding their rifles straight up and down before them, eager grins on their unshaven faces—one wearing an engineer's pin-striped cap, the other, a high-crowned, snuff-brown Stetson and a bulky buckskin coat.

Brindley and Higgins.

Yakima fired a shot. Brindley screamed and grabbed his right thigh. Higgins dove for cover, and Yakima threw himself left as another heavy-caliber slug tore up snow and sod where he'd been sitting.

Yakima rose to his left elbow, setting his jaw against the pain searing his left arm, and extended the revolver in his right hand. The man with the rifle—the bounty hunter, Wit Bardoul—was too far away for the short gun, but he fired two shots, anyway.

One shot plunked into the spindly cedar to Bardoul's left, while the second drilled a rock below him and to the right. The bounty man flinched and scrambled back behind the rocks capping the rise.

Yakima flexed his wounded arm. It felt as though the bullet had gone through without breaking the bone. Cold blood soaked his coat sleeve, adding a fine chill to the burning pain.

He rose to his haunches and looked behind him as the man on Brindley's right, Higgins, fired his Spencer from the cover of a low cedar, the smoke wafting, the bullet whistling over Yakima's shoulder and plunking into the snow twenty feet upslope.

Yakima returned an errant shot, looked around quickly. A shallow coulee lay about twenty feet straight ahead, between him and Bardoul. As Bardoul and Higgins stitched the air around him with whistling lead, Yakima bolted forward, running hard and diving.

What felt like a bee buzzed around his left ear and snapped a sage shrub.

He smacked the bottom of the depression on his right shoulder, pain hammering his left arm. He lifted his head, glanced back to where Higgins hunkered behind the snow-draped cedar.

Brindley was thrashing around in the snow, beating his gloved fists against the ground and cursing loudly.

"Come on out and get it over with, breed!" Bardoul called from the stone barricade in the opposite direction.

Quickly, Yakima thumbed open his six-shooter's loading gate, plucked out the spent cartridges, and replaced them with fresh from his shell belt.

A low rumbling sounded, as if a train were chugging somewhere in the distance.

Ignoring the sound, Yakima stretched his pistol over the depression's lip, thumbing back the hammer and aiming at the gray sombrero and broad, bearded face showing above the snow-tufted rocks capping the hillock.

Bardoul was forty yards away. Adjusting for distance, Yakima fired. The slug ground into the rock below and to the left of the bounty hunter's head, and, cursing, he jerked down behind the natural barricade.

Yakima couldn't lie in the depression forever. He had only so much ammunition. He had to make his move now, or shake hands with the devil soon.

As the man behind him fired, blowing up snow at the depression's lip, Yakima leapt to his feet and sprinted toward the hillock.

He raised the revolver, triggered a shot. Bardoul returned fire. Yakima dodged the bullets stitching the air around him, ducking and swerving, leaping cedars, extending the pistol before him, firing and trying to keep the bounty hunter from drawing a steady bead.

He fired four shots, then five.

When he was twenty yards away, his sixth smashed the shooter's rifle with an angry clang. Sparks sizzled along the barrel and over the hammer. Bardoul screamed and tossed the rifle away, as though he'd suddenly found himself holding a striking diamondback.

The rumbling grew louder, the ground shifting and

sliding beneath Yakima's moccasins. Out of the corner of his right eye, he could see something large and white seeming to plunge toward the ravine.

Not breaking stride, Yakima turned his head. A wave of snow, dislodged by gunfire from the rock face above the clearing, was rumbling toward him, bending and snapping pines in its wake.

The avalanche seemed to get caught in the back of his mind, a secondary consideration.

First, Thornton's men . . .

Fury boiling through him, Yakima pushed off the snowy ground, leaping toward the rock barrier while sliding his broad-bladed bowie knife from its beaded leather sheath on his left hip. As his left foot landed atop the wall, he adjusted his grip on the knife so that the blade angled down.

The snow was like an ocean wave, roaring toward him. He could feel its cold breath, hear the trees groaning and snapping under its weight.

Before him, Bardoul was down on one knee, snarling, his rifle lying several feet away. The bounty hunter was trying to grab his pistol from beneath his buffalo coat, but the long barrel was caught in the curly hide.

Bardoul cursed loudly, enraged eyes snapping wide, silver front teeth flashing inside the gray of his scraggly beard.

Yakima flew toward him.

The snow caught him in midleap. Before him, Bardoul was swept away in a blur, replaced with white. Yakima felt the air driven from his lungs as the snow picked him up and hurled him in the same direction as the bounty hunter.

In less than a second he was rolling and tumbling amid the snow chunks, beaten and pummeled, feeling like a cork in a raging millrace.

Chapter 23

Lying flat on his back beneath the leaden snow, Yakima swam up from unconsciousness and immediately felt as though a giant were kneeling on his chest. He opened his eyes. Rather, he *tried* to open his eyes.

The snow was so heavy, pressing on every inch of his body, that he could hardly lift his eyelids. It didn't make any difference. All he could see through the slits was darkness.

Panic raking over him, he sucked a breath. His lungs expanded only a hair, drawing snow up his nose and down his throat. He choked, tensing, feeling the panic grow, sending a ringing through his ears as his heart pitched like a bucking bronc. He jerked his legs and arms, trying to get some space around him, room to breathe.

But it was like trying to swim through wet adobe. He could move only a couple of inches.

Somewhere above, as though from a long way through water, Faith was calling his name.

Yakima's heart pounded harder. He bunched his lips and funneled his strength into his right leg and right wrist, drawing the wrist up along his thigh, then angling it up and, grinding his foot into the snow for leverage, lifting that arm from the shoulder.

Grunting with the effort, choking at the snow in his mouth and nose, he began raising his arm against the leaden weight above.

"Yakima!" Faith screamed, bounding into the knee-deep snow blanketing the ravine in scalloped drifts and chunks. She whipped her head around at the pine branches protruding here and there like human limbs from the snowslide.

From the rocks fifty yards away, she'd watched the avalanche sweep into the ravine, literally erasing Yakima just as he'd leapt toward the bounty hunter, Wit Bardoul. She'd sloughed through the snow to where she'd last seen the two men, and now she saw only the tops of rocks protruding from the crusty snow chunks.

"Yakima!" she shouted, turning her gaze toward the pines at the ravine's far side, in the direction the snow would have swept him. "Can you hear me?"

She continued calling his name as she trudged through the knee-deep snow, turning her head frantically from right to left, breathing hard. Finally, just as hopelessness began to wash over her, a crackling sound rose behind her.

She spun around, hair flying. Thirty yards away, near the edge of the ravine, a gloved hand protruded from the snow, forming a fist, snow capping the glove. The hand disappeared. A moment later, it reappeared with a crusty rasp, snow flying out from around it.

"Yakima!"

Faith scrambled over and dropped to her knees. She squeezed the fist and began scooping the snow away from around it, trying to gauge where his head would be. She dug deep, scooping the snow toward her until a red-tan shape appeared.

Yakima's face rose from the snow as though from the surface of a lake.

"Hahhhh!" he grunted, bolting up to a sitting position, spitting and blowing snow from his mouth and nose. He tipped his head back and took a deep, grating breath.

Faith leaned toward him, placed her hands on both sides of his head, and pressed her cheek against his shoulder. "I thought you were gone!"

He sucked another breath, then another, the hoarseness slowly leaving his voice, his breath evening out as oxygen pumped through him freely once more. She could feel him shaking, saw the blood-soaked left coat sleeve and the small, ragged hole. His legs were still covered with snow. She began brushing it away.

"We have to get you warm. I'll build a fire."

She pulled away, but he grabbed one of her arms. "Where's Bardoul and the others? You seen 'em?"

"No." She looked around, frowning. "They're under the snow somewhere. Best place for 'em." She placed her own hand over his as he clutched her forearm. "Come on, Yakima. You're shaking like a leaf."

"Wait." He released her and stood, snow flying off of him. His wet buckskins clung to him. The snow stuck to his coat and breeches in white patches, already crusting in the cold air.

He began to, slog through the snow, his wet hair flying around his head, the wounded left arm hanging straight down at his side.

He stopped, staring into the trees, then moved down the slight slope toward the edge of the ravine. Faith followed him. When he stopped, she sidled up to his right shoulder, followed his stare.

Ten feet away lay Bardoul. Only his head, neck, and

about six inches of chest protruded from the snow. His greasy pewter curls swirled lightly in the breeze and his brown eyes were glassy with death.

His head was tilted against a small pine, as if he were just resting there. Yakima's bowie knife protruded from the left side of his neck. Liver-colored blood bathed his neck and shoulder, staining the snow around his head.

Yakima stepped forward and placed his good hand against the man's forehead, bracing himself as he dislodged the bowie knife with his right. It sprang free with a wet sucking sound, blood stringing onto the snow.

Faith felt her stomach roll up, and she turned away sharply, covering her mouth, trying hard not to vomit. Yakima cleaned the knife in the snow, sheathed it, then put his right arm around Faith's shoulders, drawing her to him, leaning unsteadily against her.

She shoved against him, semi-supporting him as he looked across the snowslide glistening wanly in the opalescent light, back toward the trees where he'd first spied Thornton's hostlers. They were probably under the snow somewhere.

He was shaking harder now from the damp chill and blood loss.

"I saw a cabin through the field glasses," he said, urging her forward. His voice shook slightly. "We'll go there . . . build a fire."

They slogged through the snow, heading for the horse and the mule staring at them from the rocks above the slide.

"A *big* fire," Yakima said, laughing dryly.

He dropped to a knee and had a hard time, even with Faith's help, climbing out of the snow. When they made it to the paint and the pack mule, they were both breathing hard, Yakima doing all he could to keep from passing out.

Faith helped him onto his horse, then mounted the mule. Slouched in his saddle, Yakima looked around, his vision blurring, but he managed to take a reckoning, then touched his heels to the paint's ribs.

"I think we should stop and build a fire," Faith said as they made their way through a branching ravine.

Barely able to keep his chin above his saddle horn, Yakima shook his head. "Up this high . . . storms move in fast. Cabin's best."

The cabin he'd seen through the field glasses had looked abandoned, with no smoke ribboning up from the chimney, no stock in the adjoining paddock. As they brought their horses to a halt at the edge of a clearing and stared at the cabin before them, the place indeed looked derelict under the good foot of snow mantling its sod-and-log roof. To the right, fifty feet from the cabin, snow-tufted sluice boxes snaked down to a rocky wash, sections of the contraption collapsed and buried.

"Come on," Yakima grunted.

He gigged the horse forward.

At the front door, he half fell from his saddle, awkwardly shucked his Winchester from the boot, and stepped through a knee-high snowdrift to the front door, glancing with satisfaction at a low woodpile hunkered against the front wall and peppered with bird tracks and mouse droppings.

He nudged the timbered door wide with his rifle barrel and surveyed the sparse furnishings arranged around the earthen floor. The snowdrift continued over the threshold for four feet. Shuffling through it, Yakima looked into the gray shadows, spying a sheet-iron stove and a bed beyond the table formed by four pine stumps and peeled poles strapped together with shrunken rawhide.

"Nice little den," he called over his shoulder, setting the

rifle against the wall near the stove and collapsing onto the bed of braided rawhide. He rolled onto his side and hunkered down in his damp coat, shivering. "I'll build a fire in a minute."

He closed his eyes for a lot longer than he'd intended. When he opened them again, the room was warm, almost hot, and Faith sat at the edge of the cot, nudging his right arm and tugging at his soggy four-point capote.

She was calling his name gently. ". . . have to get you outta these wet clothes, and I gotta have a look at that arm . . ."

A fire thudded in the stove, making the iron creak and groan. A pan of snow sat atop the stove, sending steam tendrils to the low rafters, from which sod roots hung like spiderwebs. The snowdrift had been swept out of the cabin, the door closed, their gear piled here and there on the floor. The cabin had obviously been occupied by miners—mining gear hung on the walls, and on a shelf by the door were a scale and pestle for rough assays.

The veins had probably pinched out and the miners had abandoned the place in disgust, leaving their implements for anyone else who wanted to try their luck.

Yakima looked at Faith sitting beside him. She'd removed her own damp clothes. A blanket draped her naked shoulders, partly exposing her full, pale breasts, which swayed and jounced as she tugged at his coat.

He heaved himself up to a sitting position and winced at the pain in his stiff left shoulder as she pulled his coat off his frame. Soon she'd removed his boot moccasins and every stitch of his damp clothes, and he lay naked upon the cot. She rolled him this way and that as she padded the cot with blankets, then draped a fur robe over him. His body felt like cold rubber. He heard his teeth clacking lightly. The robe wrapped him like a cocoon.

"You're a good nursemaid, lady."

She'd peeled the robe back to inspect his arm. "Looks bad."

"Bullet went all the way through. I don't think the bone's broke."

Her breasts were in his face. He could feel the warmth of them, smell the moist, floury fragrance. A nipple grazed his cheek as she leaned close to inspect the gelled blood in the wound.

He lifted his arm and reached a finger to the nipple, but before he could touch it, the fatigue, his inner chill, and the warm cabin conspired to pull him toward the still depths beneath the day's raging current.

He woke a couple of times, barely, when she washed and dressed his wound. She prodded him awake again to spoon some hot canned tomatoes into his mouth, then again when she climbed under the robe and rubbed her warm breasts against his back, the nipples raking him like tender flower buds. She pressed her lips to his back, then snuggled against him.

Faith slept then, too, fatigue washing over her. She hadn't been out long, however, when she opened her eyes.

She lifted her head and stared over Yakima's right shoulder at the front door. She'd forgotten to turn out the lantern and snuff the two candles burning in tin cans. Dim light shuttled shadows to and fro. Yakima snored deeply.

Had his snores awakened her?

In the paddock, the mule brayed softly. Then she remembered it was the braying that had roused her, and the wooden rattle as the two mounts shoved against the dilapidated corral poles.

Faith slipped quietly out from under the robe and off the

bed, adjusting the robe over Yakima once more before pulling on her jeans and slipping into her fur-lined moccasins.

Under the heavy cover, Yakima breathed deeply, sound asleep.

She didn't want to wake him. The horses might only be stirring at a raccoon or some other night creature. Besides, he needed to sleep. It was her turn to take care of him.

She didn't take the time to button her shirt, but donned her coat, securing one button over her chest, then grabbed her carbine. As she headed for the door, she glanced at the lantern. She'd leave it burning, so any possible intruders wouldn't know she was onto them.

Cracking the door, she peeked at the glittering yard, over which a billion twinkling stars arched, then stepped out and quickly, softly latched the door behind her. She stood quietly, looking around and listening, her breath puffing around her head.

Fifty yards ahead, the horse and mule stood like statues inside the corral, staring into the snow-dusted scrub before the cabin. Faith hefted the rifle in her hands, swallowing her fear, then turned to her left, crouched beneath the window, and stole along the cabin's east side.

At the rear of the shanty, she slowly rammed a fresh cartridge into the Winchester's breech, gritting her teeth against the metallic scrape, which sounded as loud as a blacksmith's hammer in the quiet night. Then she tramped through the snow to the cabin's west rear corner.

She looked straight out from the shack. Nothing there but the ruins of an old corral protruding above the snow, a small stone springhouse and, beyond, a low, cedar-studded bluff.

She peered along the cabin's west wall to the front. About halfway between her and the yard, a pile of unsplit pine logs—about five feet high, six feet wide, and covered with a good foot of pristine snow—abutted the cabin wall. Faith bent low and ran to the pile, doffed her hat, and edged a look over the top, hearing the soft scratching of a mouse somewhere within the loosely piled logs.

She waited, listening intently and sweeping her gaze along the front yard, holding the rifle in one hand, her coat closed with the other.

The cold pushed against her like an icy bath, burning her lungs. She shivered, hoping against hope that the mule had only spooked at some harmless beast. An elk or a moose, maybe. Even a black bear or a wolf she could handle.

Just don't let it be men.

Chapter 24

In the corral, the mule bobbed its head and brayed. At the same time, a shadow moved at the far side of the yard. Faith watched a man stumble out of the brush and, rifle held across his chest, begin trudging toward the cabin across the snow-scalloped yard, a hitch in his gait.

Faith's back tightened painfully, and she hunkered low, but not so low that she couldn't keep an eye on the man from around the woodpile's right edge. He was medium tall, with a blanket coat and a billed hat tied to his head with a muffler. The cuffs of his duck trousers were stuffed into the high tops of his mule-eared boots.

Recognizing him, Faith almost snorted despite her fear. Yakima had been right. Thornton had sent Brindley along with Bardoul. The third man was probably Ace Higgins. She remembered how the two hostlers had ogled her lasciviously, too bashful to speak but not too timid to undress her with their beady eyes, snickering at their own secret jokes.

Now the chuckleheads were scurrying around in the middle of the night, trying to bushwhack her and Yakima.

Faith glanced around, looking for Higgins while wondering how the pair had survived the avalanche.

In the yard before her came the rustle of snow and the

raking of Brindley's labored breaths. She looked around the woodpile. The lumpy-coated hostler was moving more slowly now as he approached the cabin.

Faith took one more glance around. Maybe Higgins had died in the avalanche, she thought as she moved around the woodpile. She had Brindley in full view about thirty yards out from the cabin.

She thumbed the rifle's hammer back, raised the stock to her shoulder, sighted down the barrel.

Brindley turned his head toward her, as she took up the slack in her trigger finger.

The report flatted out across the silent night, its echo sounding like a chill wind funneling through a narrow canyon.

Brindley grunted. His right foot flew out from under him. As he threw the rifle out to his side, his other foot swung up, and he fell on his back, arms akimbo. He drew several sharp breaths, lifted his right arm, like an injured bird trying to take flight, and dropped it.

"What the *fuck*?" sounded a voice somewhere above Faith.

Heart thudding, she levered a fresh shell into the rifle, stepped out away from the woodpile, and spun toward the cabin. Her left foot came down on an icy patch, and she fell.

At the same time, a gun flashed above the snow-tufted roof. The bullet chunked into the snow just behind where she'd been standing. She thrust herself up onto her butt, raised the rifle, and aimed at the bulky, buckskin-clad silhouette of Ace Higgins staring down from the roof at her, mouth agape beneath the brim of his high-crowned hat.

Faith's Winchester sneezed.

"Ughh!" Higgins dropped his rifle and grabbed his belly. He stumbled back, then dropped to his knees. His hat tumbled to the roof, rolled, and dropped to the ground. "Christ!" he cried, his eyes pinched with disbelief. "I come all this way to git kilt by a *whore*!"

Faith glared up at him, her upper lip curled. "I ain't a whore no more, Ace."

Higgins looked down at his gut. Blood gurgled out around his hand and between his fingers. He lifted his head to stare once more at Faith. "Once a whore, always a whore!"

Leaning forward, he pitched over the roof's edge, knees bent, his hands clutched to his belly. He looked like a meal sack tossed from a barn loft.

He hit the ground with a muffled thud, rolled onto his right side, groaned, and lay still.

A gun hammer clicked loudly. Faith turned to see Yakima standing at the cabin's front corner, extending his cocked revolver at her—a spare he'd taken from the freighters. He wore his four-point capote and boot moccasins and not a stitch more. His hairless, tan, well-muscled legs were bare.

"I was taking care of some pesky varmints," Faith said.

Yakima depressed the Colt's hammer with a soft snick, lowered the revolver, and walked over to where Ace Higgins lay dead, blood blackening the snow around his belly.

When he'd inspected Higgins, he pulled Faith to her feet, then walked out and crouched down beside Brindley. Faith strode halfway between him and the cabin, and stopped, holding her rifle across her thighs.

"Wonder how they made it out of the avalanche."

"Probably didn't get caught in it." Yakima straightened. He yawned deeply. "If you're done shootin', I think I'll go back to bed." He walked to the cabin and disappeared inside.

*   *   *

He slept deeply and without dreams.

He lay on his side on the cot, the robe pulled up over his head. He'd been hearing a quiet commotion for some time, but fatigue and the painful left arm held him just beneath consciousness.

He pulled the robe down low enough that he could peek out into the cabin lit by streams of golden sunshine slanting through the fogged, grease-paper windows. The woodstove popped, blue smoke leaking out through open seams, filling the cabin with the smell of burning pine.

Faith was pouring steaming water into a corrugated tin tub sitting on the earthen floor in front of the stove.

She wore only her moccasins and a thin chemise hanging off her shoulder, exposing half of her full left breast. Her steam-damp skin glistened in the sunlight, the sheer silk clinging to her wet breasts and hips and belly like a second skin. She'd pinned her hair up, and vagrant blond wisps pasted themselves to her cheeks and neck.

When the tub was half full, she returned the tin bucket to the stovetop. Yakima watched her secretly from beneath the robe, feeling his desire grow as she turned back to the steaming tub. Kicking off her moccasins, she slid the chemise's right strap down her arm.

She slid the left strap down the other arm, and the wash-worn garment fell down her breasts, snagging on the nipples, then tumbling over them, jostling the deep orbs slightly before pooling around her waist.

Faith wriggled her hips until the chemise had fallen to her ankles. Lifting one foot into the tub, she winced. She pulled the foot out for a second, then, balling her cheeks painfully, set it down in the tub and drew the other in beside it.

Setting her hands on both sides of the tub, she slowly lowered her bottom into the water, cupping the steaming liquid over her arms and shoulders, the vapor curling up around her, wreathing her like a gauzy shroud gilded by sunlight.

She reached over, grabbed a cake of soap off the table, and began soaping herself, scrubbing hard beneath each arm, running her soapy hands along her belly and over her breasts until each one glistened with soap bubbles.

Yakima grunted.

Faith brought her left foot toward her chest to soap it and turned toward the cot. A sultry smile lit her blue eyes. "Enjoying the show?"

"You could give a man a heart seizure."

He flung aside the robe, swung his feet to the floor. Her eyes ran up and down his naked form, pausing at his crotch.

Her voice was husky, the words automatic. "Easy, partner. You need your rest."

He gripped the edge of the cot as the room pitched slightly, dimming, then brightening, and shook his head.

Her eyes were on him as he walked toward her. He stopped, let her fondle him for a moment, her hands sending a shudder through his loins.

Moving around behind her, he knelt, dropped his hands into the tub on either side of her. He ran his palms up her sides slowly, caressing, then across her flat belly and up and over her breasts. He kneaded them gently, savoring the warm, supple flesh, squeezing and fingering the nipples, which hardened under his touch.

Her head fell back on her shoulders, and she groaned as she nuzzled his neck. She moved her lips up to his, raising her hands to his cheeks, holding him gently, kissing him. Her tongue slid into his mouth, and then she rose up in the tub, keeping her lips pressed to his, turned, kneeling, and wrapped her arms around his neck.

Slowly, she straightened.

He rose with her, lifted her out of the tub, grabbed a flour sack off a chair back, and carefully dried her arms, shoulders, and breasts, then knelt and dried each leg, taking his time, admiring the long ovals of her thighs tapering to her calves and slender ankles and long, narrow feet.

Faith stepped away from him and lay down on the far side of the cot, patting the bear robe spread beside her.

He lay down, and she ran a hand across the twin slabs of his chest, then, her nipples jutting, breasts swaying, she crawled on top of him, straddling him. She rose up slightly and adjusted her position, using one hand while bracing herself with the other.

"Oh!" she cried, throwing her head back.

As she slid over him, Yakima reached up and unpinned her hair, let it spill across her shoulders.

"Beautiful," he said, as they began moving together slowly.

When they'd finished and she'd lowered her head to his, pressing her damp breasts against his own sweat-soaked chest and burying her face in his neck, he ran the tips of his fingers lightly up her side. He felt a small scar just below her rib cage and pressed his fingers gingerly against the knot.

"What's that?"

She rose up and looked down at her side. He could see the scar clearly—a small, star-shaped twist of white skin surrounded by tiny stitch marks. Yakima lowered his hand a few inches, and she rubbed the scar with her index finger, a pensive expression darkening her gaze.

She was silent for a long time. Then she turned to him and placed her hands on both sides of his face, staring down at him seriously.

"Yakima, I should have told you this already, but I

thought you'd try to talk me out of continuing to Gold Cache if I did."

He didn't say anything.

"The woman in Gold Cache I mentioned," Faith said. "I have a history with her, if you get my drift."

Yakima touched the scar on her side. "This history?"

Faith straightened, her hair tumbling down both sides of her face. Her nipples were like tender pink rosebuds.

"A few years ago, when I was first starting out, I worked for Crazy Kate Sweney at Crazy Kate's in Laporte. Makin' a long story short, Kate killed a deputy sheriff one night in the brothel, and, by accident, I saw it.

"The deputy wanted a payoff. Kate and the local law rigged the gambling tables and divvied the profits. Kate had been trying to fleece her partners. The deputy lived for a few days, and he told the sheriff he'd seen me pass by Kate's office just when Kate stuck the stiletto in his neck in a rage."

Faith tossed her hair back with the back of her hand and laughed caustically. "I was only sixteen and scared out of my wits. So when the sheriff called me into his office, I told him everything I knew. Kate fled town but not before ordering two of her bouncers to kill me."

Yakima didn't say anything. The stove popped, a log shifting with a muffled thud. Outside, birds chittered in the snow-flocked pines.

"They burst into my room the night after Kate left and shot my best friend, Mandy, while she slept, thinkin' she was me." Faith turned to stare pensively at the popping stove. "Killing Kate was my original intention."

"What about now?"

She thought for a moment, then turned to him with a slight, cunning smile. "More killing won't bring Mandy back. Now I reckon I'll settle for any ol' place of my own. On Kate's turf, of course."

"I'm not taking you up to Gold Cache to get you shot or stabbed by some crazy brothel queen."

"Have some faith." Faith grinned and rubbed her breasts on his chest, touching her nose to his and wriggling atop him seductively. "I can be right congenial when I set my mind to it. Why, I ain't hard to get along with at all."

As she wrapped her arms around his neck and kissed him hungrily, Yakima allowed she wasn't. But as they began making love once more, making the log bed creak like a firewood dray with ungreased wheels, he also speculated that there were going to be plenty of fireworks in Gold Cache.

Chapter 25

Yakima and Faith lay around the cabin for the rest of the day, resting, healing, eating, and making love. Faith cooked a large supper of sonofabitch stew and biscuits, and they washed it down with wild currant wine she found hidden away and forgotten in a hole beneath the woodpile at the west side of the cabin.

They were up before dawn the next morning.

Yakima had regained most of his vigor, and while his left arm was sore, he'd recovered most of his strength in that hand. The last stars were still twinkling in the violet western sky as they headed away from the cabin, Yakima taking the lead and booting the paint toward the timbered high reaches, heading southwest.

He rode quietly, picking his way along the old Basque shepherds' trail through the pine forest, up and over saddles, the trail marked here and there by rock cairns or cabin ruins or frayed strips of colored rawhide tied to branches. A dark mood haunted him. The closer they got to Gold Cache, the closer they came to the time he and Faith would have to part.

It was all clear to him now, and Yakima silently chastised himself for believing it could have been otherwise.

How could they stay together—a half-breed drifter who'd

never spent more than nine months in any one place in his life, tied to no one but his horse, and a beautiful white woman?

He could maybe stay with her for a time in Gold Cache, but he'd never be anything more to her there than a silent partner, a servant. The townspeople wouldn't let him be anything more. Soon, Faith would grow to despise him for his servitude and inability to become anything more, and he would hate her for being a queen in the eyes of other men.

There was no denying that Yakima loved her, and he could tell by the way she looked at him and made love with him that she felt the same. But it was easy to love each other when you were the only people around, when you'd seen the elephant together, and you depended on each other.

In Gold Cache, after the torpor of everyday life set in, their love wouldn't last more than a few weeks.

Such thoughts were as raw as the cold, dry air. They sent him reeling in gloominess, cursing the fate that set him apart while wanting only to grab Wolf as soon as he could and bolt free over the mountains, maybe hole up in some abandoned trapper's shack down south, in the San Juans.

In the spring, he'd ride east and try to pick up enough ranch work to see him through another summer . . .

Faith.

He was worried about her. Crazy Kate sounded like the genuine article, a real demon. Faith might have a powerful benefactor in the banker waiting for her in Gold Cache, but had she thoroughly considered what she might be riding into? Brothel madames could be as territorial as Texas stockmen.

He wondered if Faith's quest for revenge was clouding her judgment.

Yakima knew it wasn't any of his business. She was her

own woman. But the thought of anything happening to her was a knot of coiled snakes in the pit of his stomach. He'd die before he'd see her harmed by anyone.

In the middle of the afternoon, Gold Cache appeared, nestled in the gulch below the bench they'd been traversing, flanked and shaded by a blue-green pine ridge veiled in woodsmoke, spotted with shaft houses and ore tipples. They continued past sporadic diggings and cabins, then wound down the canyon and into the town from the north end, assaulted by the smell of latrines and rotting trash and horseshit tempered by fragrant woodsmoke wafting on vagrant, frigid breezes.

Gold Cache was about three blocks long, the snowy main street lined with smart-looking whipsawed business establishments with high, ornate false facades. Firewood was stacked nearly everywhere, draped with hides or burlap and choking the street in many places, causing bottlenecks in the wagon traffic. Cook fires burned along the street, and bearded, heavy-coated men sat around them, sipping steaming liquid from tin mugs.

Dogs barked. Burly men laughed, swilling beer on the boardwalks or woodpiles or the backs of wagons. Somewhere, a baby cried, and there was the perpetual, metronomic thunder of a mill stamping ore into dust, and the regular thuds of someone chopping wood.

A big, unpainted barn with several sprawling corrals sat at the other end of town. That's where Yakima was heading, weaving around drays and wagons, when Faith called behind him, "Hold up a minute."

Yakima turned in his saddle. Drawing the mule up close to the right boardwalk, behind which was a whitewashed bank with grilles over the windows, she leaned toward a man sitting on a bench and holding a kitten in the folds of his bulky buffalo coat. A corncob pipe sagged from the right corner of his mouth.

"Does Mr. George Underhill still own this bank?" Faith asked.

The man knocked his pipe against the bench. "Underhill died of a heartstroke last month." The man grinned devilishly, jerked his head to his right, and wheezed a laugh. "At Crazy Kate's place, don't ye know?"

Faith looked as though she'd been slapped. She stared at the old-timer. "Are you sure?"

"I helped haul him outta there, ma'am. Rest assured, he died with a smile on his face!"

When Faith had brought the mule up beside Yakima's buckskin, her face was white. "That's all right," Yakima said. "Winters get too long in these parts, anyway." Maybe she'd ride on out with him. They had no future together, but he'd feel better leaving her somewhere safer than a gold camp where a brothel madame had it in for her.

"I'm not that easily deterred," she said stubbornly, heeling the mule forward along the street.

They had ridden only fifty more feet when they'd spied Crazy Kate's Saloon and Pleasure Palace just beyond a lumber mill and across from a small hophouse. They ran their gazes up and down the ornate spruce green and yellow facade, with the scrolled porch pillars, second-story balcony, and pink curtains in the windows.

They rode on to the livery barn. Reining up at the broad front doors, Yakima slid out of the saddle, then walked back to lift Faith down from the mule.

Men milled around them, several eyeing Faith with keen male interest, smiling and pinching their hat brims. Even in her bulky coat and men's clothes, she cut a fine, delectable figure. No doubt the best-looking filly this town had ever seen.

Yakima suppressed a pang of jealousy. He opened the doors and stepped into the barn's aromatic interior, shielding his eyes from the outside glare with one hand. "Hello the barn!"

Leading the paint, he'd taken four steps inside when a fierce, bugling whinny rose from the barn's pungent rear shadows. There was the thunder of hooves beating the earthen floor and the squawks of hemp drawn taut.

"Shut up, you goddamn demon beast!" a man shouted somewhere to Yakima's right. "Jesus Christ, I never seen such a horse!"

The man appeared out of the shadows, blinking against the light behind Yakima—a lanky, long-faced man with sandy hair, a weak chin, and one arm in a sling. "What can I help you with?" he asked above the horse's caterwauling and the thunder of its hooves.

Yakima peered toward the rear of the barn, past the stalls and ceiling joists hung with halters and bridles, past the two supply wagons and the single leather buggy. His eyes were adjusting to the darkness, and now he could see a big, dark horse rearing in the hay-flecked darkness.

He glanced at the liveryman, then dropped the paint's reins, and strode slowly down the barn's main alley, moving past the wagons and into the dense shadows, smelling ammonia, greased leather, and hay.

The whinnies rose in volume until Yakima's ears ached and rang. In a stall in the barn's left rear corner, a regal black horse reared and pitched against the two stout ropes looped around its neck and tied to posts at front and rear corners of the fifteen-by-fifteen-foot stall.

The ropes were drawn taut, keeping the horse in virtually

one place while it slammed the earthen floor with its front hooves and hammered the stout rear partition with its back ones. A feed sack had been drawn up over its eyes and looped over its ears, effectively blinding the creature.

Yakima didn't need to see the horse's head to know it was Wolf. He'd know those long, corded legs and that white-splashed barrel chest anywhere.

"Wolf," Yakima called, feeling a thickness in his throat.

Instantly, the horse stopped pitching. He stood facing him, blowing into the bag, sucking it in and out as his chest expanded and contracted heavily, withers rippling. He shook his head and nickered, stamped one hoof eagerly.

Footsteps rose behind Yakima. "Mister, you don't wanna go near that horse. He'll tear your head off. I can't let him into the corral, 'cause he'll go over the damn fence. Crazy he is, plumb *loco*!" Sidling up to Yakima, the liveryman raised his injured arm. "Look how he done me. Damn near stomped one of my hostlers to mush and fine powder!"

Faith walked up behind them and peered into the stall. "Wolf!"

Yakima planted his right hand atop the stall partition and hoisted himself over.

"What I tell you, feller?" shrieked the liveryman. "That horse will take your head off!"

Yakima walked up to Wolf, who stood frozen before him. Yakima placed his right hand beneath the horse's long, fine snout. "It's me, feller." He removed the feed sack and tossed it into the straw, then stared into the stallion's inky eyes.

Wolf nodded vigorously, twitching his ears and stomping his feet. Yakima smiled as he patted the black's neck and whispered in his right ear, "I'll get you outta here soon."

The liveryman stood staring, spellbound. "I'll be goddamned. You know that horse?"

"It's his," Faith said, tears in her eyes as she watched Yakima remove the two ropes from the horse's sleek neck.

"Hey, leave those be!" yelled the liveryman. "He might be all right with you around, but as soon as you're gone—"

Yakima stopped and turned to the man, his jaw set. "He'll be all right now that he knows I'm here. Who brought him in?"

The man shrugged. "A couple fellers. Gamblers, I think. They sold him to Crazy Kate over to the main brothel in town, and I don't think . . ." His voice trailed off, and he shuttled his puzzled gaze between Yakima and Faith, who looked at each other knowingly.

Faith turned to the liveryman. "Crazy Kate?"

"She bought the horse off the two gamblers," the man said haltingly. "I don't know what she needs a saddle horse for. She never goes ridin'. Hardly ever leaves the brothel, but . . . feller, I sure would feel better if you'd leave that horse tied up like you found him."

Yakima threw the ropes in the straw atop the feed sack. "The horse is mine." He kicked open the stall door.

The liveryman's eyes widened, and he stumbled sideways out of the way, watching the horse fearfully. His angry voice trembled. "Now, goddamn it, Crazy Kate Sweney done bought him, and it's my job to keep him stalled."

"You can't buy a stolen horse," Yakima said, striding into the alley, heading for a set of double doors in the side wall. Wolf followed him eagerly, snorting and bobbing his head.

"You got papers on him?"

"Nope."

"Well, then, goddamn it, I'm gettin' the sheriff!"

"Do what you gotta mind for." Yakima lifted the wooden bar from the doors, kicked both doors open. As blue daylight flooded the barn, Yakima led Wolf out into the side corral, where half a dozen horses milled. They watched the black moving toward them cautiously.

"I'm warnin' you, goddamn it!" the liveryman shouted, following Yakima to the door but no farther.

Faith grabbed his arm. "Listen, mister, you don't want that horse around here, anyway, do you?"

He looked at her. She smiled agreeably up at him. His eyes softened. "Well, no, I don't. But it ain't my choice. Crazy Kate's payin' for his livery and feed, and—"

"You let us handle Crazy Kate. She doesn't realize she bought a stolen horse. When she does, I'm sure she'll take the matter up with the gamblers who hornswoggled her."

"If he don't have any papers on that horse, there's no damn way—" The liveryman stopped as he turned his head toward the corral. About twenty yards away, the black stallion stood facing Yakima, holding his head down as if listening intently to every word the half-breed was saying.

The liveryman glanced, befuddled, at Faith, then returned his gaze to the corral.

Yakima's lips stopped moving. He patted the horse's neck. As the horse lumbered off, rippling his withers and lowering his head to draw water from a stock trough, Yakima strode over to the liveryman and stopped.

"He'll be all right as long as you don't try to hog-tie him again. Leave him out here. I'll be back for him soon."

"Jesus Christ, I—"

Yakima stripped his pack off the paint and slung it over his shoulder, then shucked his Yellowboy from the boot. "Stable these animals, will you? I'll need my paint taken back east. You know of any freight outfits heading that way soon?"

The liveryman scratched his head, a befuddled expression on his deep-lined face. "Well, I reckon."

"Good."

Yakima flipped the man a few coins. He took Faith's arm, and they strode away.

Chapter 26

As Yakima and Faith headed west along Gold Cache's main drag, looking for a hotel that might accept a white woman and a half-breed, Faith paused on the raised boardwalk before a women's clothing shop—the only one they'd seen so far.

She looked at Crazy Kate's brothel a few buildings up on the other side of the street, then glanced at Yakima with a devilish smile. "I could use a new dress. Will you wait for me?"

Yakima looked her up and down. He supposed her soiled, smoke-blackened trail garb was better suited to the trail than to the town in which a girl sought employment. He shrugged and leaned his rifle against the wood-frame building's front wall as Faith opened the door, its bell jingling, and disappeared inside.

He squatted on the boardwalk beside the street, rolled a smoke, and watched the wagon and foot traffic, mud splashing where the fires had melted the snow. Dogs ran loose, and so did a pig, which was hazed off the opposite boardwalk by more than one broom-wielding, cursing store owner.

A good many Chinamen passed, hide coats over their traditional dark pajamas, queues hanging from hand-knit caps to brush against their shoulders. A slender Chinese girl hauled a big wicker basket to the bathhouses and barber-shops, gathering laundry. Market hunters weaved shaggy horses up and down the street, their pack mounts draped with bloody, field-dressed game.

The doorbell jingled. "How do I look?"

Yakima rose on his stiff legs and turned. Faith walked lightly down the store's three front steps, holding a black, tasseled cape away from her shoulders to reveal a low-cut purple dress with white lace around the puffed sleeves, shoulders, and bosom.

She wore a black choker set with a tiny emerald, the green stone setting off the purple dress and the sky blue of her lustrous eyes. Barely revealed by the buffeting, pleated skirts was a pair of fawn half boots with ornate gold buck-les. Her hair was piled high atop her head in rich, golden swirls.

Yakima's eyes kept returning to her half-revealed breasts pushing up from the corset like heaping bowls of freshly whipped cream. "I'll be damned."

"Does that mean you like it?"

Yakima looked her up and down once more. Someone on the street whistled. Yakima had forgotten how ab-solutely, incredibly queenlike she could look in a low-cut dress and choker. He remembered many nights at Thorn-ton's when he couldn't take his eyes off her and hated the men she led upstairs.

When he didn't say anything, she chuckled. "I'll take that as a compliment."

Ignoring the stares of passersby, she stepped back into the store, reached around the door, and grabbed three large parcels tied with string, one of which she gave to Yakima. "I bought a few extras."

"I see that."

When she'd balanced the other two parcels in her arms, she glanced at him coquettishly. "I hope I didn't keep you waiting too long, but a girl has to look her best."

Yakima snorted, hefted his rifle in his right hand, adjusted the saddlebags over the other shoulder, and clamped the parcel tightly under the same arm.

"Hey, lady, is the breed bothering you?" someone called from the other side of the street.

Yakima didn't look to see whom the voice belonged to. He'd seen them before, and it didn't do any good to look at them. He'd end up pummeling or getting pummeled senseless, and being thrown out of town. Faith looked, however, her eyes hardening.

She'd opened her mouth to respond when Yakima took her arm. "Forget it." He led her up the boardwalk, toward a hotel he'd spied when they'd ridden into town, one that looked like it might take a half-breed and a white woman.

"Please, Kate, I can't stomach any more of that tarantula juice!" pleaded the young, tawny-haired whore named Emily as, sitting at the edge of her bed on the third floor of Crazy Kate's Saloon and Pleasure Palace, she clutched a sheet about her pale, naked, sweat-soaked body. Her hair was pulled back in a loose bun, and her eyes were red-rimmed, her ashen cheeks streaked with tears.

Kate gave the greenish-brown liquid one last stir, then lifted the shot glass from the girl's cluttered dresser and turned to her. "You got two more days. The Chinaman says it won't take effect until you've had three whole days of it."

"But I don't want any more," Emily sobbed. "Kate, I want this child!"

"I ain't havin' no critters runnin' around my place, so you

can forget that right now." Kate nodded at the two brawny bouncers, Randall and George, standing before the room's closed doors, like waiting pallbearers. "Hold her down and open her damn mouth. I'm sick and tired of this bullshit!"

The bouncers, wearing the required suits with wrinkled shirts, ties, bowlers, and spats, strode quickly to the bed. Emily screamed as the men, practiced in the art of helping Ma cram her Chinese herbal concoctions down impregnated whores' throats, grabbed the girl with little fuss and laid her out flat on the bed. George held her legs while Randall, grinning evilly, thoroughly enjoying his job and the view of the naked girl's squirming body, held her arms.

Holding the thick, cloudy brew in one hand and wrinkling her nose against the rancid stench, Ma leaned over Emily. She cupped the girl's chin in the palm of her hand while squeezing her cheeks to lever her jaw open. With one quick motion, she poured the "eleesir," as the Chinaman called it, down Emily's throat.

The girl choked and coughed, spitting a good bit of the foul concoction back into Kate's face. Kate slapped her with the back of her hand. "You little *bitch*!" She wiped her face with an edge of Emily's sheet. "I oughta leave that little bun in your oven, see how much you'd like that critter screamin' and chewin' your titties!"

Chuckling, the bouncers crawled off the bed and left. Emily turned toward the wall, bringing her knees to her chest, sobbing into her pillow.

Flushed with fury, Kate turned to set the empty shot glass on the dresser. Doing so, she glanced out the window, glanced away, then jerked her gaze back to the frosted pane, quickly sliding aside the curtain and staring down into Gold Cache's cramped main thoroughfare.

Her heart thudded, and she pressed a hand to her chest as

a tall, broad man in a black hat and a fur trapper's green capote threaded through the wagons and fires and vendors' tents, heading eastward while swinging his gaze from left to right along the street. He had long black hair and, from what Kate could see of his face under the hat brim, light brown skin.

Behind him, on a pack mule, rode a slender young woman in men's trail clothes and a rabbit hat. Long honey-blond hair swirled down her back. Kate couldn't see the girl's face, but even beneath the bulky winter coat the girl's willowy, full-busted body was evident. When the girl and the dark man ahead of her stopped on the street before Kate's brothel and tipped their heads back, giving the building a cool, searching appraisal, Kate saw her face.

Faith.

The dream came back to her as though someone had shoved a tintype in front of her. In the same dream, a dusky-skinned man had hovered in the shadows, atop a tall black stallion.

As the disparate pair continued along the street, Kate's heart fluttered wildly, and she stumbled back and plopped down in a chair before Emily's dressing table. She could no longer hear the girl's sobs, could no longer hear anything but a high-pitched ringing in her ears.

She sat sorting through her thoughts for several minutes while staring at the frosted window.

"Oh, gawd!" Emily howled, rising up on an arm. Her strained voice came at Kate as though from the far end of a long tunnel. "I'm gonna be *sick*!"

Kate turned to her dumbly, then rose from the chair. "Thunder pot's on the floor. Aim true or you'll clean it up yourself!"

With that, Kate staggered toward the door, steadying

herself on the furniture, her fleshy, heavily painted face bleached masklike, and left the girl's room.

Kate hurried down the hall, her amber, brocaded hoop-skirt swishing as she moved, full bosom heaving beneath her whalebone corset, and made her way down the stairs. In the saloon's main hall, several groups of men were clustered around the gambling tables.

Kate hurried to the L-shaped mahogany bar, vaguely startled by her own harried image in the mirror, black hair framing her waxy face under the bright red lipstick and pink rouge.

"Max, give me a bottle and a glass, and fetch Sebastian."

The barman was mopping the floor behind the bar, a lock of thick black hair winging over his right eye. He looked up with surprise. Crazy Kate hardly ever showed herself downstairs before evening, as the light of day did not flatter her features.

"I beg your pardon, Miss Kate?"

Kate dug her jeweled fingers into the bar top, and breathed deeply. "Set a damn bottle up here, and fetch Sebastian!" She hadn't meant to shout, and now she glanced sheepishly around the room, at the men and doxies regarding her skeptically, then returned her eyes to the swarthy barman.

Max set a bottle on the bar, then plopped a glass down beside it, glancing at the woman dubiously. "I'll fetch Mr. Kirk right away, Miss Kate!"

When Max had trotted out from behind the bar and disappeared outside, heading for the mine office, Kate plucked her bottle and shot glass off the mahogany. Ignoring the puzzled glances being shuttled her way, she made for a table before the broad front window to the right of the door and sank into a chair.

She set the bottle and glass on the table, popped the cork. Her hands shook as she splashed whiskey into the glass and peered up the street in the direction Faith and the half-breed had ridden.

She'd thrown back three full shots by the time Sebastian Kirk strode quickly past the window, clad in his bear coat and beaver hat, and pushed through the saloon's heavy door. He'd seen her in the window, and he walked over to stare down at her, the smell of smelter smoke on his clothes.

"What is it, Kate?" He removed his foggy, silver-framed spectacles. "Max said you were distraught. I dropped everything—"

"The blonde from my dream just rode into town."

Sebastian wrinkled the bridge of his nose. He appeared owl-eyed without the glasses. He'd never been sure what to make of Kate's dreams.

"Her name is Faith. She used to work for me."

"Are you sure it's the same girl you saw in your dream?"

Nodding, Kate nervously turned her glass in her hand. "She rode in with some half-breed. Somehow, they're both connected to the black horse. They were heading toward the livery barn."

Sebastian just stood there, his spectacles in his hand and an incredulous look on his pale, horsey face.

She slapped the table. "Sit down, Sebastian!"

He doffed his beaver hat and sat down to her right. Kate had Max bring over another shot glass. She filled the glass, shoved it toward Sebastian, and turned to stare out the window as if dreading a violent storm.

Watching her, Sebastian said, "What do you think she wants?"

"I don't know. I tried to kill her once."

"Oh . . . well . . ." He sipped the whiskey. "You think she's here to return the favor?"

"I have no idea what she's here for. All I know is that she's up to no good. She's most definitely a threat. I smelled camphor in the dream, and whenever I smell camphor or wormwood—sometimes mushrooms—I know the person I'm dreaming about has it in for me."

"What about the half-breed and the horse?"

"What about them?"

"What do they have to do with the blonde?"

Kate shrugged a shoulder and splashed more whiskey into her glass, slammed the bottle back down on the table. "It's unclear to me. All I know is that the blonde—"

"Yes, yes, she's a threat." Sebastian patted Kate's pudgy hand patronizingly. "But what do you propose to do about it, my dear? You can't very well send your men out and have her flogged because you dreamed about her and smelled . . . what was it?"

"Oh, shut up, Sebastian!" Kate hissed. "I didn't call you here for counsel. I know this is out of your realm. Can't you just sit here quietly and drink with me?"

Sebastian lowered his shot glass, wincing. "Isn't that what I usually do?"

"There they are." Kate was staring wild-eyed across the street.

Sebastian leaned forward, craning his neck to see out the window and around a parked freight wagon. Heading toward the saloon on the opposite boardwalk was a pretty blonde in a new-looking dress and cape, her thick hair piled atop her head.

Beside her walked what looked like a mountain man or a fur trapper. A half-breed, possibly a Metis, by the cherry-brown skin and the flat angles of his handsome face. The half-breed carried tack and a rifle, and he and the girl were both carrying store parcels.

They passed the brothel and turned down a side street.

"Heading for that Rooshian's hotel, probably," Kate said, staring at the spot where the two had disappeared. "He'll rent to a breed."

"Want me to have them arrested? Zahn will find out what they're up to." Ray Zahn was Gold Cache's town marshal and a business associate of both Sebastian Kirk and Crazy Kate Sweney. He was paid to overlook the fact that Kate's roulette wheels were weighted with lead and that her black-jack dealer was a mechanic from Omaha.

A self-satisfied smile on his lips, Sebastian threw back the rest of his drink, then reached for his hat, preparing to leave.

Kate grabbed his arm while staring out the window, blue veins throbbing in her forehead. "Don't be an imbecile."

After a moment, Kate added darkly under her breath, "It has to play out."

Chapter 27

The Russian hotelier was a short, barrel-chested hunchback with coal black eyes, close-cropped white beard, and a knee-length antelope-hide coat. He didn't bat an eye when Yakima and Faith asked for a room. He barely even glanced up from the doe he was skinning in front of his small log hotel to take the coins Yakima tossed into his bloody glove.

When he'd dropped the coins into his coat pocket, the Russian tossed a hunk of bullet-ruined meat to the cur sitting nearby in the bloodstained snow then gestured at the open, pine-timbered door.

"All da way back," he said. "Rooms in da back. You pick."

The place was nearly as rustic as the cabin in which Yakima and Faith had spent the previous two nights, though it owned a mahogany backbar with a baroque mirror that had obviously been hauled in from much fancier digs and that looked about as at home in the small log shack with greased-paper windows and iron stove as would a crystal chandelier in a two-hole privy.

Either the Russian's hopes for prosperity here in Gold Cache had already been dashed, or he was still hoping . . .

Yakima and Faith chose the largest of the six rooms in the

back, all of them boasting musty Indian blankets for doors but reasonably large and with solid beds with pine-log legs, grass-filled mattress sacks, and real goose-down pillows. When they'd gotten their gear situated, Yakima built a fire in the stove in the corner, and he and Faith napped together under the hide robes naked, too exhausted from the long ride even for love.

When he woke forty-five minutes later, Yakima got up and dressed quietly so as not to wake Faith. He took a long drink of water from his canteen, chunked another log into the stove, and sat down at the table by the shuttered window. He rolled a cigarette, then took his revolver and rifle apart and cleaned and oiled them, working by the slate gray light filtering through the cracks in the shutter.

He was reseating the revolver's cylinder when Faith groaned softly on the bed and turned her head to look at him through her mussed hair. She wrinkled her nose. "What's that smell?"

"I think there's a pigpen behind us. You should be stayin' over at the Denver."

"Without you? Never." She rolled onto her back and crossed her arms behind her head. "Besides, I grew up in a place like this."

She'd never told him where she'd come from, or what had led her to whoring. He couldn't help nudging the door a little, now that she'd cracked it. "In Colorado?"

She shook her head. "Chugwater Buttes, Wyoming. God-forsaken place. Pa was a rancher, though I never saw many cattle, mostly tumbleweeds. The water stank like that pen over yonder."

She scratched her head thoughtfully. Outside, the wind howled under the eaves. "When Ma died, he shipped my brothers off to an Englishman neighbor, and I went to the preacher who had a little chicken farm. I wasn't there long before the preacher started visiting me in my room off the kitchen, if you catch my drift. Told me to keep quiet or I'd go to hell." She glanced at Yakima, an ironic glint in her eyes. "You know, I believed him?"

Yakima snapped the Colt's cylinder home and took a drag off his cigarette.

"The preacher's wife must've figured out what her husband was sneaking down to my bedroom nearly every night for. One day she took me to town for the week's shopping and left me there. I was filled out even at fifteen, so it didn't take me long to find work at the local saloon. Had a room much like this one, a little colder and more barren, and I could burn only a few logs a day during the cold time."

She dropped her legs over the side of the cot, and stood, wrapping one of the robes around her naked body, hair curled up above her shoulders. She walked over to him, knelt between his legs, and rested her head in his lap, hugging his thighs.

"Yakima, let me go over to Crazy Kate's alone tonight. You stay here."

He looked down at her, a frown carved deep in his forehead. "Why?"

"I've caused you enough trouble." She lifted her head, stared up at him, eyes beseeching. "This is my game."

"No."

"Kate's funny about Indians. She won't let you in."

"Let me worry about that."

Faith shook her head. "Yakima, you're the only man I've ever loved. Don't let me get you killed."

He set the gun on the table, reached down, and took her naked arms in his hands, lifting her slightly, causing the robe to fall to the floor. "This is *our* deal. Remember? *Our* stake.

Besides, there's a little matter of a horse. Crazy Kate and I have to straighten that out."

Faith smiled wanly, lifted her chin. He leaned down and kissed her, then stood, picked her up in his arms. Leaving the robe on the floor, he set her down on the cot. She lay naked and dusky-skinned in the firelight.

She watched, smiling, eyes glistening behind a thin sheen of tears, as he kicked out of his boots and undressed.

It was seven o'clock and good dark in spite of the braziers and torches as Yakima led Faith across the frozen, crusty street toward the front porch of Crazy Kate's Saloon and Pleasure Palace. They climbed the steps and entered the steady, low hum of cardplayers and drinkers, miners in overalls and hobnailed boots and cloth caps dickering and laughing with half-dressed pleasure girls.

The roulette wheel clattered, and the craps dice clicked. Lantern light shunted shadows around the broad, deep room. Smoke swirled like breeze-torn spiderwebs.

More than a few eyes shifted to Yakima and the beautiful blonde as they made their way to the bar, and conversations closest to them died. They didn't have to stand at the bar long before the big, black-haired bartender with gray-flecked sideburns moved toward them, taking their measure as he cleaned his hands on his apron. Something in his demeanor told Yakima the man had been expecting them.

"Is Kate Sweney around?" Faith asked.

The barman ran his eyes over Faith again appreciatively and gave a knowing smile. "Miss Kate's in her office. Second floor. Far right end of the hall."

Faith glanced at Yakima, who arched his brows and set his elbows on the bar. He'd left his rifle in the hotel room, but he'd tucked his six-shooter back behind the capote. "Sure you don't want me up there?"

"She'd see you as a threat. I'll give a yell if I need help."

As Faith started toward the back of the room, the barman leaned toward her. "Miss."

Faith turned. The barman jerked his head at Yakima without looking at him. "No Injuns on the premises. House rules."

"He's with me," Faith said.

The barman raised his hands and canted his head, keeping his eyes hard.

Yakima smiled. "You didn't make the rules, but you sure as hell better break 'em. I'm not goin' anywhere as long as the lady's upstairs."

Two big men in three-piece suits and bowler hats, wielding bung starters in their hamlike fists, had moved around behind him while the handful of miners standing nearby had shuffled away. Yakima had watched the pair in the periphery of his vision. The barman slid his dark eyes to them.

They moved in fast, one on each side of Yakima, raising the hide-wrapped mallets. "Nice and easy now, breed," said the taller of the two.

Out of the corner of his left eye, Yakima watched the man reach for his left arm. Yakima swung swiftly, smashing his left forearm into that of the bouncer. The man grunted, stepped back, and raised the bung starter behind his shoulder. Before he could bring the hide-wrapped club forward, Yakima lunged toward him, ramming his own head into the man's chest. The man's bung starter continued over Yakima's head, connecting with his partner's wrist.

The second bouncer screamed as he grabbed his injured wrist, his own mallet hitting the floor with a heavy thump.

Yakima buried his right fist in the first bouncer's solar

plexus. As the man curled up with an echoing grunt, Yakima wheeled. The second man held his right wrist down low, pain etched on his face. Snapping curses through gritted teeth, he reached inside his coat with his left hand.

Yakima lifted his right foot above his head and slammed his heel against the man's right cheek.

"Ahhh!" he cried, half a wink before hitting the floor on his left cheek and shoulder. He rolled onto his back, clutching his face, which looked like a broken clay mask, dislocated jaw hanging askew, the blood draining out of it. He howled like a gut-shot bear.

Yakima backed away from both men, his hand on his pistol grip but leaving the gun in its holster. The first bouncer was down on his side, groaning, knees raised toward his chest, hands clutching his belly. The other man lay with his cheek to the floor, too pain-wracked to move or do anything but grunt.

The bartender stood scowling over the bar, shuttling his disgusted gaze between the bouncers.

Yakima glanced at Faith, staring at him from about ten yards down the bar. He jerked his head toward the stairs. Reluctantly, she turned and headed toward the back of the room, casting cautious looks behind her at Yakima and the fallen bouncers.

The rest of the room was so quiet that Yakima could hear someone puffing on a wet cigar. Then someone chuckled, and more laughter followed. Yakima glanced around. Seeing no one else coming after him, he bellied up to the bar.

"I'll have a beer," he told the barman.

The man told the bouncers to haul themselves over to the doc's, and when they'd risen from the puncheons and staggered outside, he pulled a beer. The conversations and the gambling had started again, and one of the whores was snickering.

The barman set the beer on the bar before Yakima, his eyes hard. "Where'd you learn to fight like that, breed?"

Yakima shrugged, sipped the beer as if to judge its quality, then sauntered over to a table to the left of the front door. He sat down with his back to the wall, kicked out a chair across from him, and propped his feet on it.

Sipping the beer, he relaxed and kept his ears pricked for Faith's call for help. His eyes slowly swept the room. Near the back, near the roulette wheel to the left of the broad staircase, a face was turned toward him, peeking out around the black-clad gent dealing faro. When Yakima's eyes locked on the man staring at him, the man jerked his head back behind the faro dealer.

Yakima edged his gaze to the right, saw another man sizing him up. Sandy-haired, shorter than the first, and wearing a shabby bowler and brown suit coat too tight for his stocky frame.

Yakima stared across the room as the sandy-haired man's eyes widened. He turned away quickly.

Yakima licked the foam from his lips and smiled.

When Faith reached the second-floor landing, she cast a glance down the stairs behind her. The fight seemed to be over, and Yakima was apparently out of trouble for the moment. She turned right and strode down the pine-paneled hall lit with red and purple bracket lamps. Under her new half boots, a thick, amber-colored carpet runner muffled her footsteps.

Behind the doors on both sides of the corridor, grunts and passionate groans kept time with squawking bedsprings and the occasional hammering of a headboard against a wall.

At the end of the hall, she stopped before an unnumbered door. She lifted her fist to knock, but before her knuckles touched the oak, a familiar voice rose from the other side of the door.

"Come in, my dear."

Faith's chest tightened. What if the woman was waiting for her with a gun? Faith felt the lump of the pocket pistol inside her cape, snugged into the makeshift holster Yakima had sewn into one of the folds with a scrap of burlap. Could she get to it in time?

Faith opened the door, peeked inside.

On the other side of the carpeted and wallpapered office, Kate sat behind a broad cherrywood desk adorned with two elaborately scrolled pink lamps. Before the desk, turned sideways to look behind him, sat a middle-aged man with a bald pate and scraggly gray hair tufting out from the sides of his head. His round, silver-framed spectacles reflected the light from the fire at the right of the door.

Faith stepped into the room and closed the door behind her without taking her eyes from Kate, who stared back at her, painted lips stretching a broad, welcoming smile.

"Ah," Faith said, offering a stiff smile of her own. "Crazy Kate's sixth sense."

"Never fails."

"You were expecting me."

"Of course."

Chapter 28

Kate stood up behind her desk. She wore a cream silk gown that hung on her like a kimono, revealing a good deal of heavy cleavage. Twin raven braids were coiled up around her ears and pinned behind her head. The hair was pulled back so tightly from her temples that it slanted her eyes, making her look like some pagan priestess.

Small skulls shaped from metal hung from her ears on long chains. They glistened in the firelight.

Kate held out a hand to indicate the man sitting on the other side of the desk. "Faith, my business associate, Sebastian Kirk. He's the superintendent of Gold Cache Mining and Smelting."

The man, dressed in brushed serge and wearing a wine-colored, gold-buttoned vest beneath his claw-hammer frock coat, stood awkwardly, his bright eyes riveted on Faith. "How do?" He stuck out his pale, bony hand.

Faith strode forward and shook it.

"Join us in a drink?" Kate asked, lifting the cut-glass decanter from the silver tray on her desk. Half-filled brandy goblets sat on the desk before Crazy Kate and Sebastian Kirk, and long Mexican cigars smoldered in ashtrays.

"No, thanks," Faith said. "I won't be here long. I came

only to tell you why I was here in Gold Cache, because you'll find out sooner or later."

Kate sank back in her plush red chair, her face tensing. "And that is . . . ?"

"Not to open old wounds, Kate." Faith's voice betrayed her anger at what had happened in Fort Dodge, and she paused for a second to get a leash on it. "Though I have to admit that when I started out, I did have other intentions. But now I'm here merely to set up my own business establishment. Nothing else. I'm sure there's room in Gold Cache for another saloon."

Kate looked at the chair angled beside Kirk, who sat puffing his cigar and gazing up at Faith with appreciation in his weak, watery eyes. Kate was aware of his stare, and annoyance gnawed at her.

"You have time to sit for a spell, don't you, dear?" Kate said pleasantly.

Faith grasped an arm of the chair, slid it out a little farther from the desk as well as from Sebastian Kirk—she could feel his eyes burning into her—and sat on the edge of it, her hands in her lap. The pistol was a comforting weight under her right arm. She was glad she hadn't been frisked.

"There's room here for another saloon, of course. But why don't you come work for me? If we've buried the hatchet, let's smoke the peace pipe. I bet we can come to a financial agreement that will prove most rewarding for both of us."

"I'm not turning tricks anymore, Kate."

Kate pursed her lips knowingly. "The . . . gentleman you rode into town with."

"Yakima. We're going into business together."

Sebastian blew a smoke stream over Faith's head. "A . . .

saloon?" His eyes swept her once more, no doubt imagining what she looked like beneath the cape and the dress.

Kate caught the look. It was like a dull knife poking her ribs. She kept smiling.

"Just running a saloon would be a waste of your assets. Dear Faith, you're the loveliest whore I've ever known. Men swoop to you like coyotes to fresh meat. Why, just sitting there ogling you, Sebastian is about to unload in his pants!" Kate glanced at Sebastian and threw her head back, laughing.

Sebastian turned brick red and busied himself flicking ash from his cigar.

"I appreciate the offer," Faith said, rising. It was almost over. She would get out of here alive. "Those days are over for me."

Kate stood suddenly and walked around the desk. She stopped two feet in front of Faith and narrowed her eyes, as if trying to peer into the depths of Faith's soul, wary, skeptical. "No blackmail? No running to the town marshal with word of what I did to you in Fort Dodge? Come, now, Faith—do you really expect me to believe that?"

"It's the truth, Kate. Blackmail or running to the law won't bring Mandy back. I just want to get on with my life, and I've decided the best place for me to do that now, the best place to raise a stake, is right here in Gold Cache."

"Do you have money?"

"I'm sure I can find a benefactor among Gold Cache's businessmen." Faith's eyes flickered toward Sebastian, who quickly looked down.

Kate saw the glances exchanged and nodded crisply. "I'm sure you can."

Faith held out her hand. "Peace?"

Kate continued to study her. Finally, she squeezed Faith's

hand. As Faith turned toward the door, Kate said, "What about the black horse?"

Faith turned quickly, one hand on the knob. "Wolf?"

"Oh, that's his name." Kate acquired a cunning, speculative air as she crossed an arm over her chest, worrying an earring with the other hand.

"How did you—?" Faith stopped herself. She'd heard of Kate's psychic abilities, and they'd always frightened her. Imagine such a hideous creature with otherworldly powers. "He belongs to Yakima. A couple of drifters stole him." She took a step toward Kate, beseeching in her eyes.

"Well, your Yakima will have to take it up with them, won't he? I bought him, and I don't intend to sell him. Unless, of course, you agree to leave here and never come back."

"But I thought . . ."

"Or unless you agree to come work for me." Kate turned toward Sebastian. "Look at that, Sebastian. How much would you pay to fuck a body like that? The cape really doesn't do her justice."

Kate lunged toward Faith, reaching for the cape's black bone buttons. Faith stepped back, removed her right hand. She held the .32-caliber pocket pistol straight out from her chest and thumbed the hammer back. She lifted it higher, squinted one eye as she aimed at Kate's forehead.

"You bitch," Kate said, bunching her lips, her dark eyes hawkish. "How dare you bring a gun into my office."

"How dare you kill Mandy! How dare you try to enslave me again like you did before you tried to *kill* me!"

Faith stepped forward. Kate stepped back, the muscles in her face slackening in fear. Faith felt her fury flow like water from a broken damn.

"I swear, if you make trouble for me, I'll kill you, Kate.

I'm no longer the child I was. I'll open a brothel that'll make yours look like a child's tree house."

Faith glanced at Sebastian, who remained in his chair, leaning back against the desk, fear in his eyes. "Talk sense to her," Faith said. "If I see her within half a block of me, I'll kill her."

"Uh . . ." Sebastian stammered.

Keeping the gun on Kate, Faith suddenly saw the possibilities here. They overwhelmed her, made her giddy with power. Crazy Kate was backing away from her. She wasn't half as tough as Faith had thought she was.

Faith glanced again at Sebastian and grinned devilishly, enjoying the terror she saw in Kate's black eyes. "Who's the richest man in town?"

"Uh . . ." Sebastian swallowed. "I don't know . . . I suppose the owner of the mine . . . uh . . . Vincent Marberry."

Faith squinted down the pistol's barrel at Kate's haunted eyes. This was better than killing her. "He live here in Gold Cache?"

"Yes."

"Does he like women?"

Perspiration ran down Sebastian's gaunt features, fogging his glasses. His glance darted between the two women. "Of course . . ."

Faith's stare held Kate like a moth on the end of a pin. "Thanks."

She stepped straight back, opened the door, sent a cold, parting glance at Kate, and went out.

She closed the door behind her and, holding the cocked pistol straight down at her right side, moved quickly away. Her skin crawled, and her heart pounded. She expected the door to open any minute and for Kate to bound out, screaming and shooting or lunging with a knife.

About a quarter of the way down the hall, Faith slowed her pace, listening for the door but hearing only the sounds of drunken conversation, laughter, and lovemaking.

A calm swept over her. By the time she was descending the stairs, having returned the pistol to its makeshift holster and lifting her billowing skirts above her boots, she was smiling.

She'd won.

Back inside the office, Kate was still glaring at the door when another latch clicked to her left. She turned to see a short, devilishly handsome man with thick blond hair combed to one side step out of her bedroom. His full pink lips shaped a grin as he strolled toward Kate and Sebastian, an unlit cigarette in one hand, a battered brown Stetson in the other.

Only five or six inches over five feet tall, he was thick and lumpy, like a pugilist. He wore the clothes of your average stockman—blue shirt, red neckerchief, bull-hide vest, and denims. A tin star was pinned to his shirt.

"What the hell were you doing in there, Charlie? She might have killed me."

"Nah, she wasn't gonna kill ye, Miss Kate." He grinned, swaggering up to Kate's desk and helping himself to a match. "She was just feeling you out, that's all. Besides, I figure you can take care of yourself."

"No more free fucks, Charlie-boy," Kate said through gritted teeth, "until she's dead."

Charlie Ward had once robbed trains in Nebraska and Missouri before coming here to gamble and hide out from federal marshals. While he was frolicking with the doxies in Kate's fine digs, Kate had convinced him that he'd make a hell of a town marshal—as long as he overlooked rigged gambling tables and discouraged competition. Thus the badge he was wearing now.

Charlie lit his cigar. Puffing smoke, he blew out the match and looked at Kate, surprised. "You want me to *kill* her? Shit, that's one fine-looking piece of ass!" He laughed and glanced at Sebastian, who sat holding his drink in one hand, cigar in the other, regarding Kate gravely.

"Really, Kate, killing her might be going a little far," Sebastian said. "Why don't we just have Charlie run her out of town? Or, better yet . . ."

"Convince her to come to work right here at the Pleasure Palace," finished the marshal, grinning into Kate's face from only inches away. Being the same height, they could look directly into each other's eyes.

Though Kate had entertained the same idea, she knew now that Faith was too big a threat. Her looks and her influence on men would make her far too powerful. If she opened her own place—even just a crib behind the Russian's hotel—within months she'd be the richest whore in town.

With the backing of Vincent Marberry, Adrian Timms, or even Sebastian Kirk himself, she'd soon have the entire camp in her corset, and a bordello to rival that of Alva McQueen's Diamond Stud in Canyon City.

As old as Kate was, with sagging tits and brandy fat padding her middle, she'd be turning tricks for quarters on Burlington Avenue in Cheyenne.

No, since she obviously couldn't be scared away, Faith had to die.

"If you like your job and your free fucks and whiskey, not to mention your free *room*, Charlie-boy," Kate growled into Ward's face, "you'll arrest her. She came in here with a gun, tried to rob me. You'll haul her and that half-breed bastard outside town, kill them, and throw their bodies in an old placer digging where no one but the wolves and crows will ever find them."

Returning Kate's stare, Ward let the smile sag from his handsome face, a flush touching his fair cheeks behind his two-day growth of blond beard stubble. "All right, Kate," he said, sounding injured. "You don't have to get nasty. Consider it done."

He glanced again at Sebastian, then stepped around Kate as though avoiding a bear trap. Donning his hat and sticking his cigarette between his lips, he opened the door and left.

Downstairs, Faith took a seat beside Yakima, who kept his eyes glued on the two horse thieves playing faro at the far end of the smoky room.

"I think everything's going to be okay," she said. "The only problem is Wolf . . ."

"Wolf's no problem," Yakima said. "The men who stole him have the problem."

The dark-haired horse thief stretched his head around the faro dealer once more, his long, unshaven face turning toward Yakima. Yakima grinned and waved. The man jerked his head back out of sight.

"Who's that?" Faith asked.

"Friends I'll be buddyin' up with again real soon."

His voice trailed off as he watched a short, blond little bulldog wearing a tin star on his shirt slowly descend the stairs at the far end of the room. The marshal's eyes swept the saloon's main hall, finding Yakima and Faith and holding.

As the man sauntered toward the bar, a good head shorter than most of the other men in the room but broad as a lumber dray—he kept his eyes on Yakima. He finally turned

away as he leaned his elbows atop the mahogany and ordered a drink.

"Come on," Yakima told Faith, kicking his chair back and
rising. "We best get some shut-eye. I think we got a big day
ahead."

Chapter 29

Yakima awoke the next morning at cockcrow. It was literally a cock's crow that woke him, as there must have been a chicken coop as well as a pigpen nearby, and the rooster was announcing the first wash of slate light through the cracks in the mud and straw chinking between the wall's square logs.

As he lifted his head from the pillow, Faith, asleep with her head on his chest, groaned and scissored a leg over his, holding him down. He gently shoved her aside, evoking another, longer groan. Instead of waking, however, the girl rolled over to face the wall, burying her head beneath the quilts.

Yakima had expected trouble from Crazy Kate and the town marshal, so he hadn't undressed before crawling into the Russian's unexpectedly comfortable bed. Rising, he pulled on his boot moccasins, quietly added dry pine needles and cones to the hot ashes in the stove, blowing to coax a flame, then added a couple of small logs.

He donned his capote and hat, picked up his rifle, and slipped quietly out of the room, softly latching the door behind him.

A minute later, he stepped into the front yard of the hotel, wincing at the icy wind lashing his face, and pulled the hotel's timbered door closed before setting the rifle down and fastening his capote's top button against the chill.

Dull light illuminated the buildings along this side street—mostly dilapidated hovels remaining from when Gold Cache was still only a shack town. Most looked abandoned, though some with padlocked doors were probably being used for storage. The chill wind howled between them, whipping tar paper about and sawing under a tin roof somewhere to Yakima's right.

Nothing moved but a few vagrant snow flurries. No footsteps showed in the dusting of fresh snow around the hotel. The new-fallen snow only lightly covered the blood the Russian had splashed around while carving up the doe, so that a film of pink remained around the front door.

Yakima circled the hotel, finding no tracks or sign of interlopers. He figured that if trouble was going to come from Crazy Kate and the town marshal, whom she no doubt had on her payroll, it would have come at first light.

Maybe Kate and Faith had buried the hatchet after all, as Faith believed.

Yakima could use a quiet day. He'd curry Wolf, trim the black's hooves and reset his shoes, get the stallion ready to pull foot when he was sure that Faith would be safe here. A piece of dried-apple pie would be nice, with fresh-whipped cream and hot black coffee spiked with rye.

He moved up toward the main street, holding the Yellowboy low in his right hand, the brim of his hat bending in the wind.

When he came to the corner, he stopped beside a brick harness shop and cast his gaze to the right, toward the small stone jail hunkered at the west end of town, at the edge of a frozen creek. He could make out the hovel now, about twenty yards on the other side of a three-story mercantile.

The jail's windows were dark. No one milled around it—at least not in the open.

Directly across the street from the place, a big woman with stringy black hair and a blanket draped over her rounded shoulders split wood in front of a small frame building calling itself, succinctly, CHEAP FOOD. Smoke streamed from the chimney pipe and hovered low over the shake roof, tossed and torn by the breeze.

Low growls and scuffling sounds rose. Yakima turned left. Half a block away, in the snow-flocked sage of a narrow lot, two coyotes played tug-of-war with a skinned venison haunch they'd scavenged from a cabin yard.

Across the street, Kate's brothel, with its broad front porch and pink-curtained windows, stood silent and dark, the wind ticking snow against its west wall and shuttling an empty bottle to and fro on its third porch step.

Yakima looked to the west again. Still no movement except for the woman splitting wood.

Raising his capote collar and tugging his hat brim low, he started east up the street, deciding to check on Wolf at the livery barn. The coyotes spooked and ran off down the middle of the street, gripping the haunch between them and snarling, disappearing into the gray-blue fog of dawn.

Yakima had walked only half a block before an icy worm wiggled along his spine. He stopped suddenly and glanced back toward the jailhouse.

In the dead center of the street, about ten yards on the other side of Crazy Kate's brothel, three men stood facing him. Yakima could see only their hatted silhouettes, bulky in buckskin coats and mufflers—two tall men on either side of a short, broad-shouldered, slightly bull-legged gent in a battered brown Stetson. They were forty yards away, but even in the wan light Yakima could see the five-pointed stars on their coats.

In her dark room on the brothel's second story, Kate drew a robe around her bulky body and sidled up to the window near her bed. She slid the pink curtain aside to peer out through the frost-framed, snow-specked glass.

Below her and left, three men stood in the middle of the street, facing east. To her right, a long-haired gent in a black, flat-brimmed hat, green capote, and boot moccasins stepped off the opposite boardwalk. Holding a rifle down low in his right hand, he walked to the center of the street and stopped, facing Charlie Ward and Ward's two tall, beefy deputies.

Kate hadn't realized a soft snicker had escaped her until Sebastian stirred in the bed, under a mound of quilts. His voice was thick with sleep. "What's wrong, Kate?"

Kate smiled as she stared into the street, the soft gun-metal light reflected in her black, downcast eyes. "Nothing, dear. Everything is just fine."

On the street, Yakima felt the cold wind against his face, blowing his hair out from his shoulders. He had to dig his heels into the frozen-rutted, snow-dusted street to hold his ground.

Ward yelled, "You and the girl are under arrest, breed!"

Yakima stared at him, squinting against the snow pellets.

"She went to Kate's room last night, threatened her with a gun. You assaulted two bouncers." The lawman's lips stretched in a smile. "This is a law-abidin' town. That kind of actin' up don't cart wood around here. Now, you gonna come willin', or are me and my boys gonna have to turn our horns out?"

Yakima stood with his feet spread, the corners of his mouth raised slightly, eyes hard. "You should be more careful who you throw in with, Marshal. It's a damn cold day to die."

"That mean you and her ain't gonna come willin'?"

"Nope."

The marshal snapped his rifle across his chest, cocking it, the metallic rasp thinning out on the wind. The two deputies, one on each side of him, followed suit.

Yakima raised and cocked his own Winchester.

The three men began moving toward him, the two deputies splitting off from the marshal, forming a wedge about ten yards across, holding their cocked long guns at port arms.

"Come on, now, breed," the marshal called. "Be reasonable. You're outgunned. What's more, you're *surrounded*!"

Yakima turned quarterwise, flicked a look behind.

Two more men walked toward him from the east. One held a long-barreled shotgun, the other, a .50 Spencer with an octagonal barrel. They grinned, snaggletoothed.

These two didn't wear badges, and they had the brutish look of seasoned miners. Figuring he might need extra help, the marshal had probably deputized them last night in one of the hophouses.

"What do you say, breed?" the marshal called, within twenty yards now and closing.

"Not another step," Yakima warned, turned sideways to the street and keeping all five men in his vision's periphery.

In the corner of his left eye, the miner in the red blanket coat raised his Spencer, and aimed. The rifle barked. Yakima bounded off his heels, throwing himself backward, twisting in midair.

The large-caliber round blew up frozen mud two feet in front of the marshal, who lurched back, cursing the miner. Yakima hit the ground on his right shoulder and raised his Winchester in both gloved hands, drilling the Spencer-wielding miner through his right temple.

As the man was punched backward, dropping his rifle, another gun barked to Yakima's right, hammering the frozen turf at his left.

Yakima aimed quickly at the deputy right of the short marshal, and around whose head gun smoke wafted, and fired.

As the deputy groaned and slapped his right shoulder, Yakima leapt to his feet. He ran, ducking and zigzagging, toward the north side of the street as several bullets cracked into the frozen mud and plunked into the boardwalk beyond him, another slug pinking a window in the women's clothing store.

As he dove behind a frozen stock trough, a shotgun boomed, the blast echoing off the buildings as the double-ought buck slammed into the trough, throwing slivers of wood and ice back onto the boardwalk behind Yakima.

Several more rifle rounds hammered the trough and the low pile of split wood beside it. Yakima crawled on his knees and elbows, snaked the Yellowboy around the woodpile. In the middle of the street to his left, the surviving miner was down on his knees, thumbing fresh wads into his broken-open barn-blaster.

Yakima spat a curse and, just as the man snapped the double-bore closed, pulled the trigger. The man jerked his head up and howled as the .44 round burst through his belly and out his back, painting the snow-frosted street behind him bright red.

He dropped the shotgun and looked down, jaw hanging as he loosed another howl.

Yakima crabbed to the other end of the stock tank as two more shots drilled chunks of wood from the trough's lip, pelting his hat with more wood and ice. He peered around the end of the trough.

While the one wounded deputy was on his knees, cursing and stuffing his neckerchief into his coat, trying to pad the shoulder wound, the marshal and the other deputy ran toward Yakima's side of the street, heading for the harness shop and an open field of fire.

Yakima rose to his knees, slammed a fresh round into the Winchester's chamber, and fired first at the marshal, then at the deputy.

He'd fired too quickly for accuracy, and the first shot thudded into the ground off the marshal's left boot. The second sailed over the deputy's head and punched into a support post on the other side of the street half a block west.

The first shot caused the marshal to change direction and bolt, cursing, toward the street's other side, diving for a woodpile. The second might have clipped the deputy, who flinched as he disappeared around the other side of the harness shop, slinging his right arm out like an injured wing.

On the other hand, maybe it hadn't.

As an ejected casing smoked over Yakima's right shoulder, the deputy jerked his head and rifle around the far front corner of the harness shop. His Henry stabbed smoke and flames, the slug slicing like a hot knife along the right side of Yakima's neck.

As the marshal fired from behind the woodpile across the street, Yakima hammered off two quick rounds at the deputy, the slugs spraying slivers of the harness shop's log wall into the man's eyes.

Grimacing and screaming, the man jerked back behind the building.

Yakima waited for the marshal to drill another round his way, then lifted his head, spied the man's face and rifle barrel low on the woodpile's left side, and fired three shots—
boom, snick-boom, snick-boom, snick!

As the third casing rattled onto the boardwalk behind him, Yakima ducked down behind the stock trough again, having raked his gaze up and down the street, noting the shotgunner lying on his side, holding his guts in his hands while shouting curses skyward.

He and his partner were out of the game, but the deputy Yakima had shoulder-wounded had hauled himself out of sight. Since Yakima had only winged him, he still had all three lawmen to worry about.

As the marshal drilled two more shots and the shotgunner continued bellowing like a wounded grizzly, Yakima looked at the far front corner of the harness shop. No sign of the deputy who'd taken cover there.

Shit.

Keeping his head down and his gaze riveted on the harness shop, Yakima thumbed shells into the Yellowboy's loading gate. The marshal was holding his fire, maybe waiting for the deputies to surround Yakima. The only sounds were a distant barking dog, the ticking snow, the breeze funneling between buildings, and the wounded shotgunner's anguished bellows.

Yakima jerked his rifle up suddenly, fired twice at the marshal. As the marshal returned two shots, Yakima leapt to his feet, two sets of rounds now kicking up dust and wood as he ran around the side of the harness shop and pressed his back to the wall, sweeping his gaze from left to right.

He listened for footsteps. The deputy he thought he'd winged was no doubt trying to flank him, creeping around the shop's rear.

Keeping his ears pricked, the gunfire dying behind him, Yakima made his way to the rear of the harness shop, edged a look around the corner toward the other side. The deputy had had the same idea. He jerked back behind the opposite side of the building half a second before Yakima did.

Yakima pressed his back to the wall, pricking his ears, listening for footsteps, waiting, squeezing the Yellowboy in his gloved hands.

After a minute, snow crunched under a boot. Yakima threw himself straight out from the end of the building.

A Winchester roared, the slug plunking into the building's corner. Yakima hit the ground on his back five feet from the end of the building and snapped his rifle up, aiming quickly at the big deputy crouched at the middle of the harness shop's rear wall.

Boom!

The deputy groaned, dropped his rifle, and grabbed his throat.

The Yellowboy spoke again.

A round, dark circle appeared in the man's forehead, throwing him straight back against the wall. His hat tumbled off his head as he bounced off the wall, twisted around, and fell on his side, boots crossed, quivering.

Chapter 30

Marshal Charlie Ward, hunkered down behind the woodpile on the other side of the street from where Yakima had been shooting, worried his thumb over the grooves of his carbine's cocked hammer and stared at the gap between the harness shop and the women's clothing store.

It had to be well below freezing in spite of the lightening eastern sky, but sweat streaked his forehead and rosy cheeks. His heart pounded and his feet felt like putty.

He'd had enough of this shit. That goddamn half-breed was hell with a shooting iron, and he didn't seem to have any fear!

It had been about two minutes since Ward had last heard shots rise from behind the harness shop. If his deputy, Kenny Slocum, had killed the half-breed with those shots, Slocum would have called out or shown himself by now. Since he'd done neither, he was most likely dead.

And that damn wolverine of a kill-crazy half-breed son of a bitch was probably hunkered down between buildings or holed up in a woodpile or stable or stock pen, waiting for Ward to try rooting him out.

"For the love of Christ—son of a bitch gut-shot me!" the wounded miner, Homer Landusky, yelled for the umpteenth time, curled up in the street. "Someone fetch me a goddamn medico."

As Ward was thinking about silencing that goddamn caterwauling with his carbine, boots pounded the boardwalk behind him, spurs ringing raucously. The marshal's heart turned somersaults and he swung his rifle around so quickly that a log brushed his hat off his head.

"Hold on, Charlie, goddamn it—it's me!" hissed his other deputy, Dennis Gamble, dropping to one knee on the boardwalk in front of Langella's Dentistry and Tonsorial Parlor.

Gamble had lost his own hat, and his long face with its spade beard and single brown eyebrow was flushed with pain. The left shoulder of his buckskin coat was blood-stained and lumpy from the neckerchief the deputy had stuffed into the wound.

Gamble winced and raked his eyes across the street. "Any sign of that bastard?"

"He's that way." Ward blocked out the miner's persistent cries and surveyed the other side of the street, spying no movement, hearing no sounds but the breeze and a dog that had started barking back in the pines when the shooting began.

Ward turned to Gamble, tried to hide his terror. "Go on up the street, circle back through the alley. We'll surround the son of a bitch."

Gamble's eyes and lips were pinched with fury. He nodded. "You got it, Charlie. Can't wait to drill some hot lead through that son of a bitch's heathen heart!"

He lurched forward and ran, crouching and jerking cautious looks across the street, heading eastward up Main. When he was fifty feet away, Ward again stretched a glance across the street.

"For godsakes," the miner bellowed, again causing Ward to grind his molars, "I'm losing my goddamned innards!" He started bawling.

Ward jerked his carbine toward the miner, planted a bead on the man's forehead obscured by his breeze-whipped pewter hair, and fired. The bullet plunked through the man's right eyebrow, jerking his chin up. His back stiffened, and then he sagged to the street, like an exhausted man lying down for a long-awaited nap.

The miner's hands slid away from his bloody belly and flattened out beside him, and his entire body was still and quiet at last.

"I swear," Ward muttered, ejecting the spent shell from his carbine, seating a fresh shell, then off-cocking the hammer.

He donned his hat, rose, looked around, and, with sweat dribbling down his cheeks and neck and into his coat, chilling him deep, he turned and stalked westward along the boardwalks, holding the carbine down around his thigh. He strode heavy-footed, shoulders slumped, head down, snow dusting his battered hat brim.

He was halfway up the porch steps of Crazy Kate's brothel when three shots flatted out at the other end of town. A hoarse cry sounded. Ward turned, saw nothing but the lightening eastern sky and the snow, coming down harder now that the temperature was climbing.

The silence following Gamble's cry was funereal.

Ward winced, imagining the end the deputy must have come to, then continued up the steps. He crossed the porch and pushed through the door.

"What the hell do you think you're doing, *Marshal*?"

Ward stopped just inside the door, one hand on the knob. He glanced to his left, where a small group was spread out before the window—Crazy Kate, Sebastian Kirk, three whores in rumpled nightgowns and robes, the bartender, and two gamblers who'd been hanging around for the past few days, getting fleeced at every game they tried.

Dressed in a silk wrapper as black as her hair, Kate glared at Ward savagely.

Ward curled his upper lip, slammed the door, and sauntered toward the bar on the right side of the room. "What's it look like?" He lifted the hinged bar top, let it slam onto the mahogany, then took a brandy bottle from a shelf. "I'm havin' a drink."

He plopped the bottle and a shot glass onto the mahogany, and plucked the cork from the bottle. "Anyone join me?"

Kate turned toward him, obsidian eyes large as horseshoes. "Is that savage *dead*? Is the *girl*?"

"Who knows?" Ward splashed brandy into his glass. "All I know is I'm still kickin', and your whores ain't purty enough, and my room ain't posh enough, and your whiskey ain't *good* enough, to push the issue with that *creature* out there."

Ward lifted his glass, glanced around it at Kate. "I'm goin' back to rustlin' and robbin' stagecoaches. Live longer. Cheers." He threw back the brandy.

His head was still tipped back on his shoulders, eyes closed, savoring the burn of the liquor at the back of his throat, when Kate jerked her head around wildly. Spying what she was looking for, she raked the Colt Navy from the holster on Alvin Pauk's right hip and aimed the heavy gun with both hands at Ward.

The whores gasped, grabbing each other's arms and that of the bartender, shuffling back to the far wall.

Still groggy from sleep, Sebastian Kirk gaped and said, "Kate . . ."

Alvin Pauk and Leo Salon, who'd been up all night playing faro and Red Dog, merely glanced at each other warily, and blinked.

The marshal opened his eyes and dropped his chin. Seeing the gun in Kate's hands, watching her thumb the hammer back, he opened his mouth and screamed at the same time the Colt barked.

It sounded like a cannon blast in the close quarters, acrid powder smoke wafting around Kate's head.

The bullet ripped through Ward's right ear and cracked the mirror behind him. "Ahhch!" He staggered against the backbar, cursing and clutching his ear, blood oozing between his fingers.

One of the whores shrieked as the bartender sucked air through his teeth.

"Jesus *Christ*!" exclaimed Leo Salon.

Sebastian Kirk was instantly awake. "Kate!"

Coughing and wincing against the powder smoke, Kate stepped forward, keeping the gun extended in both hands, again thumbing back the revolver's trigger.

"No, wait!" cried Ward.

His voice was drowned by Kate's second shot, which took the short lawman through his upper chest, smashing a pyramid of shot glasses on the bar behind him and spraying the shards with blood.

One of the whores loosed a quivering screech. Ward twisted around, fell against the backbar, knocking glasses and bottles to the floor with a roar of shattering glass. He staggered sideways and fell with one last curse and a thump that shook the entire room.

Kate wheeled with the gun in her hands. The barman, Sebastian, and the two gamblers leapt straight back, eyes snapping wide. "You *men* get out there and kill that savage!"

Alvin Pauk's voice trembled. "Now, look, ma'am . . ."

"Kate," said the bartender, walking stiffly toward the bar behind which Charlie Ward had fallen, "you're . . . outta your mind."

The man wheeled toward her suddenly, as if realizing his mistake and raising his hand to shield his face. "*No!*"

Kate drilled a round through his chest, sent him spinning, then tumbling down against the base of the bar.

Kate spun toward the three remaining men in the room as the whores, clumped together as though glued, shuffled sideways toward the staircase at the room's rear. "Now, I've got a thousand dollars for the man or men who'll bring me that savage's head and the head of the girl. For any nancy-boys in the room, I have a *bullet!*"

A female voice rose behind her. "I've got one for you if you don't drop that gun, Kate." There was the metallic snarl of a rifle being cocked, and Kate's back tightened as she turned her head to one side.

"Don't turn around," Faith said, walking out from behind the far end of the bar, holding the Winchester carbine in both hands.

She'd heard the shooting and slipped through the brothel's back door. Knowing that Kate would be orchestrating the assault from the brothel, she intended to help Yakima by putting the madame out of commission once and for all.

She wore her trail gear—denims, flannel shirt, and blanket coat. She wasn't wearing a hat, and her hair, still mussed from sleep, tumbled about her shoulders. Her blue eyes were hard, jaw taut.

Sebastian, the two horse thieves, and the whores stared at her skeptically.

Kate held the gun against her right thigh. It shook faintly.

Faith lowered the Winchester's barrel and squeezed the trigger. The rifle boomed, rattling the remaining bottles and glasses on the backbar and blowing a chunk of wood from the puncheons a foot to the right of Kate's left slipper.

Everyone in the room jumped as the concussion rocked the house.

Kate gasped and, without turning toward Faith, flung the pistol onto the table three feet to her right.

Faith glanced at the whores gathered on the right side of the room, between the piano and the big potbellied stove. She jerked the carbine's barrel toward the stairs. Holding their robes closed, fear etched on their faces, the girls ran to the back of the room and up the stairs, their terrified breaths echoing faintly.

Faith stepped forward, sliding the rifle's barrel back and forth between Kate and the three men gathered about ten feet from the front window, in the middle of the room.

There was a table between the men and Kate. Kate's gun was on the table. Faith approached the table and stopped, aiming the rifle barrel at the middle of Kate's back as she extended her left hand toward the revolver.

She nearly had her fingers curled around the worn walnut grip, when Kate wheeled toward her, screeching like ten dying cats. The madame nudged the rifle barrel aside, and grabbed the forestock in both hands.

She swung Faith in a circle, thrusting a foot out to trip her. As Faith's back and head hit the floor, her jaws snapping together, Kate wrenched the rifle out of her hands with such force that Faith felt as though her arms had been pulled from their sockets.

Shrieking even louder—a high, keening cry—Kate aimed the carbine at Faith, holding Faith down by planting one slippered foot on her chest.

As the bore yawned in Faith's face, Kate shrieking and glaring wildly, looking like a witch loosed from the boiling bowels of hell, Faith squeezed her eyes shut, bracing herself for the shot.

Pop!

Kate stopped screaming. Faith opened her eyes.

Kate stared down at her, the madame's head canted sharply left, lower jaw hanging. A nickel-sized hole shone in her right temple. As blood dribbled to the edge of the wound, it caught the gray light from the front windows and streaked down Kate's forehead toward her brow, like a heavy bead of quicksilver.

Faith turned to where Sebastian Kirk stood nearby, a smoking pistol in his hand, still aimed at Kate.

Kate exhaled heavily. The carbine dropped from her hands to land with a clattering thud. She sagged to the side and was dead before she hit the floor in a heap.

Yakima heard the thud half a second before he bounded through the brothel's front door, quartering around to his left, extending his cocked Yellowboy straight out from his right hip.

The two gamblers shuffled back, snapping their nervous gazes to him and jerking their hands shoulder high, palms out.

The tall, pale gent wearing only a plaid robe and black socks was aiming a single-barreled, silver-plated, pearl-gripped derringer somewhere off to Yakima's right, toward the bar. Smoke curled from the barrel. It was the peashooter's report Yakima had just heard.

Yakima followed the man's dark gaze.

Beside a table and an overturned chair, Faith and Crazy

Kate lay side by side on the floor. Faith was on her back. For a second Yakima thought she was dead. His pulse hammered in his temples. Then he saw her chest rising and falling heavily.

He looked at Kate. Blood pooled on the floor beneath her head.

When Faith sat up, Yakima turned to the three men before him. The tall, bald gent looked stricken, his fringe of hair sticking out like wires around the lumpy, pale crown of his head. He set the derringer on the table, shuffled toward Kate, and knelt down beside her.

Yakima returned his gaze to the two men who'd stolen Wolf, aiming the Winchester at the heart of the shorter, blond-haired gent in the shabby bowler. He tightened his jaw and set his mouth to speak, but stopped when he heard a dribbling sound.

He lowered his gaze. Urine dribbled down from the inside of the blond's right trouser leg to pool on the floor beside his undershot stockman's boot.

Yakima looked at the man's bleached face, lips bunched, eyes twitching. He seemed ready to cry.

Yakima turned to the taller, dark-haired gent in the wine-colored vest. He wasn't pissing his pants, but he looked nearly as scared as the blond, eyes bugging, hands shaking.

"You boys go on back to cow country. Stay there."

The blond loosed a held breath. He stuttered, "Y-you ain't gonna kill us?"

"Give me time, I might change my mind."

Keeping their hands raised, the pair shuffled out the door and were off and running.

As the tall, bald gent knelt beside Kate, Faith climbed to her feet and ran to Yakima, buried her head in his coat. He lowered the rifle, raked a hand through her hair, pressing her head against him.

"You all right?" he asked.

Keeping her cheek pressed to his chest, she nodded. She looked up at him, blue eyes glowing in the gray light from the window as she touched a finger to the slight gash along his neck. Her worried, questioning gaze moved to his.

"I've cut myself worse shaving." He turned when he saw the bald gent straighten, lifting Kate's lumpy body in his arms. He grunted as he carried the dead woman toward the back of the room. Halfway to the stairs, he stopped.

He turned and looked at Faith. "You wanted a business, young lady. I reckon you have one."

He ambled into the heavy shadows at the back of the room and started up the stairs.

Yakima went to the bar and grabbed a bottle and two glasses. He strode back toward Faith, who stood staring at the staircase, and sat down. He filled each glass to the rim.

"I don't know about you, but I could use a drink."

Epilogue

One month later . . .

On the second story of the brothel that had once belonged to Crazy Kate Sweney, in the broad four-poster bed he shared with Faith, Yakima opened his eyes and stared up at the dark ceiling.

He hadn't slept much all night. The dawn light pushed through the room's two street-facing windows, vaguely limning the bed and the several chairs, dressers, and fainting couches, the fancy lamps and candle tapers adorning tables.

The room smelled of lavender soap and perfume.

Faith had come a long way in a short time, gotten exactly what she'd wanted. Their journey was over. Thornton wouldn't bother her here. She'd made too many friends, and she'd hired a big Irish bouncer named Marley who would make sure no one laid a hand on her.

Yakima glanced at her, lying curled beneath the quilts and the silk comforter, turned away from him, her blond hair fanned across her pillow. He wanted to reach out and touch her, but he didn't want to wake her. Instead, he slowly peeled the covers back from his chest and began sliding his right leg toward the floor.

As if sensing his movement, she groaned and turned toward him, sliding a hand across his chest, pulling him back down to the sheets and resting her head on his belly, hugging him.

"Don't get up. It's early."

"Sun's on the rise."

He felt her smile against his belly, slide her hand to his crotch. He grunted. She kept her hand down there, gently squeezing, caressing, pumping, teasing him with her palm. His blood rose, and he awakened fully.

Finally, she turned away from him, thrust her naked bottom against his hip.

He slid her hair back over her right shoulder, snaked his hand around her side, and cupped her right breast. He fingered the nipple until it stood pebbled and erect, and then he cupped both her swelling orbs, squeezing and kneading, until her chest rose and fell sharply with desire.

She groaned and slid her hand over her hip, finding his erect member, and, turning slightly forward and spreading her legs, guided him into her.

Grasping her hips in his hands, he thrust gently in and pulled slowly out. She moaned and sighed, reaching behind and wrapping her arm around his head, caressing his cheek with hers, nibbling his chin. The bedsprings sawed quietly, growing only slightly in pitch and volume as the lovers' passion grew.

When they'd spent themselves, he pulled away from her. She gasped, then sighed and scissored her legs into his, her thighs powdery smooth and warm against his own. Thrusting her slender back against his chest, she snuggled down in the sheets, and in a minute her breathing grew deep and slow.

Asleep.

Yakima lay there a moment, until his own breathing slowed and his heart beat regularly again. Finally, he slid away from her. She groaned softly but did not awaken.

He dropped his legs to the floor and rose slowly.

He turned back to her, mounded beneath the covers. His heart felt heavy, his belly raw. He leaned down and kissed her cheek, letting his lips stay pressed to the butter-soft skin for several seconds, savoring her, before he pulled his head back, straightening, letting one finger trail through her silky hair.

His old Shaolin mentor, Ralph, had once said, "Some wolves are not born to the pack."

While Faith slept, Yakima dressed quietly by only the pearl light pushing through the windows' pink curtains. He'd packed his saddlebags and cleaned the Yellowboy the night before, after Faith had gone to sleep. He shrugged into his four-point capote, his gloves stuffed in the pockets, and donned his hat.

He moved slowly to the door, his boot moccasins whispering on the thick carpet, and picked up his rifle from behind a chair. He plucked his saddlebags off the coat hook, slinging them over his left shoulder.

He turned to look back at Faith buried beneath the covers, then opened the door slowly, slipped into the hall, and gently closed the door behind him.

He was halfway down the broad staircase when he saw a pale-robed figure sitting at one of the saloon's tables. He stopped before the table, where the pregnant dove, Emily, sat with her legs propped on a chair, a beer mug half filled with milk on the table before her. Her face was a misty oval in the dusky shadows, her chestnut hair piled loosely atop her head.

"Couldn't sleep?" Yakima asked.

"Got the morning flu again," the girl said, eyes sweeping him curiously. "Goin' hunting?"

"I'm pullin' my picket pins." He headed for the door between the room's two front windows, milky in the first wash of dawn. "Good luck, Emily."

"Does Faith know?"

"She knows."

He went out and looked around from the porch, wisps of woodsmoke touching his nose. The high mountain chill wrapped around him. A dusting of fresh snow glowed softly against the dawn shadows, like sugar in a dark bowl.

Across the street, the bulky woman with stringy black hair was splitting wood, as she did every morning, before her tiny eatery. A red fox crossed the street on Yakima's right, moving at a brisk, stiff-legged trot, glancing at Yakima with vague interest before disappearing into the snow-dusted sage of an empty lot.

Yakima descended the steps and started down the middle of the main street, there being no wagon traffic at this hour. At the end of the street, he opened the livery barn's doors and disappeared inside.

He reappeared a few minutes later, throwing both doors open with a wooden bark and a grating squawk of rusty hinges. He led Wolf outside, the tall black saddled and bridled and arching his neck eagerly, vapor jetting from his nostrils. Dropping Wolf's reins, Yakima went back into the barn and led out a buckskin packhorse—a deep-bottomed gelding that he'd bought two days ago, along with a wood-framed packsaddle and heavy hemp-and-burlap panniers.

The paint mare was probably back with Jeff Ironsides by now. Yakima had paid two freighters he'd deemed trustworthy to lead her back down the mountains.

Yakima scrutinized the packsaddle once more, tugging

and shifting the overstuffed pouches. He adjusted the buckskin's bridle before grabbing Wolf's reins, toeing a stirrup, and hauling himself into the saddle.

He gigged the stallion westward down the main street, trailing the buckskin, and pulled up before the spruce and yellow brothel leaning back against the pine-carpeted northern ridge. FAITH'S SALOON AND PLEASURE PALACE, read the letters splashed across the second-story facade.

Yakima looked at the windows on the far right end of the second story.

Some wolves are not born to the pack.

Yakima cursed. He pinched his hat brim at the window, grunted, "Good-bye, Faith."

He gigged Wolf westward along the street, booting the black stallion into a trot, the buckskin keeping pace behind him.

In the bed upstairs, Faith lay curled as Yakima had left her. She stared unseeing at the pillow beneath her cheek.

"Farewell, Yakima."

GRITTY HISTORICAL ACTION FROM

USA Today BESTSELLING AUTHOR

RALPH COTTON

JACKPOT RIDGE	0-451-21002-6
BORDER DOGS	0-451-19815-8
GUNMAN'S SONG	0-451-21092-1
BETWEEN HELL AND TEXAS	0-451-21150-2
DEAD MAN'S CANYON	0-451-21325-4
GUNS OF WOLF VALLEY	0-451-21349-1
KILLING PLAIN	0-451-21451-X
THE LAW IN SOMOS SANTOS	0-451-21625-3
BLACK MESA	0-451-21382-3
BLOOD LANDS	0-451-21876-0
TROUBLE CREEK	0-451-21792-6
GUNFIGHT AT COLD DEVIL	0-451-21917-1
BAD DAY AT WILLOW CREEK	0-451-21998-8

Available wherever books are sold or at
penguin.com

S909

Penguin Group (USA) Online

What will you be reading tomorrow?

Tom Clancy, Patricia Cornwell, W.E.B. Griffin,
Nora Roberts, William Gibson, Robin Cook,
Brian Jacques, Catherine Coulter, Stephen King,
Dean Koontz, Ken Follett, Clive Cussler,
Eric Jerome Dickey, John Sandford,
Terry McMillan, Sue Monk Kidd, Amy Tan,
John Berendt…

You'll find them all at
penguin.com

*Read excerpts and newsletters,
find tour schedules and reading group guides,
and enter contests.*

Subscribe to Penguin Group (USA) newsletters
and get an exclusive inside look
at exciting new titles and the authors you love
long before everyone else does.

PENGUIN GROUP (USA)
us.penguingroup.com